Curtain Call:

A Death Metal Novel

I0612658

Nathan Squiers

Published by
Lurid Leopard Press
a division of
Tiger Dynasty Publishing, LLC
www.tigerdynastypublishing.com
ISBN-13: 978-1-940634-03-6
ISBN-10: 1940634032

ALSO BY NATHAN SQUIERS:

A HOWL AT THE MOON
*S(a)TAN
*FORBIDDEN PAINTS ON A WICKED CANVAS
THE CRIMSON SHADOW SERIES
**THE FIGHTER

*A prequel to the Crimson Shadow series
**A prequel to Scarlet Night (by Megan J. Parker)—COMING
SOON

Proudly dedicated to all those who live by their own soundtrack as well as those who are still looking (your tune will come)!

ACKNOWLEDGEMENTS

If I were to make an album of all those who deserve credit for this book in some form or another I'd no-doubt wind up with one of those unreasonably long, 18-disc collections that you see advertised on late-night television. Even then, I'd probably not have enough time or space to adequately praise everybody or flat-out forget a bulk of A-listers just because my mind is fractured like that...

But here we go, anyway!

As always, a very special and loving thanks goes to my fiancé and fellow author, Megan J. Parker, who jabbed a pitchfork in my ass a few years back to put this very book out in its first release.

That pitchfork, I'm proud—though pained—to announce, has gone nowhere in that time.

A standing ovation goes out to my family & those who, though not of my blood, are just as much my family (if not more) who have, in some way or another, offered up their own individual brand of support; from optimistic cheers-to-motivating jeers and those who did me the favor of simply not getting in the way (never underestimate the benefit you serve by NOT being a hurdle).

This release of "Curtain Call: A Death Metal Novel" was made all the gnarlier with the contributions of the musical mastermind and close personal friend, Steve Perman. Between multiple levels of editing & consultations with Steve, this book has seen well over a dozen professional gazes all for the sake of turning it into a true rock show (any hiccups at this point are my fault entirely).

Then, of course, I'd like to cast out a "ROCK ON" to both Jennifer Warrick Davis (of The Mystical World of Books Reviews) and the annual Blogger Book Fair Awards for helping to make *Curtain Call's* sexy cover that much more pretty with your kind words & awards (winner of both 2013's best occult AND best paranormal thriller?? HELLS-TO-THE-YEA!!)—you've both brought a true and eternal blush to the deepest, darkest crevices of my core.

Also throwing down the love for my readers with The Legion for all the excitement and support from the get-go—you're the reason I do what I do; The Literary Dark Emperor loves you all!—as well as my colleagues with Tiger Dynasty Publishing for being EXACTLY who I need them to be as well.

To all those who didn't make the lyrics, know that you're present in the rhythm; this book (and many—if not all—of my other titles could never have been without all of you).

Rock out, write on, & eternal love for The Legion <3
Nathan Squiers
(The Literary Dark Emperor)

THEY CREEP

In the walls and under the floors.
(They creep)
Up the stairs and through the doors.
(They creep)

In the forest or in the street.
(They creep)
Padding along on silent feet.
(They creep)

They're the scourge of all dreams;
The source of all screams.
They flourish from our pain.
These terrible frights
That plague all our nights.
They'll leave you completely insane.

They're the thoughts that make you tick.
That make you fret;
That's their trick.

They're the scourge of all dreams;
The source of all screams.
They flourish from our pain.
These terrible frights,

That plague all our nights.
They've driven us insane.

(They creep)
(They creep)
(They creep)
(They...)

PALE ANTHEM

A half-filled cup,
What do you see?
A horrid life?
Or serenity?

Now what if some cruel fucker,
Came and drank the rest?
Can you still find the good inside?
Does it even exist?

And this is the mindset,
That we teach our young:
Enjoy all the potential,
Before it is all gone.

And all the laughter we once knew,
Has become a painful sin.
All that's left is all the tears,
That we fight to keep within.

And so we take that empty glass
And smash it on the floor.
We let the shards into our lives,
So we can finally feel once more.

Fight for the right to live!
Fight for the right to laugh!
And when someone gets in your way,
Empty their fucking glass!

Prologue

"ALRIGHT, EVERYBODY," the announcer's voice paused and allowed a squeal of feedback to pass, "GIVE IT UP FOR THE BLOODTONES!"

The audience's roar overwhelmed the booming voice's dying echo as a pair of fog machines began to pour a thick mist across the stage. With the ghostly wisps crawling across the stage floor, a series of backlights came to life and the five silhouettes of the band's members came into view. The cheers grew louder in response.

A soft percussive buildup began, mingling with the audience's cries and soon surpassing them. The sharp crash of a cymbal shrieked and a spotlight beam shot down a split-second before an explosive impact on the bass-drum, giving the audience their first look at William Jones—perched behind his 19-piece custom drum set—as he raised his tattooed arms over his head before bringing them down to begin the song. Though he had done his best to reign in his messy brown hair several renegade strands pulled free from the elastic and fell in front of his green eyes. Ignoring the minor inconvenience, he pinched the ring at the left corner of his lip between his teeth and drove on.

A deep series of heavy thrums and growling twangs joined in then and resounded across the arena. At that moment two more spotlights shone down and illuminated Derek Sumner—stooped over his brick-red 5-string Fender Jaguar bass—and the band's rhythm guitarist, Brian Rains. As Derek's nimble fingers galloped across the strings his bowed head and gold-dyed hair bobbed methodically to the beat; his black, sweat-glazed skin shimmering like obsidian under the intense light. On the opposite side of the stage, Brian worked the strings of his Warlock guitar; its blood-red body the exact shade of his swaying Mohawk.

Rampaging on, the bass-drum thundered again and another spotlight brought David, their lead guitarist, into view; his long, black hair partially covering a pair of gray-blue eyes that stared out at the audience with animal ferocity as his fingers stalked across the neck of his sandy-brown Ibanez Super Strat.

As the intro's buildup climaxed Brian leapt into the air and Derek swung his bass out like a medieval warrior; a growling feminine voice calling out to the audience.

"LET ME HEAR YOU FUCKING SCREAM!"

The energy in the arena reached climactic heights and the audience's shrieks doubled in effort as the final spotlight turned on. There, on the edge of the stage, Rebecca Gespon came into view, perched and gazing out over the crowd. Though she was the smallest member of the band, what Bekka lacked in stature she more than made up for with enthusiasm; an enthusiasm that often had her band-mates struggling to keep up. Her bright blue eyes shimmered, fed by the roar of the crowd. Tossing her bright purple hair to the side, she brought the microphone to her black-painted lips and let loose a howl that trumped the combined cheers of the audience.

That sound—that raw, exuberant energy—was her entire purpose of being.

As the tempo shifted, Bekka stood and wetted her lips; bringing the microphone to her mouth.

"SLITHER AND SHAKE!
WITHER AND QUAKE!
NOTHING TO LEAVE,
EVERYTHING TO TAKE!"

Will slammed down on the cymbals and started an aggressive assault on the toms. His feet came down again and again on the pedals as he set the pace.

"COIL AND STRIKE!
TOIL AND STRIFE!
EVERYTHING'S THE SAME,
WHEN SCORED WITH A KNIFE!"

With Derek pumping out a strong bass-line, David jumped in with another riff; his fingers a blur on the neck of his guitar as Brian leaned in towards his own microphone, letting out a deep growl that overlapped with Bekka's voice.

"WITH THEIR VENOM WE TAKE CHANCES!
WITH THEIR FLESH WE SEEK ROMANCES!
WE DARE NOT HONOR SECOND GLANCES,
AS THEY ENGAGE IN SERPENT DANCES!"

The two guitarists moved together towards Brian's microphone as Derek slapped a chord sharply with the side of his thumb before leaning towards his own mike stand; all three syncing their voices to join with Bekka's.

"FEAR!
(SLITHER AND SHAKE)
REVERE!
(COIL AND STRIKE)"

As they finished, Brian took a step back and David returned to his mark. Bekka, looking over her shoulder as she rocked the mike stand on its base with the beat, locked eyes with Brian and grinned. They were all harmonized; both in body and in mind.

Their performance was going perfectly!

"THEY MOVE AS ONE!
TOGETHER AS ONE!
NEVER FORGETTING:
THEY'RE FOREVER AS ONE!"

As Brian advanced on his microphone Bekka withdrew from hers and let her body succumb to the music—her tiny body thrashing with the beat—as her band-mate's growling voice returned.

"SO FAR FROM THE FANG,
BUT FOREVER TOO CLOSE!
BLESSED BE,
THE OROBOROS!"

Bekka continued moving to the music as she returned to her microphone; her and Brian's voices once again synchronizing.

"WITH THEIR VENOM WE TAKE CHANCES!
WITH THEIR FLESH WE SEEK ROMANCES!
WE DARE NOT GIVE THEM SECOND GLANCES,
AS THEY ENGAGE IN SERPENT DANCES!"

The crowd shrieked and hollered and thrashed before them; their combined mass taking on a serpentine shape that complimented the song's lyrics all-too-well. Soaking in their cheers, Bekka approached the edge of the stage and turned, smiling at her still-performing band-mates and spreading her arms a moment before allowing her body to fall from the stage. Somewhere in the distance the faint shout of an angered security guard could be heard, but it was too late.

The raised hands of the crowd caught and supported her, and as she allowed her body to be taken out into the sea of music-lovers she stared up at the arena's rooftop and took in the kaleidoscope of lights.

That was when she first spotted them.

At first she mistook them for plastic bags—possibly some trash that had fallen victim to a sporadic air current. However, focusing on them, she could see from the way they darted between the rafters that there was some sort of consciousness driving them. While there were already too many to count she was shocked to see that more were coming; emerging through a dark, shifting tear that faded rapidly behind them. As the rift vanished, the beings' colors—vibrant shades of blues, reds, and greens—became brighter. The beautiful display was short lived, however, and before Bekka could react they converged above her and began their descent.

JUST AS WELL

This will be the final hour.
(It's just as well)
Keeping with the sacred needs.
(May we rot in Hell)
A moment that'll be forever ours.
(It's just as well)
Lost within the cosmic reeds.
(It's just as fucking well)

As bitter-sweet
As the Devil's teet.
You'd better believe
It's worth it in the end!

Crying!
(I can't stop crying!)
These fucking tears of blood!
Dying!
(You're all dying!)
In the resulting flood!

As bitter-sweet
As the Devil's teet.
You'd better believe
It's worth it in the end!

It's just as well.

It's just as well.

It's just as fucking well.

BURNT

There is an eternal fire that grows and spreads.
I can't help but stare into it.
So much chaos hidden within its charms,
Such danger in its beauty.

I stepped into the flames.
Despite your desperate calls.
And I was fucking burnt.
Within its scorching walls.
Now I'm little more than ash,
And your calls still go unheard.
You wretched, horrid piece of shit.
Now we're both burnt

You never cared for me at all.
Just the piece of me you owned.
And now I've taken that piece back.
And left you all alone.

Burn, you motherfucker,
In the fire you have wrought.
The fire that has burnt me,
Is the hatred that you've taught.

I stepped into the flames.

Despite your desperate calls.
And I was burnt! It's all your fault!
Within those scorching walls.
Now I'm little more than ash,
Just a burning memory.
And I hope it burns your heart to know.
Just what you did to me.

We're both burnt.
(burnt)
And I hope you burn forever.

PART ONE:
CHORDS & CHAOS

SPIDERS

We zip 'bout our lives,
Like hordes of blinded flies.
Clinging to our comforts,
Until the day we die.

(For every fly there is a spider.
For every life there is an end)

Death's plan for us is wondrous;
A spectacular design!
Inescapable.
Twisted.
Divine.

They creep and crawl like nightmares,
Though we never can awake.
And with our bodies cold and bound,
Our essence they will take!

(Their web will take us all!)

Zipping 'bout our lives,
Like hordes of blinded flies.
Just waiting for the moment.
That we hear all the spiders' cries.

Arachnid legs!
Arachnid Legs!
Scraping in our ears!
Their toxic bites scorch our minds;
They spindle threads with all our fears.

They're creeping, crawling nightmares!
And we never can awake!
And with our bodies cold and bound,
Our essence they will take!

A DARK MIRROR

In a dark mirror,
I see all I am not.
I see what I will never be.
And know what I forgot

There's danger in reflections.
They reveal forbidden facts.
Within their insidious connections
Are hideous attacks!

(DAMN)
If there's not more to see!
(DAMN)
If it's not taking me!
(DAMN)
If I don't want to be
The creature that it's making me.

Shine on
(Hone sin)
Shine on
(Hone sin)

ONE

The two guitarists stumbled into their apartment; their instruments knocking against the doorframe as they entered. David, the first past the threshold, stuffed his keys back into his jeans and navigated down the narrow hallway and into the small living room. Brian, only a few steps behind him, cursed as his guitar case banged against the wall once again.

"I swear to fucking Christ! We need to get out of this piece-of-shit shack!"

David sighed and shook his head as he stood his

guitar case in the living room closet, "We don't have the money for it."

Brian scoffed but knew better than to try and argue. After all, it wasn't the first time he'd brought it up only to be shot down. Still shaking his head in defeat he approached the closet with his own case and tried to fit it inside the cramped space.

He swore again.

David ignored his fit as he dropped himself into his spot on their ratty couch.

Finally giving up on the closet, altogether, Brian leaned his guitar against the wall and joined David on the couch; the worn-out cushion sinking under him and forming an uncomfortable pocket. They were silent, both staring straight ahead at their dated television.

Brian sighed, "Don't suppose we could at least afford a new TV?"

"Never watched enough of it to care," David said with a shrug.

Brian threw his head back, exasperated, "God dammit! I know that you're fine with the simple things—or whatever you like to call it—but we're better than this!"

David shrugged again, "I don't see a problem with how we're living."

"Yea, yea!" Brian scowled, "I should move in with Will. *He* knows how to live!"

David smirked and cocked his head, "And what if he *bit* you?"

"And what if you *ate* me?" Brian shot back.

David laughed at the question and settled further into his spot. Sneering, Brian tried to do the same; rolling his shoulders into cushion to try and get comfortable.

"The least we could do is get a decent couch."

"This conversation is over," David leaned his head back and closed his eyes.

"Whatever you say, boss," Brian grumbled, "I mean, I'm not the one that sleeps on the damn floor! I just thought you'd be happy with a piece of furniture that doesn't smell like one of your cousins took a *piss* on it!"

David's eyes shot open and the corner of his lip lifted; an angry snarl beginning to rumble inside of his throat.

Eager to change the subject, Brian teased one of the studs in his lip, "So… uh, how do you think we did tonight?"

David's glare softened and he finally shook his head at him, "You're some piece of work, you know that?"

Brian smirked, "So I've heard."

David sighed, "I think we did well. It was probably one of our best so far."

Brian teased the piercing a moment longer, "What about Bekka?"

"What *about* Bekka?" David arched an eyebrow at him.

Brian felt his cheeks go hot, "I… I don't know! I just thought she seemed a little—y'know?—twitchy or something."

David frowned, "Twitchy?"

21

Brian nodded, "Yea. Especially after the first song; after she dove into the crowd."

David shook his head, "I didn't notice anything." He smirked, "But, then again, I don't watch her like you do."

Another wave of warmth flooded Brian's cheeks and he looked away to try and hide his blush. "So much for the keen observational skills of a predator," he sighed and pulled himself from the sinking cushion and headed for the kitchen, eager for an escape from the conversation, "I'm gonna go nuke myself some dinner. You want something?"

"I'm not too hungry," David answered behind him, "Maybe just a few of those Hot Pockets."

Brian laughed and shook his head, "Right. Sure."

As he left the living room and flipped the light switch he was greeted by the loud and angry hum of ancient appliances. The kitchen, like every room of their apartment, was a miniature mockery of what it should have been and in no way suited to prepare a decent meal. Fortunately for them, however, neither knew how to cook.

Though he'd succeeded in fleeing from the taunting eyes of his friend, Brian couldn't help but continue pondering Bekka's strange behavior as he went about preparing their dinners. He was surprised, despite what David had said, that he hadn't noticed. While he knew that his friend didn't have feelings for her, he *did* have a tendency to watch over her with the nearly obsessive manner of an older brother...

... or a loyal guard dog.

Back in high school, David had been the loner; others

often avoiding or even teasing him for being quiet and nervous around others. Despite the opinions of her peers, Bekka had shown no reluctance in first approaching him and offering him her—and, by association, Brian's—friendship. Though hesitant at first, David's shyness melted away immediately when their small-talk turned towards music.

As it turned out, the class misfit was a closet-case heavy metal fanatic and Brian, who had been playing guitar for most of his life, soon after found himself teaching their new friend how to play the guitar. Their friendship had been sealed the moment David's fingers first touched the strings.

That summer, during a sleepover at Bekka's—after several hours of videogames and binge-eating had driven the three to pass out in the living room—Brian and Bekka had awakened to discover David's secret.

At first they were terrified by the bestial snarls; afraid that some feral creature had somehow gotten inside the house. After a terror-filled moment of uncertainty, they found that the source was David—still asleep in her father's recliner. They had watched, horrified, as their friend kicked and pitched in his sleep; his already-misshapen body twitching violently as his bones snapped and reshaped themselves. Groaning and whimpering in pain, David lashed out at whatever had been haunting his dreams with discolored arms that bulged with new muscle. As his mouth parted to let out another snarl, they realized that even his face was being affected by the change. Howling again in pain, he'd shot upright in the chair as his eyes—bright and cat-like—opened wide and locked on them.

Nobody had said anything; Bekka and Brian too terrified and their friend too embarrassed. Then, slowly, David's body began to shrivel and pale; his bones reshaping once again as they returned to normal.

"That"—Bekka had started, breaking the silence—"was the *coolest* thing I have ever seen!"

Both Brian and David had nearly collapsed.

As the tension in the room had subsided, David told them that he'd had a nightmare. The two, caring little about his dreams, demanded to know what they'd witnessed. Reluctant to disclose his secret, David was slow to answer, but finally explained that he was a "therion". When the term was met with more confusion he'd sighed and used a more understood term…

"Werewolf"

The microwave chimed and Brian pried it open with a nearby screwdriver set aside solely for that purpose. Tossing the Hot Pockets on a paper plate, Brian cursed as a glob of molten cheese burnt his palm. Still grumbling, he picked up his own plate of chicken Parmesan with his free hand and started back towards the living room.

After handing David his food, Brian sat and stared at his own plate with the realization that he'd made himself a meal he wasn't hungry for.

David grunted before swallowing a mouthful of food and cleared his throat, "Why don't you give her a call if you're still worried?"

Brian shook his head, "And what if I'm wrong? I'd look like a total ass!"

Looking away, David shrugged and stuffed the last half of one of the Hot Pockets into his mouth, "Suit yourself."

Brian sighed. It was late anyway. She was probably already asleep. Furthermore, if something *was* wrong, he was sure that dragging her out of bed to talk about it was the last thing she wanted to do. He sneered at his untouched plate of food and passed it over. Confused, David looked up at him as he pulled himself from the couch.

"You aren't hungry?" He asked, making no attempt to hide his hopeful tone.

Brian shook his head, "All yours, buddy."

Once inside his bedroom, Brian navigated through the darkness—ignoring the broken light switch by the door and relying on memory to guide him. He paused along the way to pull off his boots and peel himself out of his shirt and pants. Free of the minor discomforts, he palmed the surface of his dresser and picked up the first CD case his hand touched. Taking his mystery prize with him he ran his hand across the countertop until his thumb found the "POWER" button of his old, broken television. Though more-than half the screen had gone black years ago, a dull, gray glow emanated as power surged through it. Opening the case, Brian repeated his blind button-search with his old stereo, eventually finding and pressing the "OPEN" button and feeding it the CD. As the tray retreated and began to scan the disc he lay down on his bed as the haunting opening to Dir en Grey's "Ouroboros" crept through the room.

TWO

"COME ON, SWEETHEART! JUNIOR'S GONNA BE READY FOR HIGH SCHOOL BY THE TIME YOU'RE OUT OF MY FUCKING WAY!" Will honked his horn at a woman with a stroller.

Bekka frowned, "Will, stop it! She has the right-of-way!"

"My ass!" Will growled through gritted teeth, "She's abusing her rights as a pedestrian!"

Brian shook his head, "Dude! The light's still red! Chill out!"

"Bitch is lucky I don't plow through her and her spawn!" Will's rant continued.

David sighed and rolled his eyes, "Just relax! We're almost there."

"He's right, Will," Bekka's voice was calm as she reached over the seat to squeeze their driver's shoulder, "It won't be much longer."

Brian rolled his eyes and braced himself as the van jolted forward with the changing light. He had taken the seat next to Bekka in the second row of Will's van, leaving the back open for David and their equipment. Derek, riding shotgun, stayed quiet through the ordeal as he puffed on a cigar and stared out of his window at the passing scenery.

Like always, practice was held at Will's—the only member of the band with both a vehicle and enough space to fit everyone comfortably. While he had taken his fair share of abuse it was no secret that the others were jealous of his luxurious, stone-walled mansion. Resting atop a tall hill, the estate was framed by two willows in the front yard, which Will paid to keep maintained. As the van rocketed around a bend in the road the pair of trees came into view and everyone let out a relieved sigh.

"Home-sweet-fucking-home!" Will said as he turned into his driveway and started up the hill; the hanging branches audibly brushing against the roof as they passed under them.

"Indeed," Derek said, breaking his own silence, "It's a miracle we're still alive and not being arrested for your reckless driving."

Will grinned as he parked the van in his garage and pressed the remote to close the door, "You got something to do with that, magic-man? Hmm?"

Derek shook his head, "There isn't a spell strong enough to protect us from you."

Will cackled and slapped Derek on the back; his usual, good-natured attitude quickly returning, "You got that fucking right!"

Brian rolled his eyes again as he helped himself out of the van; Bekka and David not far behind.

Several years earlier—a short time after the three of them had decided to start their own band—they had come across Derek during a walk through the city. Bekka was the first to notice the nearly inaudible, melodic sounds and had looked up to notice a boy their age sitting on his stoop and absently plucking at an old bass guitar.

He had been wearing a Bob Marley tee and a pair of loose-fitting, cut-up jeans; his ears pierced and stretched to the size of pencil erasers—a pair of white plugs occupying the space and contrasting with his black skin. As he played his head swayed and his braided hair swung to-and-fro.

"You're very good," Bekka had finally said, unsure of how else to get his attention.

His fingers continued to dance across the frets as he looked up and smiled back at her, "Thank you."

"How come I've never seen you at school?" She'd asked.

Still playing, he'd motioned with his head towards the door behind him, "My grandpa home-schools me."

For some time they had stood there, too nervous to ask the question they all had in mind but too captivated and hopeful to leave. Instead, they sat down and listened as best they could.

"I'm Bekka," she introduced herself a short time later when she had finished her soda, "This is Brian and David."

Only then had the young man stopped playing; freeing a hand to shake theirs, "I'm Derek."

With the mood lightened, Bekka had taken the opportunity to ask him what they had wanted to all along.

"You're in a band?" He'd asked, his voice raised with new interest, "What do you play?"

"Brian and David play guitar and I sing," she'd answered, "Though I *can* play the piano."

Derek frowned at that, "Why don't you, then?"

"Doesn't go well with heavy metal," Brian had explained for her.

Derek frowned, "Metal, huh?"

The three began to see their chances crumble under the weight of his skepticism.

"Yea," Brian jumped in, hoping to turn the tides, "But we're trying to create our own sound. We just don't have a bassist or a drummer."

Nodding at this, Derek had looked down at his bass as though it would provide him with the answer. After a long, tense moment he smiled and shrugged, "Can't hurt to try, I suppose. Though, it's going be hard without a drummer."

"I know. But it's been so hard finding anybody who can play worth a damn," Bekka had said.

"I might know a guy," Derek had offered, his smile returning, "He plays every now-and-again at the bar my Grandpa works at." He frowned and looked away for a moment and shook his head, "But you probably won't want him."

"Why?" Bekka frowned, "What's wrong with him?"

"He's just… different," Derek had said, dodging the question.

Bekka smirked, "That's fine; 'different' doesn't bother us."

Derek sighed at that and gave his bass a few light taps with his thumb, "I guess you can try. Just remember that I warned you."

That night, answering to an invite from Derek, Will had showed up, pulling into Bekka's driveway in a white van. As the pierced and tattooed stranger stepped out of his vehicle, David's lip had peeled in an angry snarl. Seeing their friend's reaction, Brian and Bekka's eyes darted back-and-forth between their friend and the newcomer. As Will approached, toting all of his equipment with surprising ease, he looked up and narrowed his eyes back at David.

"Isn't it against the law to have dogs outside without a leash?"

David snarled at the insult, taking a step toward Will, "Shut up, leech!" He swiveled his head then to glare at Derek,

"You invited a *vampire* to join our band?"

Despite the growing tension, Will had smirked, a fang poking out as he did, "So we gonna do this or not?"

Bekka, despite her obvious nervousness, stepped forward to put a hand on David's shoulder. With her friend slowly relaxing, she'd nodded to Will, "You can set up your stuff in the garage."

The tryout had been incredible!

As Will played everyone stared, awe-struck, at the blur that his hands had become as he belted out a solo. With all the attention on Will the three of them had been startled when Derek—who had taken the opportunity to plug his instrument—joined in with a smooth bass-line.

It wasn't long before all five were plugged-in and joining the effort and The Bloodtones were born.

Brian waited as David finished pulling their instruments out of the back of the van before pulling the sliding door shut. Still sitting behind the wheel, Will continued his playful joking with Derek; the effects of the sun poisoning rapidly wearing off. As it had turned out, sunlight wasn't instantly fatal to Will and others of his kind, but— through some complex biological process that Brian never cared to remember—exposure was unpleasant and, when prolonged, dangerous.

"That's it! I'm getting tinted windows!" Will boasted as he pushed open his door, the rusted hinges howling like bad punk-rock.

Brian smirked, "Long as you're splurging, why not

just get yourself a new van?"

Will scowled and patted the van on the hood, "And what would become of this good ol' girl?"

Brian shook his head, "Who cares! It's a rusted piece-of-shit!"

"'She'!"—Will corrected—"And *she* is a finely tuned and loyal machine!"

"*She* is an outdated, gas-guzzling waste of parts!" Brian said.

Will narrowed his eyes at him.

David cleared his throat then, "Are we going to practice or whine about our only mode of transportation?"

"You two can fight to the death later," Derek mumbled around his cigar, "I know I'll have fun watching that."

Bekka let out a nervous sigh, "C-can we talk for a moment?" They all looked at her, surprised by her meek tone, and she blushed under their collective stare, "I... I have something I need to tell you guys."

"Sure," Will smiled, "Band meeting it is, then!"

With no argument, they all stepped out of the garage and into Will's basement. As Will and Bekka started up the stairs Brian, Will and Derek paused to set down their equipment before following; nobody saying a word as the nervousness Bekka's tone had instilled grew.

Though Will presented himself as what people would expect from the drummer of a heavy metal band, the inside of his home was a different story. Where most would expect stained and broken furniture and walls littered in horrific and morbid movie and music posters there was, instead, an expensive, matching living room set and several meticulously-framed and carefully-hung photographs dating back several decades. In each corner of the room a series of speakers had been installed that were wirelessly connected to a large and up-to-date entertainment system that was displayed proudly ahead of them as they emerged from the basement.

Grunge, it appeared, was not powerful enough to pull Will away from living the good life.

Brian smirked at the sight and shot David a look, "*This* is how it's done!"

David only shook his head and continued past him.

Derek, the last one up the stairs, carefully slid what remained of his cigar into a metal tube to save and let out a heavy billow of thick, pale-brown smoke as he reached into the back of his jeans' pocket and retrieved a shiny flask, "So what's this all about?" He asked, unscrewing the top and taking a quick pull. As he did, the acrid scent of liquor and peppermint filled the room.

Brian sneered and turned away.

Will allowed himself to fall back into a wide, leather armchair and looked up at Bekka; concern edging across his normally carefree face, "Yea, what gives?"

David, despite the expensive collection of furniture surrounding him, sat on the floor and curled his legs underneath him.

Brian watched as Bekka's eyes took in each of them

one-by-one. Finally, her eyes came to rest on him and her lips curled in a slight smile.

Bekka sighed, "Last night—during our performance—something happened to me."

"While you were crowd-surfing?" Derek asked, still standing with the flask in his hand.

Bekka chewed her lip and nodded.

Brian frowned, looking first at her and then the others; nobody seemed surprised. Even David—despite what he'd said the previous night—seemed unaffected by Bekka's news.

The lying bastard!

"So what happened out there?" David asked, cocking his head to one side.

Brian scowled, "Did some perv take a grab at your ass?"

Will laughed, "When does some perv *not* take a grab at her ass?"

Derek shook his head, "Perhaps we'd like to let her finish?"

Once again all eyes were on Bekka, who shifted uncomfortably under the renewed limelight.

Brian took a step towards her, "Bekka?"

Still shivering, Bekka smiled weakly and gave him a reassuring nod, "Some... some *things* came out of the ceiling when I was offstage."

"What do you mean?" David asked.

Brian frowned, "What kind of things, Bekka?"

Bekka shook her head. "I don't know. They looked like neon jellyfish," she looked down, "I know that sounds *insane*, b-but I don't know how else to describe them."

"'neon jellyfish'…?" Will raised a pierced eyebrow and chuckled, shaking his head, "What sort of trippy shit did you score?"

Bekka's nervousness vanished as her eyes narrowed at him, "I wasn't on drugs!"

The others' eyes widened at Bekka's outburst. Though they all knew she avoided drugs and alcohol like the plague, it was unusual for her to get upset when others joked about it. Will, the most surprised, held out his hands and nodded.

"All right. Drug-free trip. That's cool, too."

Bekka made a face and Brian thought that she was about to cry and he started towards her again. Before he could take another step, though, she shook her head, stopping him.

"At first"—she continued with the story—"I thought it was just the lights—you know, playing tricks on my eyes. But then they…" She shook her head.

"Bekka, what happened out there?" Brian asked.

"They… went inside me," Bekka confessed in a whisper.

Everyone was silent for a long time.

Will shook his head, as confused as everyone else, "So you were raped by the neon jellyfish?"

Bekka's eyes shifted to him and turned to daggers, "So help me, Will, I will *rape* you with your god-damn drumsticks!"

Derek took another calm swig from the flask, "It's alright, Bekka. We're just having a hard time understanding."

Will grumbled and nodded.

David shook his head, "Did these things hurt you?"

Bekka held a hand over her sternum. "They felt… like water balloons," she laughed nervously and shook her head, "Water balloons shot from a bazooka. It hurt like hell! But by the time I was back onstage I didn't feel a thing.

Derek studied her, "You didn't feel *anything*?"

Bekka shook her head, "No. I was just—I don't know—nervous."

Brian looked at her, "Nervous?"

Bekka nodded.

"Nervous about what?" David asked.

Bekka fidgeted, "That somebody was after me."

Derek narrowed his eyes, "That *who* was after you?"

Bekka only shrugged.

Brian gave her a reassuring smile, "It could've just been nerves. I mean, we *have* been under a lot of pressure lately. Maybe the stress is just starting to get to you. Maybe…"—he frowned, knowing how the others would react to what he had to say,—"maybe we should take some time off."

"Are you out of your fucking mind?" Will roared, shooting out of the chair, "Are you forgetting how hard we've worked to get this far?"

"Will's right," Bekka said; strength and determination

returning to her voice, "We can't sacrifice all of our efforts just because of this."

Brian glared at Will before looking at Bekka, "But you just said—"

Derek shook his head as he returned his flask to his pocket, "Either Brian's right and this whole thing is stress-related or it's something worse. Either way it's in our best interests to be careful."

David pulled himself from the floor and rose to his full height, "I agree. Either way this deserves our full attention."

"This is insane!" Will growled, "Do you all *really* think that it's going to be that easy; that we can just drop off the grid and then pick up where we left off?"

"Exactly!" Bekka said, the last traces of fear and doubt disappearing, "Whatever this is, it's not going to get any better just sitting around doing nothing!" She locked eyes with Brian, "I'd go crazy!"

"You promise that you'll be alright?" David asked.

Bekka nodded, "I promise."

"So suddenly it meant nothing?" Derek's arms were crossed in front of his chest, "What happened to the fear and panic we all saw a moment ago?"

"Derek," Bekka blushed, "it was just scary." She shrugged and smiled at him, "And nothing's happened since then."

Brian scoffed, "So you just want us to ignore all of what you've told us?"

Bekka frowned, "I just don't see any reason to give up doing what we love for something that I might've just imagined."

Though he was clearly displeased with the situation, Derek remained silent. Slowly, as the rest of them came to a unanimous decision, everyone turned their heads to face Brian.

"Well?" Will pressed, "Does his royal Mohawked highness have any more objections?"

"Fine!" Brian sighed and turned away, "We'll ignore it! But the moment this gets worse—and we *know* that shit like this *always* gets worse!—then we take a break and figure this out!"

"Yea, yea! Shrinks, psychics, and séances; the whole nine yards!" Will walked past, heading for the basement, "Now can we *please* get to practicing? I suddenly feel the need to hit something repeatedly!"

Getting all five band-mates downstairs proved to be a slow and tedious process; one involving a line to use the bathroom and another to raid Will's refrigerator. Derek— whose tastes in liquor were a more exotic—was disappointed that all their host had to offer was imported beer and expensive wine. The resulting argument served to entertain David, who sat by and watched as he chugged one of Will's beers. Despite his friend's enjoyment, Brian thought otherwise and stormed from the kitchen with an angry and disgusted sneer as he popped the top to his Coke.

By the time they had all finished and gotten downstairs and plugged in, more than an hour had passed.

Everyone watched, impatient, as Derek—who was still shaking his head at Will's limited tastes in alcohol—adjusted his shoulder strap to a comfortable length before plucking a string to begin tuning. The sound rumbled, rich and heavy, and before it had completely faded another string was plucked, followed by another. Derek's eyes remained closed; the bassist relying solely on the sound of the previous note to adjust the next.

Brian, like everyone else, relied on their electric tuners to get the job done, and had long-since finished. Derek, however, found this a cheap and "soulless" method. Finally, when he was finished, he opened his eyes and looked down at the bass' golden-brown body with admiration.

Brian raised an eyebrow at the scene; no matter how long he'd known him, Derek had some unsettling quirks.

"Is the magic-man done with his ritual yet?" Will teased.

Derek smirked back at him and rubbed absently at one of his earlobes, which had been stretched over time to allow jewelry over an inch thick to hang therein, "Still a riot every time I hear it, Will."

"Are you girls going to chatter all day or can we do this, already?" Bekka spoke into her microphone to emphasize her point.

Brian idly plucked the C string and sighed, "Yes, please let's."

Laying a fingertip on the still-rattling cymbal to silence it, Will gave an exaggerated salute, "Ready when you are, captain!"

"Alright, boys," Bekka's voice started to turn to a growl in anticipation, "let's see if you can keep up!"

THREE

The band's otherwise quiet and composed lead
guitarist was the worst of the five when it came to drinking.
While Brian wouldn't allow alcohol in their apartment, he
had little control of David's addiction outside of their home.
That being the case, when Will made the suggestion that
night of Pauly's Pub—the bar Derek's grandfather worked
at—David all-but freed his inner beast with excitement and
nearly broke his Gibson trying to stuff it in its case. While the
others thought that David's reaction to the promise of getting
wasted was hilarious, Brian and Bekka shared a defeated sigh

and reluctantly climbed into Will's van.

After all, it beat walking home.

Derek rode up front with Will, who tapped his fingers against his steering wheel in rhythm to the stereo. In the back, David bounced like an excited child. And in the middle, sandwiched between them all, Brian and Bekka traded annoyed sighs at the scene around them.

Before the van had come to a complete stop in the parking lot, David was tugging at the door. Will laughed at this and, as he finished parking, unlocked the door for him and sent him off with a high-pitched "go get it, boy". Shortly after, Derek and Will, still laughing, went through the doors; the sound of their giddiness fading as the door slammed shut behind them, leaving Brian and Bekka alone in the lot.

"Fucking assholes," Brian grumbled as he reached into his jacket and pulled out his pack of Marlboros.

"They're just trying to have a good time," Bekka said, her voice giving away her own repulsion.

Brian nodded, rolling his eyes, "If you say so," he grumbled as he lit up a cig and took a long drag, "So now you're defending their alcoholism?"

"Not everyone who drinks is an alcoholic," Bekka frowned, narrowing her eyes at the cigarette.

"Oh yea?" Brian raised an eyebrow at her, "So when did you start drinking?"

Bekka blushed, "Well, I didn't say it was *my* idea of a good time... but 'to each their own', right?"

"There's better ways to have a good time!" He spat

out the words along with tiny bursts of smoke.

Bekka coughed and Brian frowned and adjusted himself so he was downwind, "Didn't you say that you were going to *quit* those things?"

Smirking, he shrugged and flicked an ash before returning the cigarette to his mouth, "To each their own, right?"

Bekka frowned, "So you still haven't told them, huh?"

"What good would it do?" Brian asked.

"It might help them to understand; maybe they'd even cut back for your sake," she smiled.

"Or it might make them pity me and get all weird around me," Brian countered, "Besides, I don't need to give them a reason to not get drunk."

Bekka frowned at him, "You *kill* yourself with those damn cigarettes and you expect them to believe that you don't approve of drinking for *health* purposes?"

Brian took the cigarette between his fingers and held it up in front of him, "This isn't going to kill me."

Bekka put her hands on her hips, "Oh?"

"Nope." He returned the cigarette to his lips and made a show of taking another drag, "The *cancer* will."

"And what do you think *causes* the cancer, retard?" She argued.

"With my luck? Everything else," he laughed.

Bekka glared and drove a fist into his shoulder, "Not funny, asshole!"

Brian yelped from the punch and laughed, "Hey! Ow!

What was that for?" The sight of Bekka's sad face caught him like another punch and his laughter stopped, "What's the matter?"

"You... you don't *want* to die," she locked her tear-filled eyes with his, "do you?"

Blowing out twin trails of smoke through his nostrils, Brian shrugged, "It'd be easy to find another rhythm guitarist."

"God dammit, Brian! That's not funny!" Bekka yelled, hitting him again.

Brian bit his lip and looked down at her; the Marilyn Monroe stud on the right corner of her upper lip quivering. Unsure of what to do, he pinched the cigarette between his teeth and reached out to put a hand on her shoulder.

"Hey. I'm sorry. I didn't mean to—" His apology was cut short as the single light over the entrance flickered and buzzed, flashing brighter before dying out and throwing the two into near-total darkness. As they backed away from the bar and deeper into the parking lot, the nearby streetlights did the same, burning brighter for a brief moment before going out entirely. Brian frowned and glanced at Bekka, "Do you think it's a power outage?"

Bekka shook her head and motioned back towards the bar; the lights inside still shining brightly.

Confused, Brian flicked his cigarette to the ground and crushed it under his foot, "I swear if this is some kind of joke—"

"Who could joke like this?" There was fear in Bekka's

voice.

Brian frowned, "Come on. We should get inside."

"But you hate—"

"It's fine. C'mon. I'll get you a cranberry juice."

The roar inside the bar spilled out into the darkness as they stepped inside; an old jukebox buzzing and whining around an indecipherable song. Through the bustle of the crowd, they spotted their band-mates sitting at the bar. Will was sitting ramrod-straight on his stool as he finished his beer and pushed the stein forward for a refill. Next to him, chatting with the bartender, Derek sipped casually at what Brian could only assume was an exotic and overly complicated concoction. Finally, sitting at the end of the bar and hunched over the counter, David chugged from a pitcher. After a moment he paused and sat up long enough to let out a belch that shook his whole body and threatened to topple him off his stool. When he was certain that he would remain upright, he returned to the pitcher and emptied it before setting it beside Will's. Brian scowled at the sight of his already-inebriated friend and leaned towards Bekka.

"How many do you think he's had by now?"

There was no reason to worry about Derek—an enthusiastic-yet-responsible drinker—who had long-since learned his limit and was not afraid of admitting that he'd had enough. The same could be said for Will who, despite his seemingly endless thirst, was biologically guaranteed to be sober at the end of the night since vampires could not get drunk.

Werewolves, however, could.

She shook her head, taking in the spectacle of David's impatient ramblings at the bartender, "I shudder to imagine."

The two of them were halfway through the bar when the jukebox skipped and began to whine. Bekka and Brian turned, startled, and watched as a series of sparks began to shoot out from the plug that fed the malfunctioning machine. The already distorted sound of "Free Bird" turned into an unbearable screech and, as the patrons began to shout and curse, one of the busboys ran out and yanked the plug from the wall.

With the howling machine rendered silent and peace returning to the bar everyone cheered and applauded their pockmarked young savior. Staring out at the crowd and blushing, the busboy looked out at his adoring audience before making a show of bowing. Responding to the calamity, the bar's manager was quick to find a dolly and drag the jukebox to the back room.

"What the hell is going on?" Brian frowned as he and Bekka closed the distance to join their friends. "Hey! We need to get out of here!"

David smiled at the sight of them and grabbed Brian's shoulder, "Oh man! Did you guys see that?" He slurred.

Will narrowed his eyes in the direction of the retreating jukebox and shook his head, "I'll admit, that *was* new."

Derek, the only one that seemed to be paying attention, turned to Brian, "What's going on?"

Growing ever-more nervous, Bekka pointed with a shaky hand towards the door, "S-something weird happened out there."

"I don't know if you were paying attention," Will pointed towards the door the jukebox had disappeared into with his thumb, "but something weird just happened in here!"

David, still holding Brian's arm, nodded, "Did you see it?"

"Yea!" Brian said, prying off the drunk werewolf's hand, "We saw it! We need to get out of here! Like, now!"

Will frowned at him, "What are you talking about? That old machine's been here longer than *me*! It was bound to go to shit sooner or later!"

Brian growled, "No, god dammit, something's wrong! All the lights—"

Will leaned in his barstool to look over Brian's shoulder, "The lights look fine to me."

Brian turned to look outside where, sure enough, the lights in the parking lot were shining brightly.

Bekka shook her head, growing frantic, "But it's true! Something happened out there!"

"You're right," Derek spoke up, setting down his drink and standing out of his stool, "Something *did* happen, and it followed you in here!"

The others stared at him.

"But I don't *want* to leave yet!" David whined, reaching for his newly-filled pitcher and knocking it over.

As David cursed about his drink Will smirked at him, "I'm with Rover! I'm not about to let some crappy, old machine scare me away! I'm having fun!"

Derek turned and glared at them, "We are dealing with powerful energies! And I can't promise that it'll be a machine that dies the next time they decide to show themselves! Now let's go!"

Both the vampire and the werewolf grudgingly rose from their seats, but before they'd even started towards the door a shelf of liquor bottles behind the counter started to explode one-by-one.

"Out!" Derek whispered to the group, "Now!"

Nobody argued.

"What the hell was that?" Will demanded as they hurried towards the van.

"It's Bekka!" Derek answered, taking his seat.

Will started the van and scoffed, "Are you serious? I've never seen her do that before."

"It's not intentional, you moron!" Derek spat, "Just get us the hell out of here!"

Will frowned, shifting into gear and starting to pull out of the space, "Did you just call me a—"

"Shut up and drive!" Derek held his gaze on Will for a moment before turning in his seat, "Bekka, you need to relax!"

"What?" Bekka whimpered, "What did I do?"

"I don't know *how*, but you're casting spells!" Derek explained.

Brian looked up at that, "What?"

"But I don't *know* magic!" Bekka pleaded; her eyes wide. As her body trembled, the van lurched and the passenger-side window cracked.

"Relax!" Derek shouted.

"JESUS-FUCKING-CHRIST"—Will tightened his grip on the steering wheel and tapped the brakes in an attempt to regain control as the car jolted again—"DO WHAT HE SAYS!" The van lurched again and rocketed forward as he lost control of the accelerator.

Not knowing what to believe but wanting the chaos to end, Brian put his hand on Bekka's leg and gave it a squeeze. "Bekka, just breathe," her frantic eyes shifted to him; panic filling her features. Forcing himself to smile for her benefit, he gave her a reassuring nod, "It'll be alright, I promise."

Nodding, she closed her eyes and slowed her breathing, setting her head on his shoulder.

Another hiccup under the hood shook them and threatened to topple the van before everything went calm.

FOUR

The rest of the drive had been easy enough after they got past whatever Bekka was doing. They'd gotten her home without any further incident, and after a great deal of reassurance on her part they'd let her get out and go inside.

A short time later Will was pulling up to Brian and David's apartment building. By that point, David's inhuman anatomy had metabolized almost all of the alcohol in his system and he had, thankfully, sobered up. Werewolf or not, however, he was not beyond nature's wrath.

"Do we *need* to have that on?" He snarled as the first

static-laced whines issued from their TV.

Brian glanced over at his friend, who by that time had buried his face in his palms and was rubbing furiously at his temples with his index fingers. He shook his head and got back up to turn it off.

Bekka's concerns, as it turned out, weren't just in her head and though he had predicted it, it did not stop him from regretting it. At least insanity could be treated and medicated.

"So what do you think?" He asked, glancing over towards his hung-over friend.

"I think," David stopped rubbing his temples and let out a whimper, "that I'm never going to drink again!"

"Uh-huh. Heard that one before," Brian rolled his eyes, "And I was talking about—"

David rolled his eyes, "I know what you were talking about."

"Then answer the damn question."

David sighed, "I don't know."

Brian frowned, "How can you not know? Aren't you a part of the supernatural world? Isn't this stuff, like, second nature to you people?"

"Excuse me?" David glared at him, "You think I'm an expert on *magic* just because of what I am?"

Brian leaned back, "Judging from your tone…"

"Exactly!" David sat up, "I'm as much an expert on what Bekka's going through as you're an expert on the lifestyles of African tribes!" He shook his head, "Besides, my kind rarely gets involved in this sort of stuff. We're not magical creatures by nature."

Brian nodded slowly, disappointed, "It just doesn't make any fucking sense!"

David nodded as well, "You think Bekka's started practicing magic?"

"And not tell *anybody?*" Brian shook his head, "I don't think so!"

David shrugged, "It's not really any of our business what she does in her free time."

"Well she'd tell me that much!" Brian said, looking away.

David chuckled and suddenly groaned in pain and clutched his head again, "Just because you're crushing on her doesn't mean she's obligated to keep you in the loop, you know."

Brian's face went red and he looked away as he poked at the studs in his lip with his tongue.

David sighed and shook his head, "Look, Bekka *is* our friend. She trusted us enough to at least tell us about what happened at the concert. That alone should tell you that she's being honest with us. Besides, whatever's going on has got her scared and wanting answers, and I don't think she'd be willing to keep anything from us that could shed some light on the situation. For the time being, though, I don't think there's anything anybody—least of all you or I—can do about it."

Brian looked at his friend and nodded. He didn't

want to agree with the idea that there was nothing they could do, but it was an inescapable truth. Whether or not he chose to accept it made little difference.

"And now, for my next trick," David blew out a pained breath as he stood and walked on shaky feet towards his room, "I'm going to go split my skull and give birth to the antichrist!"

Brian laughed, "You silly drunk!"

"Never again," David promised, "Not ever!"

"Yea. I'll hold you to that," Brian said as he rose from the couch and headed to his own room.

He'd never told David about his feelings for Bekka; not directly anyway. Instead, he chalked up his friend's awareness as the result of some animal instinct and hoped that he'd be decent enough to not mention it around the others—assuming, of course, that they all hadn't figured it out as well.

What a nightmare that'd be!

He sighed and closed his eyes, the darkness behind his lids not much greater than that in his bedroom.

Sleep took him...

There was music in the distance, though he didn't care enough to focus on it.

Besides, there were other things to think about.

Instead he just stood on the edge of the road, looking out at its concrete length. This was it; the place it had happened, though it didn't help to know by looking at it. After all, it was just a street.

Just a damn street!

Every last shred of evidence had been removed; every stain washed away. Every last one...

Except the ones that lingered in his memory.

He sighed and studied the street, tracing his eyes back-and-forth over its surface for any tell-tale signs. He had time, and he wasn't about to force things into motion. This was, after all, the peaceful part of his dream.

He knew it well enough by now and accepted it as it came.

Still, it was only just a street.

Even in his own dreams he couldn't see it as anything more chaotic—more substantial—than a simple stretch of road.

But he hadn't been there to see it as anything more...

He hadn't been there.

Feeling the familiar tug, he turned to face the doorway from his old home that was waiting behind him. Though its hinges had creaked loudly in life; in his dream it was eerily quiet as it swung open for him.

He took two long strides inside before pausing to allow little Bekka—only seven years old in this memory—to skip by; her dirty-blonde hair tied back in a pony-tail and bouncing with each step. A moment later he turned to see himself as a small boy chasing after her and he couldn't help but smile at how happy she had made him even then.

Though he knew it wouldn't work he walked across the lawn towards the house and tried the front door, hoping the dream might allow him to see the events that were transpiring on

the other side, but the bitter cold knob wouldn't even turn for
him. Stepping back, he waited, knowing now what was going on
inside but unable to watch it for himself.

The dream would only show him what he knew; only
what he'd seen for himself.

Finally the doorknob turned and the home melted away,
leaving only Bekka's mother. There were tears in her eyes and
even before she delivered the news to little Brian his lip was
quivering with realization.

"... drunk driver..."

Brian's eyes opened and he sat up. His body was cold
and clammy; his hair damp and matted. He didn't need to
check his cheeks to know they were soaked with his tears.
Sighing and shaking his head, he waited for the lingering
message from his dream to fade as it told him again and again
of the dangers of alcohol. When it continued its haunting
echo he stood and left his room—hoping the memories
would stay behind.

Maybe, the thought, a few hours of playing his guitar
would drown out the memory.

FIVE

The caller ID—located conveniently next to their cordless phone's empty charger—told Brian that the call that had dragged him from his not-so-cozy slumber on the couch had been from Derek. He growled, blaming David for the missing phone, and began to uproot the living room in an effort to find it. A moment later, David opened the door to his bedroom and stared out at him through tired, slanted eyes.

"I can't find the fucking phone!" Brian said in response to the questioning stare.

"Did somebody call?" David asked.

Brian nodded, "Derek."

David considered and stepped into the living room, "Did he leave a message?"

Brian rolled his eyes, "Does he ever?"

The two froze as the phone started to ring again.

Brian growled, "Help me find it!"

The two spread out and began to search for the source of the sound, hoping to catch it before they lost the sound again. Moments passed—more muffled rings mockingly resonating—until it once again went silent.

Brian growled again, "Fucking hell! Can't we keep track of anything? It's not like we're sitting on so much goddam living space!"

The answering machine made a sound as it picked up the call and began recording then and the two turned towards it, disbelief etched on both their faces as Derek's voice came through.

"Uh... yea, kind of wish you guys would pick up the damn phone, but whatever."—there was a heavy sigh followed by a rustling—"Listen, about what happened last night—with Bekka, I mean—I might have an idea of what's going on. So if you can, come over to my place when you get this."

The two stared a moment longer at the answering machine as Derek hung up on the other end.

"Well," David started, "I guess we should get ready."

Brian nodded, "Guess so."

After almost twenty minutes of shoulder-to-shoulder discomfort on a crowded city bus, Brian and David finally reached their stop. David, eager to be free of the cramped space, shoved his way through with an animal fury that had people glaring after him as he past.

Brian's methods weren't much different.

From there, it was an easy two block walk to Derek's.

Shortly after, as they came up to Derek's grandfather's house, they were only slightly surprised to find Will's van already parked at the curb.

"Bekka's here too," David announced after a sharp inhale.

Brian nodded. He didn't doubt his friend's superior sense of smell nor did he doubt that Derek would want to tell everyone what he had to say. They were barely on the second step of the front stoop before the door opened and the two were greeted by Will, who squinted down at them in the sunlight.

"You want to hurry-the-fuck up?" He demanded. The two, knowing better than to argue with a sun-poisoned vampire, nodded and quickly stepped inside and allowed Will to close the door. A heavy, relieved sigh issued from their drummer, "So, you guys know what any of this is about?"

Brian frowned and shook his head, "Derek only said it had something to do with Bekka in his message."

"He left a message?" Will's voice was mirrored the same shock they'd felt earlier, "Holy shit! This must be big!"

"That's what we were thinking, too," Brian said, "So where is everyone?"

"The kitchen. Derek said he wouldn't say anything until you two got here."

David frowned, "He knew we were coming?"

Will shrugged as he led the way down the hall, "I don't question the magic-man and neither should you."

Both Brian and David considered this a moment and nodded. With nothing left to say they turned through an open doorway and stepped into the kitchen. Moderately lit and large enough to fit everyone comfortably, the walls were decorated with different sized jars filled with peppers and oils and mysteries. The wallpaper, which must have at one time been yellow, had become a light and neutral shade and peeled slightly at each of the four corners. The entire room was comfortably warm, smelling of spices and exotic tea.

Derek stood by the sink, slowly and methodically dunking a teabag into a large, steaming mug. Though his back was to the entrance, he held up his hand in a greeting to them as the three entered. At a circular table in the middle of the room, Bekka sat with an open can of Coke clutched in both hands. Her eyes shifted up from her soda to the three as they came in and a soft smile swept over her face.

"I'm glad you could make it," Derek turned to them and motioned with his cup towards the table.

Taking the cue, they all sat down and looked up at

their bassist expectantly. With only four chairs at the table, Derek was forced to stand, though this didn't seem to bother him as he took a sip of tea and against the counter.

"So what's the deal?" Will asked, breaking the silence.

Derek sighed and set his mug down beside him, "I had a dream last night."

Will scowled, "Oh yea? I had one too, I was in the middle of a blood bank and Megan Fox was giving me a sponge bath! You want to take a wild guess who woke me up from—"

Before he could say anything more David held up his hand to silence him.

Bekka looked down sadly and Brian frowned; he couldn't blame her for feeling disappointed. He, too, had been hoping for something a little more solid than just a dream.

Derek clucked his tongue and shrugged as he looked from one band-mate to another, "If nobody thinks this is worth listening to then you're all free to leave."

A moment passed and nobody moved.

"So what happened in your dream?" Bekka finally asked.

The question floated in the air, growing sour with each passing moment. Derek looked down and scratched the top of his head, a deep frown creasing his features, "You died."

Bekka's eyes widened.

Brian glared, "I'm hoping this has a little more depth

to it, magic-man!"

Derek nodded as he began to explain, "We were back at the arena and you were crowd-surfing again. Only this time, as you were carried out by the audience, I *saw* what you had seen!" He sighed and paused to sip his tea, "I watched the beings you described as they ripped and tore into our world. And at the end of their struggle was the perfect hiding place for them. You."

"'hiding place'?" Bekka frowned, "Hiding from what, exactly?"

Derek shook his head, "I'm not sure. After they entered you the crowd carried you back to us, but when you reached the stage you were…" He shrugged, not bothering to say the last part again.

Brian slammed his fist on the table, "This is bullshit! You called us over here just to tell us something that you *knew* would scare us even more? What gives, asshole?"

David nodded and reached over to rub Bekka's shoulder, "I agree. We might not know what's going on, but there's no reason to assume that it's going to end that way. We don't even know what those things are."

"Or if they're even real!" Will pointed out, glaring at Derek, "Look, I've been around for a shitload longer than any of you soft-hearts, and I've never seen or heard of anything like what you're talking about!"

Derek frowned, "I'm not saying that the dream was a premonition! But we *do* need to be careful!" He returned Will's glare, "Not to sound cliché, but just because you haven't heard of it doesn't mean that something doesn't exist. Even a hard-head like you should've learned that much by now!"

Will's eyes flashed bright and his lips parted, his fangs beginning to extend, "I wouldn't talk to me like that, witch-boy!"

"Enough!" Bekka stood and slapped her hands on the table, "You're all right," she looked at Derek. "Whatever this is, it *is* real—there's no denying that now—and, like you said, it might be dangerous," she turned her attention to the others, "But that doesn't mean that I'm doomed! Most of all, we need to remember that this *is not* Derek's fault!"

Derek sighed and nodded, "Look, my grandfather might know something. I'll ask him tonight after Will drops me off from practice."

Brian frowned and shook his head, "Whoa! What was that about 'practice'? What happened to taking some time off? We all agreed that when the shit hit the fan—"

"Please, Brian!" Bekka looked at him, her eyes pleading, "Don't take my music away from me. Especially not now!"

Derek bit his lip, "Like I said, I'll talk to my grandfather about any possible solutions." He turned to Brian, "We've gotten through a lot together, and the music *has* always been there to keep us strong."

Brian frowned at Derek, "What happened to being careful?"

"Nothing's happened to being careful," Derek assured

him, "I just don't see what you would have us do otherwise."

Brian glared at him a moment longer before shaking a finger in his face, "You had better hope for your sake that whatever solution you come up with doesn't end with Bekka dying!"

Derek stayed calm, his gaze never shifting from Brian's, "I swear to you, Brian, if she dies, it's because I died fighting against it."

Will made a show of yawning loudly, "Oh boy! Is this the part where you two kiss and have an 80s workout montage? If so, can you keep it PG-13 for my stomach's sake and hurry it up?" He stared between the two of them for a moment, "No? Awesome! Now what does everyone think of watching some movies on my new HD-TV?"

Bekka let out a relieved sigh, "Only if you promise we can watch a comedy."

SIX

The tap sputtered as Brian turned on the faucet and he waited on the stream a moment before holding his glass under it. Back in the living room, David was already on the couch; their instruments stuffed away in the closet and defying all laws of special relations. The audio from the TV bled into the kitchen and Brian recognized the sounds of the late-night news as he sipped his water.

Movies and practice at Will's had been normal and uneventful.

No fires started.

No equipment exploded.

No mystical beings emerged to take them all away.

Despite these things being excellent for their metal image, it did little for them if nobody was around to see it and even less if it got one of them killed. He lingered more on these thoughts as he refilled his emptied glass for a second helping.

In the other room, the muffled sound of the phone ringing made him pause; the tell-tale sounds of David's efforts in finding the elusive device mingling with the television.

"Oh fucking hell! Don't do this to me!" He muttered to himself, "No more goddam drama for tonight, I beg you!"

Finishing his drink, he set the glass down in the sink and plodded back into the living room just in time to watch David victoriously yank the still-ringing phone out from under a fold in the rug behind the couch.

Brian stared for a moment; how the hell had it found its way there?

David smirked at him—dragging out his victory celebration a little longer—as he answered the phone, "Hello? … Yea, he's right here." He handed Brian the phone, "It's Bekka."

Blushing, Brian accepted the phone and cradled it to his ear, "Hello?"

"Brian," Bekka's voice sounded relieved, "can you come over?"

"Come over?" Brian played with the words, wondering if he was hearing them right. He looked over at the time, seeing it was nearly eleven, "You mean now?"

"Y-yea. If it's alright with you, I mean."

Brian glanced over at David and was rewarded with a thumbs-up, "Uh, yea. I guess that's not a problem. Just give me twenty minutes."

"Thanks, Brian. I really appreciate it."

"Don't worry about it. I'll see you in a bit." Hanging up, he turned to David, handing him the phone.

David raised an eyebrow, "So… ?"

Brian shrugged, "I'm not sure. She didn't say what was wrong, just that she wanted me to come over."

David smirked and nodded.

Brian frowned, "What are you thinking?"

"*I'm* thinking of going for a run," David answered with a shrug, "I think the real question is, what are *you* thinking?"

Brian felt himself blush again and glared, "Dude!"

"I'm just kidding, man!" David shrugged, "She's probably just scared and wants some company."

Brian was packed, out the door, and on the street in less than ten minutes. With everything he needed stuffed into an old backpack and slung over his shoulder, he was surprised at how easy it was to walk; he'd long-since forgotten what it was like to travel without his guitar.

Though the late-Spring night was comfortable enough to enjoy the walk he was eager to get to Bekka's and kept his pace swift. If David was right and Bekka *was* scared and lonely, he didn't want to leave her to suffer through it alone for too long.

When he arrived to the entrance of her apartment building she was already waiting in the lobby with a fantasy novel to keep her busy. As he pushed through the doors she looked up from her chair and smiled; dog-earing her page and standing to greet him.

"Thanks for coming."

Brian shrugged, "Like I said over the phone, don't worry about it."

She smiled at him and led him to the elevators and pressed the call button. Though she lived on her own, the building was owned by her parents. When she'd decided to move out several years back, they'd offered her one of the upper-level suites. While the others saw this as a remarkably kind gesture on their part, Bekka liked to joke that they'd done it to keep tabs on her. While it wasn't expected of her to pay for her living expenses, she nevertheless made sure to mail a check for what she could to them each month.

Regardless of what amount she parted with, however, she was still getting the place at a steal.

The elevator stopped at her floor, opening up to a long hallway and, just a short ways down, her apartment. Inside, red-and-gold wallpaper featuring spiraled floral designs stretched for a short distance before opening up into the living room and, at the far side of this, the most beautiful view of the city Brian had ever seen. As things worked out, Bekka's suite occupied one corner of the building and, as a result, two of the four walls were, instead, large, reinforced windows that allowed those inside a view of both the western and southern reaches of the city. On the wall next to them was a large, electric fireplace and over this hung a flat-screen TV that Will had gotten her for her last birthday and, in the middle of the room, a black leather sectional couch.

Brian sighed and shook his head as he took all this in, "Why is it that David and I are in a stuck in a dump when you're living like a queen?"

Bekka giggled and shrugged, "Mommy and Daddy *do* treat me well."

"Yea they do!" Brian rolled his eyes, "And David won't even let me spend a fucking nickel! I swear we could be sitting on millions and I wouldn't even know it!"

Bekka giggled again.

Brian smiled at the sound before coming to his senses, "So what's all this about?"

Bekka frowned, suddenly looking embarrassed, "I was just lonely."

Nodding, Brian silently cursed David's intuition as he lowered himself onto the couch, "Well, now you've got company."

She smiled and nodded, sitting beside him.

For a long while neither of them said anything and Brian, succumbing to the comfortable couch and his exhaustion, let his eyes begin to close and, before long, began to doze off.

"Brian?" His eyes opened at the sound of Bekka's voice only to droop once again, "Brian!"

This time he sat up, dazed and confused, "Huh? What is it?" Bekka's lips curled upward at his reaction, though the rest of her face remained serious and concerned. Brian, blinking away the rest of his confusion, frowned as he realized that he'd nearly fallen asleep.

Bekka frowned and looked down. "There's something that I need to tell you," she confessed.

Brian studied her a moment, "What's that?"

"I missed the bus from Will's earlier," she blushed, looking back up at him.

Brian stared at her a moment, confused, "Oh. Okay. So how did you get home?"

"That's the thing!" She explained, her voice still shaky, "I caught up to it four stops over!"

Brian's eyes widened and he shook his head, trying to mentally calculate what she was telling him, "Four stops? Bekka, there's no way you could've—"

"But I did, Brian!" She moved closer, her eyes beaming with excitement all of a sudden, "I probably could've made it all the way back home on foot, but catching the bus just seemed more fun."

Brian shook his head and held up his hands, "Hold on. Just hold on! You *must* have bummed a ride off somebody?"

Bekka shook her head, still smirking, "Completely on foot, I assure you."

"Bekka, this isn't funny!"

Bekka's smile gradually melted away and she nodded, pulling her knees to her chest, "I know. It really isn't. But it's still the truth! I didn't even get tired or even feel winded! But god damn if I hadn't just sprinted around half the city in less than fifteen minutes!"

"Bekka, this doesn't make any—"

"There really is something in me, Brian. I can *feel* them now. It's like that moment just before you fall asleep—that moment when you're not awake anymore but you're not asleep, either—and your mind is so empty that it's like you don't even exist at all?" She sighed and wet her lips, "Have you ever thought about what a strange, cosmic twist it is that *you*—your consciousness, I mean—got to exist? It's like that, Brian—that awesome, bewildering thought that I am me—only now, it's like there's more than just the one mind being thankful for that opportunity!" She looked at Brian, whose face showed a mixture of confusion, fear, and worry. She sighed, releasing herself from her coil, and shook her head, "Never mind. Even I know how crazy that sounds. I'm… I'm just really glad I'm not alone tonight."

Looking at his friend a shudder worked its way through Brian—rippling through his guts like a parasite. He remembered what had happened at the bar and in the van, and the story that Bekka had told them about the things that had entered her. If they were real, they were working quickly.

However, as he dared once more to look her in the eyes, he could see his life-long friend still vibrantly shimmering therein. Whatever was happening—wherever this whole mess was leading—it *was* still Bekka.

"You're never alone, Bekka. You need to remember that. I'm not about to lie and tell you I understand, but I know that this—me being here for you—is what I'm supposed to be doing."

It had been a while since David had gone for a run, and with Brian out of the apartment and nothing else to distract him he wasn't about to ignore the opportunity.

After nearly twenty minutes—had it *really* been that long?—he finally found the old acoustic guitar that Brian had given him in the back of his bedroom closet. A few of the strings were broken, and he took his time to replace them properly before tossing on a ratty shirt and a pair of cut-off jeans. Finally, when he was sure that everything was ready, he grabbed his bag and stepped out into the streets.

It was late, and though the city lights did a good job of keeping the stars hidden they couldn't snuff out the bright, crescent moon. This grabbed and held David's attention for a moment, and as he stared into the sky he felt some of the tension he'd collected since his last run disperse.

He knew he'd relax more once he started running.

With his guitar strapped across his back and his bag clutched in his hand he felt something like a traveling street performer, and from the looks he was getting from the late-night pedestrians he supposed he looked like one, as well.

A short while later, he reached the entrance to the park and left the sounds of the late-night city traffic behind him. As he passed by the man-made lake and the nearby fish-hatchery he inhaled deeply, relishing in the clean, natural scent. It was good to be out of the bustle of the city; it helped remind him who he was.

It helped remind him *what* he was.

Continuing on, he left the path and entered the neighboring woods; the dense forest already beginning to beckon to him like a drug. Once out of the human element, he let the bag slip from his hand and cast his nostrils upward; testing the air to be sure it was safe to let his guard down. When he was satisfied that the area was clear, he pulled the guitar gently over his shoulders and set it down and began to strip.

A breeze picked up—or, at least, became noticeable—as his shirt and pants came off. As the last of his clothes came off, he retrieved the guitar and began stuffing his clothes into the empty bag and hung it on a nearby branch.

Then he began to transform.

It was the first time in nearly two months that he'd freed himself from his human skin, and the first shift in his skeletal structure was nearly enough to make him change his mind.

He had forgotten how excruciating the process was, and the time that had passed had only made him that much more sensitive to it.

As he continued he became overwhelmed by a burning sensation as his metabolism kicked into high gear to facilitate the process. Still trying to cope with the fire under his skin, he was forced to his knees as his skull cracked and reformed itself. Through it all his entire body—along with the pain of its reshaping—itched with the sudden growth of new, thicker hair. The aches and pains continued as his muscles grew to nearly three-times their original size; some inflating gradually while others exploded into their new size. Gritting his teeth against the mixed sensations he dared a glance at his bulging left arm, which had begun to darken like a spreading bruise.

His ears tingled momentarily before the sounds around him became louder; the call of the night-bathed woods coming in sharper and clearer. Soon after his already superhuman sense of smell was boosted and his eyesight shifted, allowing him to see every detail of the forest. Though his body was still wracked with agony, he began to laugh.

He'd forgotten how liberating this form was!

When the change was finally complete he let out a heavy breath; the last of the pains fading away as he did. Only then did he start out, following the long-remembered path to the blackberry patch.

Securing the guitar to his back with a clawed hand, he began his run.

SEVEN

Brian was awoken the next morning by the soft, buzzing ring of Bekka's phone as it vibrated against her glass coffee table. Cursing the far-too-comfy couch once again, he reached over his head and picked up the phone and checked the caller ID.

It was their manager.

He sat up and answered it, "Got tired of keeping quiet, eh Bill?"

There was a pause.

"Brian? Uh... did I call the right number?"

"Yea, you got it right. I was just chilling at Bekka's."

"Uh-huh."

Brian sighed, "Look, Bill, it's not like that!"

"Bet you'd like it to be though. Am I right?" Bill laughed.

Brian felt himself blush, "Is there a purpose to this call?" He asked.

"Yea. Of course there is!" Bill responded, sounding hurt. As their manager explained Brian's eyes got wider and wider with excitement. "Look, I *know* this is short notice and all, but it's good money and even better publicity. You think they'll be in."

"I'm sure of it!" Brian said, making no attempt to mask the excitement in his voice, "Hold on! Let me go get Bekka! I'm sure she's going to want to talk to you about this!"

Brian didn't wait for a response as he set the phone down and hurried towards Bekka's room, nearly tripping on his own feet in the process. As he approached her door he heard the sound of her mattress squeaking under shifting weight and he smiled. At least he didn't have to worry about waking her up.

He gave a gentle knock.

Silence.

He frowned and knocked harder.

Something clattered as it toppled over behind the door.

"Bekka?" Brian frowned, "Is everything alright?"

There was a muffled cry followed by a whimper.

Without a second thought, Brian seized the handle and tried to push the door open to no avail; it had been barricaded! Determined, Brian rammed his shoulder again and again against the door, ignoring the growing pain in his shoulder as the door opened inch-by-inch. Throwing his whole body against the door, something on the other side shattered and the door swung open and slammed against the wall.

Brian, frozen in shock, took in the whole horrific scene at once. The broken window and shards of reinforced glass littering the floor and the strange man in the ruffled brown suit perched over Bekka on her bed. Though he wasn't very tall, he had an intimidating air around him. His left leg was coiled beneath him for leverage while he stood on his right, his large hands working to fit around Bekka's thin neck. The chair that had been propped against the door lay in pieces on the floor, and though the man made no attempts to hide his intentions, Brian's entrance *had* distracted him. Letting out an angry growl, the man turned to face him; his wiry gray hair writhing about his head.

"Son of a bitch!" Brian started to charge to the bed and Bekka's attacker.

The man's eyes narrowed at him—enraged at intrusion—and as Brian continued toward him they rolled back in his skull; his pupils disappearing behind the top of his lids and exposing the veiny whites. Shaking with rage, the man withdrew from Bekka stood, his mouth stretching wide in a horrifyingly-impossible grin—the sounds of the stranger's jawbone separating making Brian step back—as he let out a chattering roar.

Bekka, finally free of her attacker's grip, scuttled back until she was pressed against the headboard. Glaring, Brian bent down and retrieved one of the broken legs of the chair. Though he'd never before had to ward off an attacker, Brian was sure he'd find some way to stop the intruder with it.

The stranger's inhuman howl stopped as his left shoulder jerked and his head began to shake; his twisted features soon becoming a blur.

"I've called the police, motherfucker!" He bluffed. The man's shaking face stilled and the white eyes narrowed and Brian lifted the chair leg in front of him, "I'm warning you!"

For a moment the man paused, looking at the weapon. Turning away from him, he smirked at Bekka, who whimpered and flinched under his stare.

"You can't hold onto them forever, girl!" The voice was high-pitched and forced, reminding Brian of bagpipes. Still smirking, the man turned and stepped towards the broken window, his shoes crunching in the broken glass with each step. When he'd gotten to the edge, he turned to face them once again and saluted before allowing his body to fall backwards through the window.

"Oh my...!" Bekka let out a cry at the sight, cupping a hand over her mouth.

Dropping his weapon, Brian hurried to the window and peeked over the edge at the carnage below. A moment passed as Bekka slipped on her shoes so that she could safely navigate through the broken glass so she could see for herself. She stared for a long moment, clearly confused, before her eyes widened. Brian, seeing her reaction, looked back down at the body, wondering if the strange attacker had somehow survived the fall. This, however, was not the case, and he turned back towards Bekka—staring in shock and confusion at the corpse on the pavement below.

"What's wrong?" He asked.

She frowned, "You don't see it?"

Brian looked back at the body—still motionless; still dead, "What?"

"That!" She pointed at the body, "It looks like one of those things from the concert!"

"You mean…?"

Bekka nodded, bringing her hand up to her chest.

Brian shook his head, "I honestly don't see anything."

Bekka's darted upward—following the invisible specter—until she finally allowed herself to blink.

"What happened?" Brian asked.

"It's gone," she confessed, frowning, "It just floated over him and then disappeared."

Brian nodded, though he couldn't begin to understand what she meant. At that moment he wasn't sure he *wanted* to understand. Stepping back, he studied the shattered window and the glass beneath his feet, "He came through here…" He frowned, shaking his head, "How could he have broken through the window and *not* woken me up?"

Bekka bit her lip, "It didn't wake me up, either." He looked at her, surprised. She shrugged, "When I woke up he was standing over me. I don't think he *wanted* us to wake up."

"That doesn't make any sense, Bekka!" He looked back down at the body and the crowd surrounding it before turning away from the window, "Did he say anything to you?"

Bekka was close behind, "Only what you heard."

"Yea," Brian thought back, "What do you think he meant when he said that thing about 'holding on to them'?"

"How should I—"Bekka started and then bit her lip, "Do you think this has something to do with *that*?"

Brian nodded, "I really do." He sighed and shook his head, "Look, this is serious! We need to figure this out! I'm going to tell Bill that we can't take the gig."

Bekka raised an eyebrow, "What gig? When did you talk to Bill?"

"He called a second ago and woke up me. Said he had a show lined up for us," he shook his head, "But there's no way I'm—"

Bekka shot him a look, "Brian, a superhuman psychopath tried to choke the life out of me before I was even awake! If there is *any* opportunity I can take to turn this day around, you bet your ass I'm going to take it! I'm going to get on the phone with Bill and tell him we're in!" She started towards the door, stretching her neck as she did, "Ow, shit! Dammit, I think that bastard might've torn one of my piercings!"

Brian frowned and sighed, still not happy with the idea of performing under the circumstances, "I'll check it for you."

Bill had hung up by the time they made it to the living room, and while Bekka was eager to call their manager back, Brian was at least able to convince her to let him check her neck first. Giving him that much, she sat down and pulled her purple hair up so that the back of her neck was exposed. Leaning in close, Brian examined each of the three bars that ran horizontally up along her nape. Finally he shook his head and pulled away.

"They're a little red, but I don't see any tears."

Nodding, she stood up and let her hair down again and smiled at him, "Thanks again."

He shrugged, "Don't worry about it. It's nothing."

"It's something to me! God dammit, Brian, you probably..." She shook her head, "You *did* save my life back there. Anyway," she smiled wider and clapped excitedly, "we've got a gig!"

Brian rolled his eyes but nevertheless fell victim to Bekka's infectious smile and exuberance, "Yea. We got a gig."

EIGHT

It wasn't long before the police were knocking on Bekka's door. Brian stayed still and quiet, deciding it would be both in his and Bekka's best interest if he kept himself out of the questioning process. While the other members of their band viewed his distaste for cops as an "authority issue", and while he didn't wholeheartedly disagree it *was* a bit more complicated than that.

But, then again, the others didn't know the details behind his parents' death.

Bekka did her best to tell the truth without actually

telling the truth; bending—and even ignoring—certain details that would no doubt land her in a padded cell. By the time the two officers had left they knew that Bekka had been woken up by the man who attempted to strangle her before being startled by Brian and jumping out of the window.

When they were finally gone Brian let out a stale-tasting sigh of relief, and he wondered how long he'd been holding his breath. Bekka, knowing what their presence had done to his nerves, went to the kitchen and emerged a moment later with two root beers.

"Thanks." He popped the top and took a long sip.

"It's nothing," Bekka smirked, doing the same and letting out a hard belch.

Brian made a face, "How lady-like."

"You know you love it," she smirked and took another drink, "So what do you think?" She asked, her tone turning uncomfortably serious.

Brian frowned, freezing in mid-sip, "About?"

Bekka shook her head, "About everything that's happening! About what we just went through! About what we're going to do next! Fucking hell, Brian, can we talk about this?"

Brian looked at her and noticed that the can was shaking in her hand. He set down his soda and leaned forward, clearing his throat, "I think…" He sighed and looked down, stuck. He never had been a thinker; never had needed to be, "I think we need to tell the others about this. Derek might have learned something, and even if he didn't he seems to understand it better than anybody else." He paused to let out a heavy breath, "And—fucking hell, Bekka!—I still think we should take some time off!"

Bekka shook her head, "Like I said before, no matter what happens we can't let it hurt our career! We've worked too hard for all of this to fuck if up now!"

"But this is serious!" Brian argued. Though Bekka was shorter than him by more than three inches she suddenly seemed a great deal more intimidating and Brian shivered, "Bekka…"

"I know you're scared," Bekka's eyes were fierce and determined, "and believe me when I say that I'm scared too. But I'm not going to be any safer if we don't perform. We need our music!"

"But what about what's been happening to you?" Brian tried to keep the growing shakiness out of his voice.

Bekka smiled, "So far all they've done is fuck with a bar and help me catch a bus. How bad can it get?"

Brian sighed and shook his head, "Oh shit don't make me think about that!" He took a deep breath and looked at his friend again; seeing the determination in her eyes, "Alright. Fine! Just give me tonight, then."

Bekka narrowed her eyes, "What?"

"Let me call Bill and tell him we can't do the gig tonight. It's just a small show!" He put a hand on her shoulder, "There will be other gigs. All I'm asking for is tonight."

Bekka looked at him for a long, quiet moment before

she finally shook her head, "Fine! Reschedule! But we'd better get somewhere with all of this! No dicking around!"

Brian smiled, already reaching for the phone, "You got it, no dicking around!"

Their excuse to Bill was simple enough: Bekka had a stomach bug.

With the easy stuff out of the way, the two discussed—in hushed tones, what Brian had planned—if what he was thinking could be called a "plan". By the time they'd gotten back to his and David's apartment, they had done a great deal of talking but hadn't really gotten further than "ask Derek".

David was asleep on the couch in a pair of shorts and a sweaty-looking shirt balled up and tucked under his head; his left arm hanging over the edge of the couch and clinging to his acoustic guitar.

"Huh," Brian took in the sight, "I thought he'd lost that old thing."

Bekka giggled.

Brian rolled his eyes and grabbed a pillow from the nearby chair and hurled it into David's face, "Wake up, fuzz-nuts! We need to have a band meeting!"

The pillow found its mark and David shot up with a snarl. For a moment he looked lost and angry and it wasn't until he saw Bekka that his lip lowered and hid his bared teeth. As his ferocity melted away, it was replaced by a look of confusion.

"What is it?" He asked, sitting up. The shirt that had been his pillow was snatched up and pulled over his head.

"Somebody tried to kill Bekka!" Brian declared, "Somebody not human."

David's eyes widened and a deep snarl crept up his throat, "What? Who?"

"Some suit that decided to swan dive out Bekka's window," Brian arched an eyebrow at David, who was still shaking with rage and growling; his "run" the night before had reawakened the animal in him, "He's dead now, but we don't think it's going to stop there."

Still growling, David stormed off to his room and emerged moments later in a fresh pair of pants. Fastening his belt, he looked up at Brian and motioned towards the phone with his chin, "Call Will." He ordered, "Have him meet us at Derek's."

Brian nodded, already starting to dial, "Should I ask him to pick us up?"

David shook his head, "I'm not about to sit around and wait for him!" He turned to Bekka; taking long, quick steps towards her and looking her over, "Are you alright?"

Bekka nodded, "Just a little shook up."

David took this in for a moment, "Brian said your attacker wasn't human. Any idea what he could have been? Vampire? Therion?"

Bekka shook her head and shrugged, "He was so strong and fast. I guess he could've been a vampire, but something in the way he moved makes me want to say he wasn't."

"The way he moved?" David cocked his head.

Bekka nodded, "Like his body wasn't his own; like every step was forced. It was almost robotic."

"Almost like a fucking freak-show!" Brian called out as he hung up the phone, "The guy was a lunatic!"

"What about the thing I saw?" Bekka looked at him angrily, "Was that just the crazy leaving his body?"

Brian frowned and licked one of his lip rings.

David cocked an eyebrow. "Something left his body?"

Bekka nodded, "It was one of those things I saw the night of the concert!"

David looked at her for a moment in disbelief and then turned his gaze towards Brian, "You see this thing?"

Brian shook his head.

Bekka shot a glare at both of them, "God dammit, it *was* there! I swear I fucking saw it!"

"If that is the case," David started, "why would they attack their own?"

Bekka didn't have an answer.

David nodded and looked at Brian, "Is Will on his way to Derek's?"

"Not happily," Brian chuckled.

David nodded, "Then we should head out too."

The streets were bustling and crowded; people pushing and shoving against the three as they navigated through the streets. Forced to stay close, they walked shoulder-to-shoulder in an effort to avoid getting separated. Though the bus stop wasn't a long ways away, the congestion of pedestrians made the process of getting there a difficult one. Forced to remain silent about their predicament, they pushed forward in silence.

"I don't see why Will couldn't have picked us up!" Brian yelled over the din of the city.

David growled for what must've been the hundredth time that hour, "Because the streets are crowded and we'd be waiting forever!"

Bekka sighed and shook her head, "The bus…"

David frowned and looked down at her, "Something wrong?"

"We'll explain later," Brian promised as they stopped at a crosswalk and waited for the light to turn.

"Did something bad happen on the bus?" David pressed.

Brian glared at him, "I already told you we'd tell you later!"

David bared his teeth, "Later is not good enough!"

Brian gave him a look, "It's not you we're trying to keep out of the loop!" He motioned towards all the people around them.

David sneered and looked up as the light changed for them and they stepped into the street.

The engines of stopped cars rumbled at the red light and though the three were free of the crowded sidewalk, the small swarm of people that had forced them to huddle together seemed to decide that then was the right time to cross the street as well. Brian frowned and glanced at Bekka, who almost looked like she was drowning in the sea of people. In an effort to keep her spirits up he gently bumped her with his shoulder. Her sea-blue eyes shifted to face him; a soft smile tugging at her lips. At that moment, looking back into her eyes, he lost track of everything else.

Then he heard the revving engine and looked up to see a green pickup truck as the driver shifted into gear and began to run the light.

"What the hell?" David took a cautionary step back.

"Run!" Brian screamed.

David grabbed Bekka's hand and took off for the other side of the street. Brian, running right behind them, stumbled in his haste and went down in the middle of the street; the truck's squealing tires growing louder. Brian sucked in a breath and looked over his shoulder, prepared to see the grill of the heavy-duty vehicle coming at him, but was surprised as it shot by him and made its way after David and Bekka.

"BEHIND YOU!" He cried out, fighting to get to his feet.

David, hearing the warning, turned his head to see what was happening. Too afraid to stop running, Bekka pulled free of David's grip and sprinted onto the sidewalk and towards a newsstand. Wide-eyed, David dove to the side as the truck passed by and caught his shoulder with the side-view mirror, sending him corkscrewing to the ground.

Ignoring the pedestrian they'd just hit, the driver continued after Bekka; the truck jumping the curb and roaring down the sidewalk. As people cried out and ran for their lives away from the vehicle both Brian and David pulled themselves to their feet and sprinted for all they were worth after it.

As she reached the newsstand Bekka, unaware of the situation, turned around and stumbled back when she saw that she was still not safe. The newsstand clerk, trying to get a clear view of what was causing the commotion, suddenly caught sight of the approaching truck and jumped over the counter in an effort to clear himself from its path.

Brian ignored the fire growing in his lungs and pushed on, "BEKKA! NO!"

The two guitarists didn't stop their pursuit.

Not even as they watched the truck barrel into their friend did they allow themselves to slow down. Soon after that the truck collided with the stand, throwing newspapers and magazines into the sidewalk and street. Positive that Bekka had been crushed between the truck's grill and the stand, their eyes went wide with shock as they watched her jump onto the hood and cartwheel over the cab. Bekka landed the maneuver, looking more surprised than hurt as she steadied herself in the truck bed. As Brian and David watched in horror, the truck swerved sharply and tilted before rolling onto its roof, dragging Bekka beneath it as it went.

Brian and David didn't hold back as they shoved their way through the crowd of gawking onlookers—most of which yelled out insults or commented on their lack of manners. From their angle, they could see that the truck's driver had died in the crash; his neck sharply bent away from his body and resting against the roof. Seeing this, Brian was suddenly less hopeful for Bekka's fate but nevertheless hurried around to the vehicle's rear and dropped down to his hands and knees to peer under the capsized truck bed. He gulped, trying to force his eyes to adjust to the darkness, and felt his head go light. Looking up at David, he motioned towards the back of the truck as he once again looked into the darkness for Bekka's body.

For the first time since he'd met him, David forgot all about hiding what he was and as he gripped the tail-end of the truck and hoisted it as high as his superhuman strength would allow the onlookers cried out and backed away.

Ignoring the scene they were creating, Brian glared at David, "Higher, god dammit! Don't fucking pussy out on me now!"

David groaned and pushed harder, the truck groaning and lifting up onto its hood as it rose upward, "Do you see her?"

Brian's eyes went wide, "Oh god… no!" The body

underneath—covered in chipped plastic, bent metal, and shattered glass—was more mangled and misshapen than the driver had been. A sharp heave caught in Brian's throat and he stifled it as he crept under the bed to get a closer look. Though he'd never considered himself the praying type, he muttered over and over again to himself, hoping that any deity that might exist would hear and make things better than they looked. As he got beside Bekka's body he noticed how bad her injuries really were. Her head was twisted nearly all the way around, several of her vertebrae clearly visible under bruised and broken skin. Her right shoulder had come out of the socket and the arm was broken in at least three places. Her right leg had suffered a similar fate—several noticeable breaks including a compound fracture and a sharp, jagged bend just under her knee.

Brian—tears pouring down his face—turned his head away from the carnage as he threw up on a pile of car parts and blood. With the smell of bile mixing with the growing scent of death, Brian heaved once again and was startled to hear a sharp gasp followed by a gag from Bekka. His neck turned back to his friend's body and he watched in horrified relief as her eyes fluttered opened.

"H-huh?"

"Bekka?" He stared in disbelief.

"Hmm?" Her response was calm and casual, "Oh, ouch!" She shifted as though her injuries were no more than a minor ache.

Brian continued to stare, not sure what he should do.

"Hey," David's called down, "Is she alright? Somebody's called an ambulance! It should be here any minute!" There was a hopeful pause before, "Hello?"

Bekka's beaten brow furrowed in confusion, "Ambulance? What happened?" She seemed to drift for a moment and then her face went white with terror, "Oh god! That truck! Did it hit somebody?"

Brian nodded, his lip quivering.

Bekka frowned, studying him, and then looked around at their surroundings. Then she looked down at her body; her eyes widening and her mouth gaping in horror, "OH GOD! OH GOD! I'M GOING TO DIE! NO NO NONONONO!" She cried, letting out a hard sob, "Brian! I don't want to die!"

Brian stammered, not knowing how to respond.

"I don't wanna die!" Bekka clenched her eyes shut, "I don't wanna die!"

Something popped then and Brian passed it off as something mechanical breaking free from the truck. A moment later there was another—wetter and more organic this time—and then a sequence of snaps. Confused, he looked at his still-crying, still-whimpering friend and took in a shocked breath as he watched her body twist, pivot, and shift as it returned to its original form. Frozen in amazement, he watched, the entire process—taking no more than a minute—and when it was over the only evidence that remained of what had happened was her torn and dirtied clothes.

"... wanna die! I don't wanna die! I don't wanna..."
Bekka continued to chant behind closed eyelids, unaware of
what had just happened.

Brian moved forward then, gripping her by the
shoulders, "Bekka!" He shook her gently to get her attention,
"Bekka! Look!"

Her eyes opened then, tears pouring down her cheeks
as she stared at him for a moment and then down at her now-
mended body. Silence washed over her, her eyes gazing in
disbelief, "But... how...?"

Brian shook his head, "Don't question it! Let's just
get the fuck out of here!"

Bekka took one last look at herself, giving parts of her
body gentle pokes. Once she was satisfied, she looked back up
at him and nodded.

NINE

It wasn't easy getting away from the scene with all the people flooding in to get a glance at the girl who had survived the crash, the young man that had brought her back, and the other that had lifted a truck to make it all possible. Some wanted pictures, others wanted to touch them in hopes of being granted their own miracles, and some felt that—despite all their assurances—there was no way that Bekka hadn't been hurt and insisted that they should wait for the paramedics to arrive. While Bekka and Brian tried to handle the horde—Bekka with a great deal more manners than

Brian—David ran into a nearby café and called Derek's house.

Their friend's grandfather answered.

"Hello Mister Sumner," David spoke slowly and clearly so the old man would understand, "is Derek available?"

"Oh he can't come to the phone right now," the old man explained, "He's hosting for one of his friends."

David silently thanked the heavens that Will had already made it there, "That's alright, sir. This is David. From the band."

"David huh?" There was a short pause on the line, "Are you the therion?"

David chuckled; for an old man, not much got by him, "Uh, yes. Yes, that's me."

"Well why didn't you say so? Let me go get Derek; I think he's expecting you."

"Actually," David spoke up, hoping the old man was still on the line, "I was wondering if I could talk to Will."

"I suppose," there was a sigh followed by a pause, "I have to say, though, I *was* skeptical about letting Derek play with you and the vampire at first, but I'm glad to see that neither of you has eaten anybody yet. You *haven't* eaten anybody, right?"

David laughed, "No, Mister Sumner, never have and never will."

"That's a good boy. I'll go get the vampire for you."

The phone was set down and some indistinct voices

in the background were heard. Then, "Hello?"

"Will! I need you to come pick us up! And fast!"

There was a heavy sigh, "Can't you guys take the bus like normal, non-driving—"

David growled into the receiver and a nearby barista looked up at him, startled. David ignored them, "Listen to me, asshole! We're in trouble out here and we need you, now!"

Hearing the seriousness in David's tone, Will changed his own, "What kind of trouble?"

"We'll explain later."

"This got something to do with Bekka?" Will asked.

"Yea," David answered, "It's got *everything* to do with her."

"I'm on my way," Will assured him, "Where are you?"

"Near a café on the corner of Fifth and Main."

"Got it! Be there in five minutes."

David frowned, "I don't think you're that close."

Will chuckled, "David, don't you worry *where* I am. I'll be there in five minutes!"

The line went dead before David had a chance to say anything else. Hanging up, he ran back to the Brian and Bekka and shoved his way through the masses, making an opening for them to get through.

"Will's on his way." he explained.

Brian frowned, "We haven't got too long!"

"He said five minutes," David answered and both

Brian and Bekka looked at him in disbelief as they pushed through the crowd. He shrugged, "Just telling you what he said."

"Miss," a woman turned to Bekka and grabbed her arm, stopping them all in their tracks, "Miss! You could be hurt! You should wait for help!"

Brian turned and shoved a middle finger in the woman's face, "Fuck off, lady! Don't make me feed you to my friend!"

The woman's eyes went wide and darted towards David, who turned his head towards her. Despite his better efforts, desperation and anger got the better of him and he bared his teeth at her.

The woman let go and backed away.

Will had said he'd meet them at the coffee shop in five minutes, and though none of them had timed him they were all surprised to find his van waiting for them when they emerged from the crowd. Though he was a reliable band-mate and an excellent drummer, Will had never before been very good with getting anywhere on time.

"First time for everything, I suppose," Brian muttered as he pulled the door open for Bekka and climbed in after her.

"What was that?" Will asked, already irritated by the sun, "You want to walk, shit-eater?"

David climbed in the passenger seat and slammed the door behind him, "Don't worry about it, Will. Just drive!"

"Somebody going to tell me what the FUCK is going

on?" He growled as he pulled back out into traffic and pulled a tight U-turn.

"Bekka just got run over!" Brian explained.

Will looked in his rearview mirror at Bekka and scoffed, "You're lookin' alright for somebody who just got run over. How was it?"

Bekka bit her lip and folded her hands together, not sure how to respond.

"We'll talk about it at Derek's! Just hurry!" Brian said.

Will chuckled, "Buddy, I feel like I've got popcorn cooking under my skin and my head's throbbing! I want out of this sunlight in the *worst* possible way! Trust me, I'm hurrying!"

Derek was waiting out front when the van pulled in. As Bekka climbed out he smiled at her warmly, "Are you alright?" He asked, starting down the steps to join them.

Bekka nodded, "Just a little shaken up from this whole morning."

Brian frowned, stepping down, "How do you know what happened?"

Derek smirked, "I don't, but you wouldn't have called for Will to give you a ride unless it was something serious. And since Bekka's been the topic of choice for the past few days—"

"Yea, yea! Aren't you just so goddam clever?" Will rolled his eyes as he stepped out of the van and hurried past them and up the steps towards the door.

"Is your grandfather still home?" David asked.

Derek nodded, "He's in the kitchen."

"Is it safe to talk about Bekka with him around?" David started up the steps after Will.

Another nod from Derek, "I've been talking to him about it already."

"You find out anything new?" Brian's voice was hopeful.

"Some," Derek turned and walked in after them and closed the door.

Brian shook his head, "We can't work with 'some'!"

Derek shrugged as he walked by, "Would you rather work with jack-shit?"

"Language!" His grandfather's voice boomed from the kitchen.

"Sorry!" Derek called out.

The old man shook his head as he blew on a mug of tea and stared thoughtfully down at a Sudoku puzzle. His skin was the color of coffee beans and a well-kept patch of dark gray hair lay on top of his head; a mustache of the same shade hanging over his lip. Over the years his face had drooped with age but he'd kept a strong, fierce pair of brilliant dark eyes; eyes that took in each member of the group before returning to Derek, "It's repulsive the way you kids talk nowadays! There are dark energies in those words, y'know!"

"Yes, Grandfather, I know," Derek said as he poured himself a cup of tea from the pot on the stovetop.

"Is this the girl you mentioned?" The old man asked as his eyes landed on Bekka.

"Yes," Derek didn't turn around as he answered, "She's still a little scared."

The old man scoffed but halfway through it caught in his throat and a coughing fit ensued, "I should imagine so!" He stood and approached Bekka, "These sorts of things don't happen every day, after all." He smiled as he studied Bekka, narrowing his eyes analytically, "Do they?"

Bekka bit her lip and nodded.

Brian frowned and shifted his weight on one leg.

The others stood by patiently and watched.

Finally the old man stepped back and shook his head, whistling, "Boy, oh boy! Whatever you got in there, there are *a lot* of them!"

"Any idea what they are?" Derek asked as he took a seat at the chair beside his grandfather's.

The old man sighed, "At first glance I'd say they were curses, but they seem more... sentient."

Derek quirked an eyebrow, "'sentient'?"

"Yes. You said that she saw them before they entered her, is that correct?" His grandfather asked.

"That's right," Derek stepped behind his grandfather and reached into his pocket and pulled out his flask. As he unscrewed the lid to pour whatever was inside into his tea he looked back towards his grandfather to be sure he hadn't seen anything, "So... do you think they could be spirits?"

"It's not like spirits to stick around long enough to possess anyone, and for this many to occupy one body..." The old man shook his head before perking up and frowning, "And I'll thank you *not* to try to sneak alcohol by me!"

Derek sighed and rolled his eyes, "Sorry."

Brian frowned, "Can you give her an exorcism or something?"

"Oh those hardly ever work, and there are far too many entities for it to be successful."

Bekka frowned, "Exorcism?" She looked back and forth between Derek and his grandfather, "Are you saying there are *demons* inside of me?"

"Oh that word!" The old man shook his head and returned to his seat, groaning as he settled in, "All that satanic music has gone to your heads!"

"Grandfather, it's not—"

The old man held his hand up for silence and Derek obliged. A bushy gray eyebrow rose in Bekka's direction and the old man leaned back, "Before we said anything, what did *you* think they were?"

"Um..." Bekka twiddled her thumbs, "I really didn't know."

"Look, not to be rude or anything, but can you help us or not?" Brian asked.

Derek's eyes narrowed and he started to move towards him; his fists clenched.

The old man held up a hand to stop him and shook his head at Derek before turning to face Brian, "And what do you think we should do?"

"I don't know!" Brian shook his head, "I don't know *anything* about this hocus-pocus shit!"

Bekka's eyes widened and she gave him a pleading look, "Brian, don't!"

He shook his head, "No! This is fucking bullshit!"

The old man gave a slow nod, "Bad energies."

"Spare me!" Brian spat.

"Hey! Don't talk to him like that!" Derek narrowed his eyes and the table began to shake, rattling against the hardwood floor.

"Settle," the old man laid a hand on his grandson's shoulder and waited until everything was calm once again.

Derek frowned but relaxed nonetheless.

David and Will shared a look and rolled their eyes.

The old man saw this and chuckled, "And what do the vampire and therion think?"

Both shrugged.

"What about Aunt Chloe?" Derek's voice was suddenly hopeful.

The old man thought, running his finger along the length of his mustache and nodding as he did.

"What's an 'Aunt Chloe'?" Will asked.

"She's a psychic," Derek answered, keeping his gaze locked on his grandfather.

Will laughed, "And we're supposed to go to her for

answers to a *real* problem?"

Derek looked away from the old man to glare at him, "She's a *real* psychic!"

Will scoffed, "Only real psychics are the vampire kind, and all they'll do for you is drain your head."

"There is a difference, you narrow-minded ass!" Derek shot, "She'll be able to look inside Bekka's mind and see what's going on. Maybe even channel some of the things inside her so we can find out what they want."

Bekka's face lit up.

David shrugged, "It's worth it to try."

Brian, still bitter, frowned and folded his arms across his chest, "Any danger in it?"

Derek shook his head, "I don't see how there could be."

"What about the people trying to kill her?" Will asked, "Shit-ton of danger there, if you ask me."

Derek frowned, "Well nobody—"

"Yes," Derek's grandfather cut him off before another fight could begin, "That *is* an issue."

"You think?" Brian said, getting another angry look from Derek.

The old man nodded, "Assuming these events are related, Chloe may be able to find a solution to both."

Will rubbed his hands together, "Great! So we going to see the old girl now?"

"Tomorrow," the old man answered.

"Tomorrow?" Brian yelled, "We finally have a chance

at some answers and you want us to *wait?*"

"Chloe is retired," Derek explained, glaring but holding back his temper.

David frowned, "Then how do we know she'll help us?"

"I'll call her tonight," Derek's grandfather said, "And tomorrow she *will* be ready to help you."

Bekka looked down, "So what do we do until then?"

Will looked at her and smiled, "How 'bout we go catch a movie? It's not like there's any trucks at the theater," he chuckled, "Unless we go to the drive-in."

Bekka smiled and nodded, "I think I'd like that, actually."

While they sat in Derek's living room and watched TV, he went on his computer—an outdated piece of equipment that Brian was sure worked solely on the owners' magic—and got the show times for the movie. Bekka, who had sat beside Brian on the couch, lasted a little more than five minutes before falling asleep and filling the room with the sound of her soft snores.

"Hey! Let's draw on her face!" Will laughed.

"How 'bout I draw my boot up your ass?" Brian replied, "Give her some damn peace!"

Will frowned and looked back towards the television,

defeated, "Just thought some humor would lighten the situation."

"And, as per usual," David said, "you thought wrong."

"'as per usual'" Will mimicked in a whiny voice, "Honestly, do you listen to yourself?"

Brian smirked and looked down at Bekka's sleeping face. For the first time that day she looked calm, and he was glad to see the nervousness gone from her features for the time being.

"Why don't you take a picture?" Will teased.

Brian glared and moved to punch the vampire in the shoulder and quickly regretted it as Will became a blur and he found his arm trapped behind his back. Cringing, Brian struggled against the vampire's hold, "Ow! Asshole! You're gonna break it!"

Will gave a fanged smirked, "Say 'uncle'!"

Brian glared, "Your mom's a scab-eater!"

"Oh no he didn't!" Will twisted his arm a little more and getting a whimper from Brian, "Say it!"

"Uncle! God dammit! Uncle!" Brian surrendered and pulled his arm away, stretching it, "You're a real douchebag, you know that?"

Will shrugged and laughed, "I wouldn't want to disappoint my fans."

Bekka opened her eyes and smirked, "Now, now. Play nice, children."

Brian's face turned red as he rubbed the cramp out of

his arm.

Will smiled and shrugged, "He started it!"

"And I'll finish it," Bekka's smile was just as wide; an eerie confidence behind it.

"I'd like to see you try it," Will chuckled.

Bekka sat up and cracked her knuckles, "Try me."

Will frowned, "Huh?"

She motioned to Brian, "Go on. Try to grab him again."

Brian frowned, "What? I don't—"

There was a flash as Will's body once again became a blur and Bekka lunged. Before the others could question what had happened Will crashed to the floor; Bekka pinning him down.

"Now," Bekka mused, easily holding down the thrashing vampire, "say 'uncle'."

Will's voice—with his face mashed against the carpet—was muffled as he began spouting a series of "awnkels".

Bekka stood up as Will dragged himself to his feet, looking more embarrassed than hurt. The others stared, the TV suddenly a very distant and unimportant distraction, before they started in with a round of applause.

TEN

Brian sighed and rolled his eyes.

It was premier night at the theater and the line stretched and writhed like an unholy thing that extended from the front doors and snaked halfway around the building. The crowd of people—bunched together in tight, chattering segments—waited their turns as the two tellers in the box office did what they could to keep things moving quickly. Huddled amidst the chaos, the five band-mates did what they could to keep themselves entertained and distracted from being bored.

"Jesus-fuck-me-Christ!" Will groaned, standing on his toes to try and get a better view, "Maybe this was a bad idea."

"Maybe you should be a little more patient," Derek said.

Will stuck out his tongue, "And what if I don't *want* to be patient?"

David sighed and rolled his eyes, "Don't get him started."

Derek nodded once and looked around him for a moment before digging into his jacket and retrieving his flask. He took a quick and stealthy pull from the end and let out a relieved sigh and handed it over to David, who looked around him as well before accepting the liquor and taking a long sip as well.

Brian shook his head, "You two are unbelievable."

"Tell me about it!" Will scoffed, shaking his head, "Patience, indeed!"

David smirked, holding out the flask towards Brian, "You want some? Might help you relax."

Brian glared at him, "I'd sooner die!"

At that moment a large group of teens gave up their spot in line to head elsewhere. The empty space was quickly filled by those behind them and the band found themselves advancing several feet.

"At least the line is moving," Bekka offered.

A coy smile spread across Will's face and he shook his head, "How is it that you—the lead singer of a *heavy metal* band—can be so optimistic? Shouldn't you be talking about maiming all those who stand in your way and eating their babies or something?"

"I prefer to save the poetic stuff for my music," Bekka laughed, "Besides, thinking that way all the time gives me a headache."

Will laughed, "With an attitude like that, I'm surprised you're not singing Country."

Bekka shuddered.

Brian couldn't help but laugh, "That'll be the day."

By the time they reached the box office the movie they'd intended to see was already half-an-hour into its showing. Forced to make a quick replacement decision, they all turned to Will. Though he pretended to be insulted by the responsibility, they could all tell that he'd been hoping this would be the case. After choosing what Brian could already tell would be a sub-standard comedy and fetching the refreshments they made their way into the theater.

As they entered, Brian stepped away from the group to take a seat in the back row. Seeing him settle in, Bekka and David followed, plopping down beside him. Derek—shaking some candy pieces into his palm and popping them into his mouth—took the next seat. Will, not noticing, had already started down the aisles and stopped when he noticed he was alone and frowned at his band-mates.

"Oh come on!" He protested, "We won't be able to see shit back there!" Nobody moved. Will scowled, "You guys suck!" He growled as he slammed his butt into a seat beside Derek, "And coming from me, that's saying something!"

"Hey! Shut up back there!" Somebody further up shouted.

Will's eyes narrowed, "You shut up, asshole! For fuck's sake, the movie hasn't even started yet!"

Brian sighed at their drummer and his antics in favor of the movie trailers. At that moment, methodically tossing handfuls of popcorn into his mouth, he was able to forget all of the chaos. It wasn't until he once again heard Will's voice speak up that he bothered to look away from the screen.

"Hey, Bekka, you alright?" Will's voice sounded unnaturally worried.

Three sets of eyes moved in Will's direction, all of them startled by his tone, then immediately shifted to Bekka, who was staring, eyes wide, at the ceiling. Once again the three shifted their collective gaze, but were rewarded with nothing more than the dimmed theater lights.

"Bekka?" Will called again.

There was no response.

Brian frowned and shook her shoulder, "Hey, Bekka! What is it?"

Her head turned towards him; her eyes seeming reluctant to look away, "None of you see that?"

Brian shook his head, "See what?"

"There are more of them," Bekka whispered, her eyes growing wider.

Brian frowned, "I think we should go!"

Everyone nodded and began to rise from their seats.

"Oh no..." Bekka gasped.

The others looked at Bekka questioningly a moment before the others in the theater rose to their feet and turned to face the five; their movements synchronized.

Until they started to advance on them.

The other movie-goers graceful movements suddenly became a hellish, free-for-all rush to see who could get to the back row first. Some ran to the aisles and started up the slight incline while others took to vaulting and hand-springing over the rows of seats; their eyes shining white in the limited light as their pupils rolled to the back of their heads.

"Shit!" Brian gasped, "Not again!"

"What the fuck?" Will looked around at the others, "What are they doing?"

Before anyone could answer the first of the attackers—a young girl with blonde hair and a pink pair of sweatpants—launched herself over three rows of seats in a single leap and came down at them with an angry shriek. Bekka's eyes went wide in shock and fear and Brian hurried to put himself between the two. The girl's war-cry stopped abruptly as she summersaulted in midair and landed gracefully on the seat directly in front of Brian, swiping at him her pink-painted fingernails.

The attack was inhumanly fast and—Brian was sure—would have taken his face off if David hadn't caught the attacker's wrist at the last moment. Brian's eyes widened at the sight of the manicured hand—curling and flexing in an attempt to reach him despite David's grip—only an inch from his face.

The other movie-goers flooded their aisle, coming in from both sides in their attempt to reach Bekka. Will hissed, baring his fangs at an approaching man. The threat went ignored—something that Brian was sure had never happened to Will before—and his eyes went from narrowed and angry to wide and confused.

More than a dozen people were on them at once, clawing and punching at everyone and anyone they could get their hands onto. The four of them took the beatings as they huddled protectively around Bekka, who whimpered and curled up in her seat. Pushing and shoving against the onslaught, they did everything they could to keep their attackers back only to have them flood back once again.

"They're not stopping!" Brian cried out.

Will growled and threw a fist into another attacker's chest, sending them to the ground, "Thanks for the update, Captain Obvious."

Derek's hands worked like a Kung Fu master's as he blocked and countered any attack that came his way. As he fought, his palms began to glow brighter and brighter, until it looked like his forearms were consumed in blue flames.

"Get down!" He shouted.

Before anybody had a chance to react to the warning, a ball of bright light exploded from his hands. As the ball of energy collided with the others, they shook from the impact, their knees buckling. Brian's eyes widened; a strange warmth filling him as it did.

The attackers didn't get off so easy.

Mouths hanging open in silent cries of pain, they were hurled away—their bodies lifted and carried off by the growing orb—sending them all nearly five yards from the awe-struck band-mates. As the blue wall shimmered and vanished, the bodies of the attackers began to drop down to the theater floor.

Derek's eyes spun and he teetered on his feet. Seeing this, Brian threw out a hand to steady his friend on the left side, only to have him start to fall to the right. Before anybody could say anything, Will was holding the unconscious bassist in his arms.

"I think it's time to go!" His voice was stern and undisputable.

"W-what about them?" Bekka stammered, motioning to the bodies strewn about the theater.

"They're alive," David assured her, pulling her from her seat.

Brian frowned, studying the still masses littering the theater, "Are you sure?"

"Yes!" Will shouted, "I can still hear their heartbeats! Now move!"

Brian nodded and hurried out the theater door with them, nearly crashing into an attendant who was coming to investigate the commotion. The teen frowned, eyeing the unconscious Derek in Will's arms.

"What's going on?" He demanded, "What was all that noise?"

"It's our friend!" Bekka explained, pointing at Derek,

"He's a diabetic!"

The attendant's eyes widened, "Oh man! Is he alright?"

Will nodded, picking up on Bekka's lie, "He'll be fine. He just needs his insulin shot."

"Then what was all that noise?"

"People in there thought he was dying," Brian offered, "Freaked 'em out."

"Should I call an ambulance?"

"No need," Bekka started past him, motioning for the others to follow, "His medicine's in the car. He'll be fine."

They rushed around the confused teen.

As they passed the concession stand, the nearby clerks' walkie-talkies sparked to life and the attendant's terrified voice came spilling out.

"Something's happened in theater five! There were a couple of kids..."

The rest of the message was lost as they worked their way out the doors and hurried to Will's van.

"Shit!" Will shifted Derek's limp body on his shoulder, "Why the fuck did I park so damn far out?"

"Hey wait! Stop!" An older man came crashing through the doors after them, "I said stop!"

Brian frowned and turned to face who he guessed was the theater's manager as he chased after them.

David stopped, "What are you doing?"

"I can handle this!" Brian promised him, "Get them out of here!"

"Brian!" Bekka started to turn back only to get scooped up by David and dragged to the van.

The man huffed in exertion as he did his best to sprint after them, heaving something into his radio as he did. Though Brian couldn't hear what was said, he recognized the word "cops". Deciding to try and go with the excuse Bekka had come up with he put himself between his friends and the approaching man.

"Hey, buddy, all my friend needs is his shot! If you just leave us—"

"Yea, his shot, huh? Bullshit! I've got a theater full of kids who've been beaten to hell and are barely breathing and you're asking me to believe that your friend's diabetes is responsible?" Seeing the others reach Will's van the man frowned, "Hey, you little shits, where do you think you're going?" He tried to get by Brian, who side-stepped to block him. The maneuver was ill-timed, however, and both stumbled and went down, Brian catching the side of his head on the curb, "Son of a bitch!"

Brian stared up at the man as the world began to spin around him. He tried to stand—to hold the manager back while his friends got away—but his body was heavy and unresponsive. Trying to shout at the man, his vision blurred and started to go black.

"You think he needs to go to the hospital?"

"He just hit his head! God dammit, give him some air!"

"Still can't believe he did that for us!"

"Shut up! He's waking up!"

"Oh, he's right! Look, his eyes are opening! Hey Brian, welcome—oops! He's gone again!"

"You dumbass!"

Brian groaned as his eyes fluttered open before realizing it hurt less to keep them closed. For the brief moment his eyes were open he was able to make out the familiar setup of his and David's living room and realized that he was on their couch. The back of his head throbbed and he lifted his arm to rub the sore spot, finding a large bump there.

"Shit!" He muttered, "What happened?"

"Bekka's a fucking monster is what happened!" Will laughed.

The drummer's loud voice and cackles sent agonizing waves through Brian's head and he clenched his eyes to fight the flood of pain, "Oh, fuck! Quiet down!"

The laughter stopped suddenly and Brian could almost feel the tension in the room rise.

"Maybe we *should* call an ambulance. He doesn't look so good," David said.

"I'd feel a lot better without all this fucking shouting!" Brian muttered, "I'll be fine. No doctors."

"You're lucky," Derek kept his voice low, "You'd either be in a hospital bed or a prison cell by now if it weren't for Bekka."

Brian let his eyes open again and he scanned the crowd for Bekka. Spotting her beside him—crouched down and looking more worried than heroic—he gave her a reassuring smile and started to sit up. As his head lifted from the pillow, the world started to spin and things started going dark again.

He decided it was better to stay lying back.

"What happened?" He asked again, his dry tongue sticking to the roof of his mouth and slurring his speech.

"Bekka-the-beast carried you home," Will answered. There was the sound of flesh slapping against flesh and he exclaimed in pain, "Ow! What was that for?"

"Don't call her that," David answered.

Brian growled and looked up at Derek, the only person who'd been able to keep his voice at a reasonable level while being straight-forward, "Don't make me ask again, magic-man."

Derek shook his head, "I wasn't awake for most of it. When I came to I was in the van. It was a moment before I realized that Bekka wasn't in it with us."

Brian frowned at this and looked to Bekka with a combination of anger and confusion.

She blushed and looked down, though he wasn't sure if it was shame or pride that he saw in her face.

"She wouldn't stay still!" Will chimed in, "We had everyone inside and I'd started off but she kept making a big deal about leaving you behind! I told her you could handle yourself, but she wouldn't listen!"

Brian looked at him, confused, "Wouldn't listen?"

Will nodded, "The crazy beast jumped out the damn van while I was doing sixty! Last thing she said was to meet her here."

Derek nodded, "She got you back here on her own."

"On her own? Shit, bitch, she *beat* us here!" Will pointed out.

Brian frowned and shook his head then quickly stopped, the resulting pain nearly unbearable, "How...?"

David shook his head, "We don't know, either." He looked at Bekka nervously and sighed, "The door was still locked when we got here, but when we got in you were on the couch and she was sitting beside you, waiting for us."

Brian nodded slowly, doing his best to avoid the rolling sensation in his head, "She's been pretty good at not making sense lately."

Bekka frowned and looked back up at Brian with concern-filled eyes, "You going to be alright?"

Letting out a sigh, Brian nodded, though he wasn't feeling very alright, he didn't want to make her more nervous than she already appeared, "Yea." He grumbled, "I'll be fine." He clucked his tongue and tried sitting up again, making it up a little more before he had to stop, "Mind telling us what happened back at the theater?"

Bekka frowned at the question. "There were more of those things," she explained, "They came in through the ceiling and went into those people."

119

Derek laid a hand on her shoulder, giving it a soft squeeze, "The spell I hit them with was a concentration of energy." He explained to her, "Whatever energies were controlling them would have been forced out by it."

Bekka frowned, "I thought your grandfather said that exorcisms don't usually work."

Derek shook his head, "It wasn't really an exorcism," he confessed, "To be honest, I wasn't even sure if it would work!"

Bekka glared, "You put those peoples' lives in danger?"

"There didn't seem to be any other option," Derek defended himself, "And I was almost certain it *would* work."

"But not POSITIVE," she pulled herself to her feet.

"Stop it," Brian's voice hurt his own head and he groaned. When the pain had subsided he focused his eyes on Bekka, narrowing them, "He did what he needed to protect you; to protect us!" He turned to face Derek, "Thank you."

The group stared in astonishment; none more shocked then Derek, who slowly nodded.

"You're welcome." He smiled.

Brian took in a sharp inhale and forced himself to sit up on the couch the rest of the way, resting his arms on his knees and breathing out slowly until the wave of nausea passed, "So," he spoke softly, "psychic aunt tomorrow."

ELEVEN

"Okay," Will sighed, watching Brian rub the back of his still-aching head as they shambled out of the apartment, "maybe the movies *was* a bad idea." They all had spent the night in the cramped apartment; squeezing themselves in the living room around Brian, who had been given the couch for the remainder of the night with limited complaints from Will. Though he had grumbled and complained about being forced to sleep on the floor, the others could tell he was just as glad that Brian was alright. Heading down the stairs, Will continued to rant, "But it's not like anybody could have known that all that shit was gonna happen!"

"Nobody was blaming you, anyway," Bekka pointed out.

"How do you think those things found us there, anyway?" He asked.

"They must be able to track their own," Derek answered.

Bekka, walking alongside Brian, frowned at that, "How would that be possible?"

Derek shrugged, "Energy isn't hard to track if you know what you're looking for."

David, walking behind Brian and Bekka, let out an aggravated growl. The animal sound reverberated in his throat on its way out and again in the narrow hall, making it sound all the more menacing.

Four sets of nervous eyes drifted towards him.

"This aunt of yours had better be of some use to us!" His eyes, usually calm and calculating, had taken on a bestial tint and the group gave him a little extra space as they descended the final flight of stairs.

Derek sighed as he pushed his way through the door and turned down the hall towards the main entrance, "Here's hoping."

"You're sure your grand-daddy can get us a meeting with her today?" Brian asked.

"If he said he'd do it," Derek assured him, "then it'll be done."

The van—free of any citations or waiting police officers— was parked out front where Will had left it the night before. Relieved by this, everyone began piling in, none surprised to find Will already sitting in the driver's seat, keys in the ignition, and seeming impatient with their less-than vampiric speed.

Brian waited until everybody was seated before climbing inside and sliding the door shut behind him. Before he was even in his seat beside Bekka, Will had started the van and, with a sharp jerk, merged into traffic. The jolt nearly sent Brian tumbling against the sliding door, only to be caught at the wrist by Bekka.

Her hand was soft and warm.

Brian felt his cheeks go hot as he stabilized himself and took his seat, looking in every direction except hers.

"So where am I heading, magic-man?" Will asked as he cut off a BMW and growled at the resulting honks.

Derek shook his head at the maneuver, "Right at the third light."

Will nodded and sighed as he was forced to once again turn into the right lane to accommodate the directions. The BMW driver made a note of driving up beside the van and flicking him off. When the third light came up, the van screeched to make the turn.

"Fucking hell, Will!" Brian cursed as he was thrown about in the back, "Keep this bucket on the street!"

"Please do," David seconded.

"Oh settle down, girls," Will shot, "This is why they

make seat belts."

"At the next light turn left and keep going for four blocks," Derek said, irritated.

Will smirked and took the turn, softer this time, "Don't sound so fed up already. It's still so early."

"Don't remind me," Derek groaned.

Brian rolled his eyes and turned his attention to Bekka, who had her hands clasped tightly together and hugged between her knees, her chin resting on her chest. For a moment he thought that she'd fallen asleep, but as he continued to stare she turned her neck to catch his gaze. She smiled at him, though he could see that she was scared, and he forced a smile in the hopes of reassuring her. They stared at one another a moment longer before a strand of purple hair fell in her eyes and she turned away to brush it aside.

"How's your head?" She spoke for the first time since they'd gotten in the van.

Brian shrugged and touched the sore spot gingerly, "Still hurts a little, but I'll be alright."

Bekka nodded, her eyes trained to the back of the driver's seat.

"How 'bout you?" He asked.

She looked up at the question as though she'd been dreading it and took in a heavy breath. "I'm alright," she answered, then shook her head and scoffed, "Better than 'alright', I suppose. I mean, I feel *great*! I know that I should be tired and sore," she shook her head and looked at her hands as if seeing something there for the first time, "I don't feel natural. I feel like nothing can hurt me; like I can do anything!"

Brian studied her, unsure of how to respond.

"Here," Derek pointed to an Italian restaurant, "Park in the alley."

Will frowned at the setting but did as he was told, "You hungry or something?"

Derek ignored the question and undid his seatbelt as the van came to a stop beside a dumpster. The others looked around, confused as well, and followed after Derek as he stepped out.

Brian jogged a few steps to get beside him and grabbed his shoulder, "What gives, man? I thought we were going to see your aunt!"

"We are," Derek nodded and motioned at the back entrance to the restaurant.

Not understanding, Brian stayed where he was as Derek shrugged his hand off and went to the door and pressed a buzzer mounted to the wall.

"DELIVERY!" A voice called out from the other side of the door and after a short moment it opened and a large man wearing a grease-covered apron and wiping his hands on an equally greasy towel stood in front of them. Looking more like a professional wrestler than a fine-dining chef, their greeter stared with an equal amount of confusion as the group looked from him to Derek. The man studied them and finally tossed the towel over his shoulder and locked eyes with Derek.

"There'd better be several crates of tomatoes in that van!"

"We're not here to make a delivery," Derek said flatly.

The man inhaled then, his chest puffing up and making him look all the more intimidating, "Then you're wasting my time."

Derek didn't budge, "We need to speak to Chloe."

Like a balloon meeting a pinhead the man's chest deflated. His eyes narrowed and his face puckered for a moment before he raised an eyebrow, "You Derek?"

He nodded.

The man smirked and craned out his neck to scan the alley, "Could *really* use those tomatoes, though." He grumbled as he disappeared for a moment, leaving the doorway open.

"Should we go in?" Bekka asked.

Derek shook his head, "Just wait."

The metallic sounds of cookware and the heat from the kitchen leaked out from the doorway, though little more than a sink and a shelf of towels were visible from their angle. Then—like magic—a tall, slender black woman emerged; a wide, immaculate smile beaming and bright brown eyes sparkling.

"Derek! So good to see you!" She cooed.

"It's great to see you too, Chloe," Derek said as the two leaned forward and embraced one another.

The group stared in silent shock at the "retired" aunt that they'd come to see. Where everyone had been expecting a crazy old woman they were instead looking at a beautiful woman no older than thirty wearing the same apron-and-towel ensemble as the man from before, though hers was speckled with what they could only hope was sauce and her hair was tied tightly back in a pony-tail.

"Wow!" Will offered, licking his lips.

Brian jabbed him hard in the ribs and frowned when there was little reaction from the vampire.

"I take it you got grandpa's call, then?" Derek asked.

Chloe's face turned serious and she nodded, "Yes. He phoned late last night; said that you and your friends were having a bit of a situation."

"That's one way to put it," Will scoffed.

Derek glared at him, but it was Chloe's bright eyes that shut him up. The woman wiped her hands on her apron before reaching behind her back and untying it and pulling it over her head. After folding it neatly, she set it down on the doorstep and motioned for them to follow her.

"Come. I'm sure your friend"—she put some emphasis on the word as she smirked at Will—"would like to be out of the sun."

As they were led inside, Will let out a heavy sigh; visibly relieved to be out of the sunlight. Chloe, leading them through the kitchen, pulled open the door to the restaurant and led them to the rows of tables. They were led past the hostess—a young brunette that both Will and David lingered on—and into a back room that, Brian assumed, was reserved for parties and other special events. Though there was a lot of space, only a single, round table was present along with six chairs spaced around it. When everyone was inside, Chloe pulled the doors closed behind them.

"Now," Chloe mused as she sat down in one of the chairs. She looked around at the band before finally settling on Bekka and pressing her fingertips together, "Quite the situation you've found yourself in, eh?"

Bekka blushed and nodded.

"Have they hurt you in any way?"

Bekka shook her head.

"But you *can* feel them?"

Another nod.

"Do they talk to you?"

Brian frowned, "What kind of question is that? Of course they don't—"

"They're trying to," Bekka confessed, blushing. "But I don't understand what they're trying to tell me," she looked down sadly, as though she'd just confessed to a crime.

Brian stared at her a moment, unsure of what to make of this new fact.

Chloe pressed her fingers more tightly together, her knuckles bending a bit like a spider's legs as she nodded. "Mmhm. They are hard to understand, I've heard. Very emotionally driven' sometimes it isn't what you *hear* but what you *feel*," she leaned forward, resting her elbows on the table's surface, "So, what've you been feeling lately?"

Bekka sighed and shook her head, "I don't know. I've been feeling…" She thought for a moment, "They're scared."

"Scared of what?" Chloe pressed.

"I'm not sure," Bekka frowned, "But I've been having these dreams."

"Oh?" Chloe's eyes lit up, "What sort of dreams?"

"In a lot of them," Bekka explained, "I'm running, but I can't see where I'm going."

"Running *after* something or running *from* something?" Chloe's voice was becoming a whisper.

Bekka swallowed nervously and Brian noticed a bead of sweat that had begun to travel down her temple, "From something."

Chloe nodded. "Please join hands," she instructed, already placing her own hands on either side of the table, palms up.

The others stared at her.

"Join hands!" She barked.

Reluctant at first, the group took the hands of their neighbors.

Chloe let out a heavy sigh, her body visibly relaxing as her eyes drifted shut. Derek was quick to mimic the process, followed soon after by Bekka and then David. Brian and Will exchanged skeptical glances.

"Will the vampire and the skeptic please join the group?" The two were surprised to see that Chloe's eyes were still shut.

After another shared glance, they closed their eyes and relaxed their bodies as well.

For a long while the room was silent and, convinced

that nothing was going to happen, Brian opened his eyes and was surprised to see that both Chloe and Bekka were facing towards the ceiling, their mouths moving but no sound being made. Between the two of them was Derek, head hanging low and swaying slightly; his cheeks flushed and face covered in a layer of fresh sweat. Brian stared at this a moment before nudging Will on his left and David on his right. The two opened their eyes and, taking in the sight, stared in shock.

"Hey!" Brian called out.

Neither of the three reacted.

David frowned and tried to shake his hand from Chloe's but seemed unable to free himself from her grip. Seeing this, Will tried to let go of Bekka's hand, finding that he was unable to, as well. The three began to panic and started to separate from one another, only to find that that, too, was impossible.

"What the fuck?" Will cried out.

"What's going on?" David snarled.

Brian shook his head, staring in horror at Bekka, whose inaudible ramblings continued to flow from her lips. Turning to look at Chloe, he was relieved to see that the psychic had seemed to regain herself and was now nodding reassuringly to them.

"They're talking to us," she explained.

"Is she okay?" Brian motioned to Bekka.

Chloe nodded, her eyes shutting once again, "They traveled a long way to get here; facing a great risk by crossing over."

"Crossing over?" David shook his head, "Crossing over from *where*?"

Brian sighed and shook his head, "I don't care where they came from! What do they want with Bekka?"

"Energy disperses without a container to hold it," Chloe's voice was raspy and distant. "They took the first available vessel they could find," she tilted her head, "They knew they'd be chased; knew that others would come to drag them back."

"So they put Bekka in danger just to take a *vacation*?" Brian growled.

"What were they trying to escape from?" David asked.

"They didn't want to assimilate," Chloe went on, "They were afraid."

Brian shook his head, "Afraid or not, tell them they need to go back! Tell them they can't have her!"

Chloe shook her head, "It's too late. They came back to feel life once again—to escape the abyss—and they're as much a part of her now as her own essence."

"NO!" Brian roared.

Bekka's body shook violently at that moment and her eyes flew open; everybody's hands unclasping and falling to their sides. She gasped as though she hadn't taken a breath during the whole ordeal and the others rushed from their seats to steady her as her body shook.

"Bekka!" Brian called to her, "Bekka, say something!"

"I… can't… breath!" She gasped, the words coming out in forced heaves as her face started to turn blue.

Will scowled, "Fuck! What's happening to her?"

"She's panicking!" David explained, "Bekka, you need to relax!"

"Chloe?" Derek's voice was soft but filled with concern, "Shit! Guys!"

The three turned their heads and went wide-eyed as they watched the psychic's eyes start to roll back in her head.

"Oh fuck me sideways!" Brian said, "No! Not now!" He looked up at David and Will, "I need some time! Stall her!"

The vampire and werewolf nodded, jumping to their feet and getting between Bekka and the possessed psychic. Derek stayed close to his aunt, calling out to her and trying to fight what was happening. Though it was clear she was losing the battle, the process seemed to be moving slower than the night before. Brian kept his eyes on the scene for a brief moment before looking back down at Bekka.

"Come on!" He urged her, "We need to get out of here!"

Tears were beginning to stream down Bekka's face. Her labored breathing, though softer, was still excruciating to Brian's ears and his mind raced for possible solutions.

"Chloe! No!" Derek cried out.

"It's got her!" David yelled.

Derek gasped, "No! Don't—"

Brian flinched as a loud, metallic sound echoed in the room and he turned to look at the scene.

Derek stared in shock and horror as Chloe's body hit

the floor; Will standing over her with one of the chairs gripped in his hands. Though the furniture had survived the ordeal, it was clear that the vampire had used it to bludgeon Derek's aunt.

Derek shot to his feet and he lunged at him, "What did you do?"

Dropping the chair, Will caught Derek in mid-lunge and held him a safe distance away, "Whoa! Chill-ax, magic-man! She was gonna go all dark-side on us if we didn't do something!"

"You didn't have to hit her with a goddam chair," Derek screamed at him.

"Okay, firstly; quiet down unless you want an audience! Second—I didn't kill her! And third—I'm a drummer; I fix everything by hitting it!"

Nobody laughed.

David shook his head, "While I don't agree with his methods, Will's got a point! The Chloe-problem is out of the way. Now let's get out of here!"

Brian looked down at Bekka, "Can you stand?"

Bekka heaved but nodded.

David stepped over and helped Brian get her to her feet and stabilize her while she caught her breath. Will, glancing down at Chloe with a slightly satisfied smirk, set the chair down.

Derek shook his head, "We can't just leave her like this!"

Brian glared at him, "And we can't just stay here!"

Derek considered this for a moment and nodded, "You guys get out of here. I'll stay here and take care of this."

"How do you plan to do that?" David asked.

Derek bit his lip, looking at his unconscious aunt for a moment, "I'll tell them she fell and hit her head." He glared at Will, "It might not be in the right order, but at least we wouldn't be abandoning her," he shook his head, "We don't need any more reasons for the cops to get called on us."

Will nodded, "Avoid cops. Good plan. Now let's go!"

Bekka took in a jagged breath and looked with concern to Derek, "Will you be alright?"

Derek nodded and smiled, "You don't need to worry. When she comes to she'll confirm my story."

David raised a skeptical eyebrow, "You sure about that?"

Another nod from Derek, "Yes! Now go!"

TWELVE

It was nearly eight hours later when they finally heard from Derek. They'd once again piled themselves into Brian's and David's apartment, trying their best to pass the time with whatever DVD they could find. Halfway through the fifth movie of the night when the phone started to ring.

Brian, who was closest to the phone, picked it up and studied the unknown number on the caller ID before answering it and pressing it to the side of his head that hurt the least.

"Hello?"

"Brian," Derek's voice was calm and composed, "How's everyone doing?"

Brian knew that by "everyone" he meant "Bekka" and, without meaning to, he glanced over at her, "Everyone's fine. How's Chloe?"

Derek sighed into the receiver, "Minor concussion—nothing too serious, though. Doctors say she'll be fine."

"Good to hear. She—uh—was honest about how it happened?" Brian was careful with his choice of words.

"Yea. She told them that she tripped when she was getting up," Derek explained.

"Well, I'm glad she's alright," Brian said, making sure the others could hear.

"We all are. I'll be over in a little bit."

"You need Will to pick you up?" Brian offered.

Hearing his name, Will glanced up, "Huh?"

"Nah. My grandfather's here," Derek answered, "I'll have him drop me off."

"Oh, he's there?" Brian bit at his lip ring, "He's not mad about this, is he?"

"Not really," Derek lowered his voice, "Said it probably saved her life in the long run."

"Well that's good to hear."

"Don't suppose you could put on a pot of tea for me?" Derek's voice wasn't hopeful.

Brian sighed, "C'mon, man, you know we don't have any of that shit here!"

It was Derek's turn to sigh then, "Worth a try.

Alright, see you guys soon."

"See you soon," Brian said, ending the call and setting the phone down.

Bekka was already facing him, concern painted all over her face, "So Chloe's alright?"

Brian nodded, "Just a slight concussion. Derek said she'll be alright."

This seemed to relax Bekka and she smiled slightly. The others, who'd been listening in, seemed satisfied by what they heard and turned their eyes back towards the television.

"So do I need to drive mister magic or what?" Will asked, not bothering to look up.

Brian shook his head, "He said his grandfather would drop him off."

Will sighed and looked over his shoulder, "Does that mean we're having another sleepover?" He asked in a whiny tone.

"Looks like it," Brian shrugged.

David nodded, "Probably for the better."

Will gave him a skeptical look.

"It'd be easier for us to keep an eye on Bekka and make sure she stays safe if we're all in one place," he explained.

"Easy for you to say!" Will growled, "It's your home! I, on the other hand, have been uprooted from my lovely living-space and am being forced to sleep *not* on my big, comfy bed! Why don't we just move our little slumber party back to my place?"

"You want to risk our lives while trying to get there?" David frowned at him.

This shut Will up.

For a moment.

"Fine!" He finally surrendered, "But I get the couch this time!"

"Whatever shuts you the fuck up!" Brian groaned as he hoisted himself from his seat and went to the kitchen for a soda, hoping that the drink would calm the nicotine monkey gnawing on his shoulder.

Returning to the living room, he was only partially surprised when the phone started to ring again. Sighing, he set down the soda and answered it.

"Hello?" He hoped his voice didn't reflect how he was feeling.

"Well don't you sound pleasant."

Brian frowned at the sound of their manager's voice, "Bill? Uh, hi. What's up?"

"Well, I tried getting ahold of Bekka, but she doesn't seem to be answering her phone."

"Yea," Brian rubbed the back of his head, "She's over here right now."

"Ah. Alright, then. That makes me feel better. How's she feeling? Better, I hope."

Before Brian could think of where the question might lead he'd answered, "Yea. She's fine."

"Great!" The exuberance in his voice sent alarms off in Brian's head, "Because I lined up another gig for you guys!"

Brian took a deep breath and did his best to sound excited, "That's great! When is it?"

"Tonight!" Bill's excitement made his voice crack. He cleared his throat, "It's not too big, but it's—"

Brian frowned, "Tonight? Oh geez, Bill, I don't know. This is kind of short notice."

Their manager had started to say something but before Brian could hear a word of it Bekka had leapt from her seat and snatched the phone from his hand.

"Bill! Yea, it's Bekka," she shot Brian an angry look before turning around and beginning to pace behind the couch. After a few seconds she smiled and nodded, "Yea! We'll definitely be there!"

Brian was only two steps in his advance and less than half a syllable in his protest before Bekka had ended the call. Plopping the phone back in its charger, she looked at him with a serious-yet-pleading face.

"I need this, Brian," she looked around at the others for a moment, "We all do! It's been a rough couple of days and it'd be good for us to just go out and play for a little while!"

Brian sighed and shook his head, "But it could be dangerous!"

"And one of those things could possess a helicopter pilot and steer into the apartment right now!" She argued, "At least there we'd be in danger while doing what we love!"

"Bekka, Brian's got a point! We really should—"

David started.

Will shot to his feet, "No, biscuit-breath! *Bekka's* got the point! We're *musicians*, dammit, and here we are, abandoning our calling and sitting like scared rats in a hole waiting for the next big snake to come at us! This is horseshit!"

David shook his head, "All those people in one place and us out in the open? I'm not so sure—"

Will was in David's face before they'd seen him cross the room, "Horse. Shit!"

For a moment David looked like he might haul off and hit Will and Brian took a step back in preparation for the two superhuman creatures to start brawling in the small apartment. As the tension passed, however, David looked over his shoulder at Bekka, whose face had twisted into a pout.

Brian frowned, seeing his roommate's expression begin to change, "Oh come on, David! You can't be serious!"

"Serious as fucking cancer," Will shouted triumphantly, "We got a gig!"

David sighed and looked over at Brian with defeat written all over his face, "It *would* be nice to get out and play."

Brian scowled, "Doesn't Derek get a say in this?"

Will smirked, already getting his things ready, "Nope! Haven't you heard? Nobody cares what the bassist wants!"

Brian shook his head and turned to get his guitar out of the closet, "I hope he turns you into a frog or something when I tell him you said that."

THIRTEEN

As it turned out, Derek was not against the idea of playing that night.

In fact…

"Are you *sure* you can pull it off?" Brian asked.

Derek nodded for the fourth time at the same question, "It'll take a little while to set up, but there's no reason it shouldn't work."

Hopping excitedly on his feet, Will's face beamed and he lunged forward and embraced his startled band-mate, "Oh, magic-man, you've made me the happiest girl at the prom!"

A happy giggle erupted from Bekka, her own face giving away her excitement. Brian couldn't blame her for this, however; their bassist's solution—assuming it would actually work—had laid all of his concerns to rest, as well. Even David, ever the calm, level-headed member, seemed eager and impatient.

"How much time do you need?" Brian took a step towards Derek, shying away from the—in his opinion—too-early celebration.

Derek thought about this a moment, seemingly calculating a complex math problem, but finally shrugged, "An hour, two at the most."

Brian nodded as he took this into consideration and took a look at the time. "The show starts in four hours." he looked sternly at Derek, "If we leave now, we'll get there in less than thirty minutes. Once we're there, we'll set up all the equipment and you use *three* of those hours to do this right!"

"But I only need one or two!" Derek seemed insulted at the idea that he'd need more time.

"You'll have three hours to work your magic and work it *right!*" Brian spoke sternly, his eyes turning into angry slits, "And in those three hours you'll take every necessary precaution. I don't want any surprises to fuck this up just because you wanted to show off and finish quickly, you understand?"

Derek stiffened his jaw but nodded, seeing how serious Brian was that his plan be carefully executed. "Three hours it is," he agreed, "But you'd better tune my bass for me!"

"Consider it done," Brian assured him.

"And on that all-too-tense note," Will moved towards the door and threw it open, holding it expectantly, "we are off!"

"Whoo!" Bekka howled excitedly.

Brian sighed, hoisting his guitar case and moving towards the open door, "This had better work."

"Oh ye of little faith," Will scoffed, patting his shoulder, "Would it kill you to show some excitement?"

Brian stopped at the vampire's touch and turned to face him, "I sincerely hope not, Will."

Bill—a balding twig of a man in his mid-thirties who, despite his ties to the metal community, was never seen wearing anything but formal attire—was already at the arena and talking with the lighting director when the band arrived. Waving a quick greeting to their manager, they started for the stage and began to prepare.

Derek wasted little time in stepping off the stage when he was sure it was safe to do so and headed somewhere private to work on his spell. Though the others knew very little about magic and were still somewhat unclear as to what their bassist had in store, he'd made it clear that he could set

144

up some kind of barrier to keep out any "unwanted energies". If everything worked out the way he'd explained it, everybody who came to the show and got through the gate would be free of any possessions.

If it worked.

Brian let out another heavy sigh as he finished hooking up his guitar to its amp and checked to make sure it was properly tuned. Once he was satisfied, he moved to the other side of the stage where Derek's bass was waiting. While he took care of his end of the bargain, he couldn't help but peek over towards where Derek had disappeared to. He wasn't sure what exactly he was looking for—perhaps a ghostly, magical glow or some other reassuring sight—but he was rewarded with nothing more than the sight of his band-mate standing backstage, his eyes half-closed and his hands moving slowly and methodically as if conducting an invisible orchestra. Not satisfied with what he saw, he quickly averted his gaze. He didn't want to imagine this not working.

It was too late to turn back, anyway.

Consumed with worry, he wasn't aware of Bill's approach until he was at the edge of the stage.

"Hey!" Their manager called out.

Everybody looked up at once.

"Hey to you, Billy-boy," Will called from the back of the stage, "Way to go on hooking us up with this gig!"

"Yea!" Bekka chimed in as she wrapped some cable and set it to the side of the stage, "We totally needed this."

David gave a gracious nod from behind his own amp.

Not wanting to seem ungrateful, Brian raised a fist into the air with his pointer and pinky fingers raised, "Yea man! Rock on!" He exclaimed, though it seemed half-hearted even to him.

The praise, while obviously welcome, clearly wasn't what their manager had come over for and frowned as he scanned the stage, "Where's Derek?"

"Taking a dump," Will offered with a straight face.

Bill stared for a moment before finally shrugging. "Whatever. Look, there's some creepy-looking guy here. Says he wants to talk to you two," he motioned towards David and Will, "I gotta know, are you guys are in some kind of trouble? You know if you are you can tell—"

"Did he give a name?" David asked, already setting his guitar down.

Bill shook his head, "Just asked for you two. Wouldn't say anything else."

Will sighed, stepping out from behind his drums and beside David. "Probably an adoring fan… or a drug dealer," he smirked when Bill's eyes widened, "Shall we?"

"I suppose," David groaned.

As the two hopped down from the stage, Derek paused in his spell and poked his head out to see what was going on. David paused, watching as Will gave their bassist a shrug before they moved fluidly past their manager. Bill, still frowning, turned and started after them.

"No!" Will turned, shaking his finger at him, "You stay!"

146

David looked over his shoulder and nodded to their manager, "We'll take care of this."

Bill stopped and frowned. Finally, he gave them a single nod and turned back to face the stage where Brian and Bekka continued to set up.

David watched and waited until he was sure that their manager wasn't going to try to follow again and turned to catch up with Will.

"You haven't eaten anybody lately, have you?" Will smirked at him.

"Funny," David muttered, taking long, cat-like strides, "I was actually about to ask you the same thing."

"Look!" Will's voice dropped to a growling whisper, "I am not fucking around here! This guy is clearly an authority and if he's here to execute us I'd like to know why!"

David shook his head, "The Council has already granted us pardon for associating with humans and, unless you're keeping secrets, we haven't broken any other laws. Just relax!"

"Relax?" Will shook his head, "*This* is not a moment to relax!"

I would like to disagree. The foreign voice echoed in both their heads as they approached the stranger.

Will shivered and groaned, "Great! An auric's come pay us a visit. So not only are we going to *die*, we're gonna get our fucking brains drained and melted!"

David frowned and nudged his friend, hoping it would shut him up. Not that it mattered, anyway, since their visitor could easily read their thoughts if he so desired. While not an expert in the subject, he was more than aware of the two different types of vampires: those that fed on blood—those like Will—and those that fed on psychic energy—apparently known to the more well-informed as "aurics".

"Gentlemen," their visitor—a tall, lanky vampire in an expensive blue suit with long, slicked-back brown hair—extended a hand and patiently waited as he took each of theirs in a tight handshake. While the gesture was a polite and formal one, it ultimately came off as threatening, "I'm glad I could have this opportunity to meet with you."

"I bet," the fear in Will's voice was thick, "Probably easier than having to hunt us down, right?"

The auric raised an eyebrow.

"Ignore him," David shook his head, "What is this about?"

"Straight to business, eh Devk?"

David winced at his true name and their visitor allowed a silent moment for it to settle.

The auric's features remained stoic as he cleared his throat and continued, "While you're correct in your assumptions that I'm visiting on behalf of The Council, I assure you that my orders are *not* to execute either of you."

Will let out a heavy, relieved sigh, "Oh, thank the god of fuck!"

"Indeed," the auric sneered at Will's choice of words.

"While I'm glad that we won't be dying tonight," David's face remained hard, "I can't help but be curious as to what you're doing here."

"I'm here," the auric explained, "to give you a warning."

David frowned, "About?"

The auric frowned, "About the company you keep."

David and Will stared.

"While I'm well aware of The Council's pardon, it is not a secret within our community of your association with the human element."

"Really? The human element?" Will scoffed, "We're in a band with *three* of the flesh-bags! It's not like we're parading our existence!"

"Be that as it may," the auric's eyes shimmered slightly with agitation, "there are those who would consider those three to be a threat to our security!"

"They're not going to tell anybody," David assured.

Will nodded, "You're damn right they won't!"

The auric shook his head. "It's not me you have to convince. This is not a threat," his gaze switched with machine precision between the two, "This is simply—as I said before—a warning. There are some—rogue and clan alike—who would consider your execution or the deaths of your humans as a service to our races."

"And what would you suggest we do about it?" David snarled.

"To put it simply, quit this life," the auric answered.

"Leave the band?" Will's eyes went wide, "Are you fucking shitting me?"

The auric's gaze turned hard, "No, Mister Jones. I'm not."

"And if we refuse?" David asked.

"In that case," the auric turned his icy stare to him, "you invite a great deal of danger on yourselves and your"—he cleared his throat again—"friends."

David nodded slowly, taking their visitor's warning into consideration.

Will turned to him, shaking his head, "You're not actually considering it, are you?"

"No," David's knew his answer wasn't convincing. After a moment he looked up at the auric, "Thank you for the warning."

Will sneered, exposing a fang, "Now, unless you've bought a ticket, I'll thank you to get the hell out of here! We're trying to work."

David kept his gaze on their visitor for a moment longer while Will turned and stormed down towards the stage. The auric watched him stomp away as if it were nothing more than the tantrum of a child and eventually turned his attentions back to David.

"You understand that if I so desired," he spoke slowly; softly, "I could change both your minds in regards to this matter."

David narrowed his eyes and bared his teeth, "Then why don't you?"

"Because," he answered in a whisper, "I'm only a messenger."

"Well your message has been delivered," David turned his back on the auric, "Now I suggest you go. We have a show to prepare for," With that he started back towards the stage. Though he didn't hear the doors open or the sound of their visitor's footsteps, when he turned he found the doorway empty.

"Fucker!" Will growled as he gave his bass-drum pedal an angry slam.

Brian turned towards them and frowned, "What was that all about?"

"Nothing!" David growled as he climbed onstage, "Nothing at all!"

FOURTEEN

"It's done!" Derek said as he emerged from backstage, his face flush and covered in sweat. Everyone looked up at him and then over his shoulder to see if there was any visible evidence of what he'd done, "What?" He asked, sounding more than just a little insulted, "You don't believe me?"

Will smiled and shook his head, giving one of his cymbals a tap with his index finger, "Oh, we believe you just fine, magic-man."

"Speak for yourself," Brian muttered as he knelt down

by his amp. The equipment had been acting funny since they'd finished setting up; though the sound check had gone through well enough there was an inescapable whine that, despite all attempts, was refusing to let up. Finally, he gave the top of the amp an angry slap and stood. They'd taken care of it as best they could without taking all their stuff apart and completely rewiring it.

Needless to say, things weren't starting off too well.

Derek frowned, "Look! I did what you asked! Even took a little extra time in constructing the barricade before I powered it up."

Everybody stared at him with blank eyes.

Brian slung his guitar over his shoulder, "I'm not even going to try to understand what that meant. Just tell me it'll work."

Derek smirked at the question, "Like a charm."

Will laughed, "Charm! Get it?" He looked around, his laughter fading, "Cuz he's…" He sighed and shook his head, "Oh never mind."

"If he says it'll work then I think we owe it to him to believe it," David said as he shrugged into his guitar.

Derek smiled at David's support and lifted his bass, checking it to make sure that Brian had held up his end of the bargain by tuning it; plucking at a few chords and testing them by ear. Satisfied that everything was in check, he got the strap over his shoulder and let the instrument hang at his waist. For a moment he said nothing as he looked around, then he frowned and looked down at the whining amps.

"Don't bother," Brian called over to him.

David nodded, "They're all acting weird. Even Bekka's mike is sounding funny."

"Will we still be able to play?" Derek asked.

"Fuck yea," Will shouted, "We're not letting a small thing like this send us packing."

Everyone glanced back at him.

"He's right," Bekka said, starting to bounce excitedly, "We didn't come this far for nothing! Besides, it's not *that* noticeable."

David, Brian, and Derek shifted their skeptical gazes to her and then looked back down at their equipment. While it *was* an annoyance, it wasn't something that would overpower them once they started playing.

"Doors will be opening soon," Bill leaned against the stage, "You guys ready to rock?"

The five struggled not to laugh at their manager.

"SEND 'EM IN!" Will hollered.

A pleased smile spread across his face before he glanced upward towards Bekka, "How are you feeling?"

"I've got a bit of a headache," she confessed with a shrug, "But other than that I feel great!"

Bill nodded and stepped back, "I'll go see if I can find you some aspirin," Behind him the sound of the waiting crowd growing louder gave away that the doors had been opened to allow them to get seated. He turned to see them flood the auditorium as though a damn had burst and, though his back was to the band, they could tell he was beaming. As the rows of seats started to fill he looked over his shoulder at the group and gave them two thumbs up, "Give 'em hell, kids!"

With that he scampered off.

"You're never going to see those pain killers, you know that, right?" Brian nudged Bekka lightly on the shoulder with the neck of his guitar.

She just shrugged and smirked, "Not anytime soon, anyway."

The lighting had been adjusted before the doors had been opened; the main lights having been turned most of the way up to allow the audience to get into their seats while the stage lights were turned almost completely down. This, however, didn't stop them from being seen and, apparently, recognized by some of the more fanatic audience members. As this happened, the dim clamor grew into a deafening roar of calls from the seats. Hearing their fans' hysteria gave the band the final boost they needed to go on.

Driven by the cheers, Bekka found herself growing impatient and paced around the stage. Brian frowned and shook his head; he knew what this meant…

"Can't we just wait for the cue?" David sighed.

"Fuck the cue," Will called out, "The Bloodtones will not be held back!"

Bekka smiled and nodded to him and turned to Derek, who nodded in return, and then to Brian, who smirked and shook his head at her.

He knew all-too-well that there was no stopping her now. It was better to join her than fight it, and—hell!—he didn't have any desire to fight it, anyway.

"Let's get this thing rolling!"

Nodding, Bekka motioned to the crew, who stared at her in confusion and signaled that they hadn't been cued yet. Rolling her eyes, she turned to Derek, who nodded and hurried off the stage and began negotiating with the crew. After a short while the whine of their amps grew audible and the crowd began to quiet in anticipation. Shortly after, Derek reemerged and gave Bekka a nod.

Raising the microphone to her lips, Bekka let out an ear-piercing howl, silencing the rest of the audience. As her animalistic call died down she let her voice take on the husky growl that her fans had come to recognize her for.

"HOW THE FUCK ARE WE ALL DOING TONIGHT?" The crowd roared and threw their hands into the air. Bekka shook her head, "COME ON! LET'S HEAR Y'ALL SCREAM!"

The roar grew thunderous; heavy boots stomping so hard that the band could feel it through the stage. Brian smiled at the reaction; the fans alone were loud enough to drown out the whine of the equipment. If things went on like this for the rest of the night, nobody would even notice the problem for what it was.

"THAT'S IT! FUCKING SCREAM FOR ME!"
Bekka roared.

The crowd went berserk as the lighting crew—
realizing that things were no longer going according to
schedule—brought down the auditorium lights and cranked
the spotlights. With the band suddenly lit properly the
screams and cries of the fans nearly doubled in effort.

Brian smirked; they'd all be hoarse for a week after
that.

Bekka nodded, inhaling sharply and crouching down
on the edge of the stage, "LET'S DO THIS!"

They were in top form that night, and as each song
came and went they grew more confident that they'd made
the right decision. They played for nearly two hours, the
audience never once settling back into their seats as they
banged and wind-milled their heads to the music. While the
auditorium didn't allow for much empty space and it was
nearly impossible to get a good mosh pit going, the crowd
more than made use of the aisles, acting in clear defiance to
the security team and their efforts.

It was nearing the end of the show when the whine
from the amps began to grow. At first it was barely noticeable,
but as time passed it became so loud that soon the band was
forced to stop playing—the pitch from their equipment

becoming too much to even try and play over.

Bekka frowned at this and turned to the audience. "Just a moment, folks," though she tried to maintain her rugged tone, her own nervous voice was starting to come through, "It looks like we were too much for the amps to handle."

This brought out a laugh from the crowd, though it was clear they weren't happy. Knowing that they would be calm and understanding for only so long, Bekka hurried beside Brian, who had knelt down beside his own amp and, with no other idea of how to fix the problem, had begun to slap the side.

The mechanical whine was unresponsive to the assault, and as Bekka moved closer it became louder. Brian frowned and looked up at her, beginning to make the connection.

"Bekka!" He started to stand, holding a hand out towards her, "Get awa—"

The lights of the auditorium dimmed at that moment as the power surged and Brian's amp exploded.

FIFTEEN

"It's a fucking miracle the entire place didn't burn down!"

"Just shut up and get us there!"

"I mean, have you ever seen anything like that? Everything just... just fucking blew up!"

"For Chrissake will you shut up and drive?"

"Never seen anything like it! Not ever!"

"Is this really that hard to understand?" David's face was bright red, only a small amount of that thanks to the heat from the burning equipment they'd left behind, "Just shut your damn mouth and get us to the hospital!"

Will stayed silent for a moment, shaking his head in astonishment. Behind them, the auditorium continued to be emptied out as firefighters and EMTs flooded inside, "Still," he muttered, "I've never seen anything like that; not ever!"

David snarled.

"Both of you stop it!" Derek spoke softly from the back seat. He'd been quiet until that moment, having busied himself by patting a burn on his left arm where his own amp had scorched him. Though it had started off as something far more severe, his efforts over time had nearly healed it; the only evidence remaining being the lack of hair along the stretch of skin and some slight discoloration. He looked up and sighed, "Anger's not going to get us there any faster."

David snarled again, ignoring the advice, and leaned forward in the passenger seat to see a street sign, "Take a right up ahead."

"I know how to get there, grumpy!" Will snapped as he took the turn.

Derek sighed again and shook his head, "She's going to be fine, you guys!"

"What makes you so sure?" David whipped his head around and showed his teeth, "She was nearly blown off the goddam stage!"

"And you caught her," Derek offered, "Probably saved her life, even."

"Yea!" Will glanced at him, "Kudos on that! I give you a ten on form and execution, but a six on your landing."

David shook his head. He *was* inwardly proud of himself for getting in the way of Bekka's path and stopping her from getting seriously injured, though his left side still hurt like hell from where he'd landed on it.

"I don't know how you can be joking at a time like this," he sighed.

Will shrugged, "It's like magic-man said, she'll be fine."

"She didn't look very fine when the paramedics were dragging her away," he countered.

Derek shook his head, his gaze pointed out the passenger-side window. "The beings inside her won't let her go that easily," He said flatly.

David narrowed his eyes and looked down, slowly leaning back in his seat. He wasn't sure how to feel about that. Sure, the things occupying Bekka's body had allowed her to survive a lot more than just a simple tumble and a few burns, but how much abuse were they willing to endure before they abandoned her and left her to die?

"Besides," Derek added, "she's got Brian with her."

Will nodded, "Fuckin' A, dude! It's not like she's all by herself in there."

Taking the final turn, the vampire brought the van to a screeching halt in front of the ER's entrance and allowed the others to exit before peeling off to find a parking spot. While Derek watched him disappear around a bend David started in through the sliding doors and shot straight towards the front desk.

"I already told you I'm fine!" Brian assured an overly-pushy male nurse. The orderly frowned as he pulled away yet again and finally, with a deep sigh, turned away and headed down the hall. Finally alone, he leaned forward, hugging his arms around his torso and letting his elbows rest on his knees, shivering from the chill that he'd felt ever since the explosion.

The ambulance ride hadn't taken very long, and for that he was thankful, both for Bekka's sake as well as his. After a few questions—most of which he couldn't answer—the paramedics went back to the task of tracking Bekka's vitals while he forced himself to watch. He couldn't directly blame himself for what had happened, though he *was* angry at himself for not having diagnosed the problem with the equipment sooner. Derek had done a fine job keeping all potential danger from getting into the auditorium, but what they hadn't planned on was the dangers that still lurked within it. Like the jukebox at the bar, Bekka's new "friends" had made short work of their equipment, and it had nearly killed them all in the process.

He shook his head again.

How could he have been so stupid?

The first explosion—mistaken for a pyrotechnic stunt—had been met with a great deal of cheering. Though it had launched Bekka like a human cannonball into David—

162

the impact of which would have probably killed a normal human—the crowd had taken it all to just be a part of the show. It wasn't until the other amps went up in flames that people began to realize that something was wrong. While the security team had organized the evacuation Bill had gotten on his cell phone and called an ambulance.

It was one of the first times Brian had actually appreciated their manager.

Bekka had looked peaceful in her unconsciousness. Despite a few burns that were speckled here-and-there, she seemed otherwise alright. He had noticed, upon their arrival, that some of the smaller burns were already healed, though he seemed to be the only one that noticed. While he still felt some concern, this had been enough to make him confident that she'd recover quickly.

The irony that the cause of the explosions was also healing her from its effects was bitter in the back of his mind as David and Derek started down the hall towards him. Seeing his band-mates brought a weak smile to his face and he shifted over to allow them to both fit on the bench next to him.

"Any news?" David asked, not bothering to sit.

Brian shrugged as Derek sat beside him. "Said she didn't look too bad; assured me that she'd be alright," he sighed, "Same old doctor-patient relations bullshit."

The sound of approaching footsteps caught their attention and they turned to face Will, who sat down on the bench next to Derek as soon as he'd reached them.

"God damn! You would *not* believe what I had to do to get a parking spot!" He groaned as he stretched out. A quiet moment passed before he turned to Brian, "So how's she doing."

Brian sighed and shrugged.

"Well then," Will sighed, "Good thing I hurried, then. I hope that old lady I clipped is alright, but I guess it couldn't have happened at a better place."

Derek frowned, "I sincerely hope you're joking."

Will only smirked.

A short time passed in silence then before David, growing impatient with every passing second, narrowed his eyes and began to approach the doorway in front of them. Brian frowned and stood to follow, knowing better than to doubt his friend's instincts. Soon after the knob turned from the other side and one of the doctors stepped out and into the hall. She was older—probably in her late forties—with light-amber hair and a pair of focused green eyes that studied the four of them skeptically. Finally, she wetted her overly-painted red lips and forced a smile.

"Miss Gespon is awake now," she informed them, "You may—"

David, obviously not caring what was being said, pushed past the doctor and went through the door with the others close behind. As they approached, a wide, beaming smile spread across Bekka's face.

"Hey, guys! Hell of a show, huh?"

Will laughed and nodded, "You ain't even kidding,

sister! That had to be one of our best to date!"

Brian and David glanced back at him, their eyes rolling in unison.

"You're almost completely healed," Derek said, not sounding surprised.

Brian faced her again, taking in the sight of her nearly burn-free body.

Bekka nodded, studying her own arms and hands as she did, "I know! It's freaking out the doctors!" She giggled.

"Who woulda thought that being possessed by demons was a miracle cure?" Will chuckled as he walked over to an IV drip and tapped at the bag, "Maybe cancer patients should try less chemo and—"

"Dude!" Derek's eyes narrowed at him.

David nodded, "Yea, man. Not cool."

Will rolled his eyes but didn't say anything more about it.

Bekka blushed and looked up at Brian, who had ignored the conversation and closed the distance between himself and her bed.

"How you feeling?" He asked, his voice clogged with worry.

Bekka smiled, though he was sure it was more for his sake. "Better than I should," she admitted.

Brian nodded, forcing his own smile, "Glad to hear it."

Though his back was to them, Brian could tell that the others were watching them. Even Will, who always saw a need to fill any sort of silences with his own personal brand of humor, kept his mouth shut and allowed them to have their moment.

Bekka's eyes still shimmered with the lingering excitement from the show, and despite the circumstances Brian found himself unable to look away from them. Somewhere in the depths of his mind he knew that the lack of conversation was probably getting awkward, but, comfortable with just staring at her, he remained silent.

And so did she.

Brian didn't bother looking away as he addressed the others. "Think we can have a moment?" The vulnerability in his voice crackled his words.

They didn't waste any time in leaving, each wishing Bekka the best as they did. On the way out Will finally seemed to become himself again and nudged Derek with his elbow.

"Hey," he was already chuckling at his undelivered joke, "you think the café has got some type-A on tap?"

The door closed, sealing their laughter on the other side.

The silence in the room grew even more noticeable when they were finally alone. Beside them, the monitors that Bekka was hooked up to issued their subtle, mechanical hums. Brian bit his lip and looked around at the setup, cringing at the sight of a probing tube that pierced Bekka's forearm just below her elbow.

She followed his gaze and shrugged. "It's not that bad,

really," she assured him, "It only hurts if I move it."

He nodded slowly, and then turned his gaze back to hers, "Bekka, I'm so sor—"

"Brian. Don't," she said, "What happened wasn't your fault; it wasn't anybody's fault. Besides," She smiled and blushed, "we both know you didn't ask the others to leave so you could apologize."

Brian frowned and looked down, feeling read, "No. I didn't."

"Then don't," Bekka's smile was empowering, "Don't paint yourself to be the bad guy this time. Just have the balls to say what you want to say."

He straightened himself as a hot blush enveloped him, not sure how to say what they both knew he wanted to say. How long had she known? He shifted his upper lip against the rings in his lower and tapped his index fingers against his thumbs as his eyes darted about the room. In the end, however, they always returned to her piercing eyes.

Damn it! Those eyes!

He shook his head to clear it and knelt down beside her, "I..."

She smiled at his reaction and nodded, reaching her hand out to take his, "I know, Brian. I've known for a couple of days now."

"B-but how?" He stammered.

Bekka shrugged as best she could with the medical equipment restricting her. "I'm not sure," she blushed, "I've just felt it."

Brian stared, not even trying to pretend to understand.

"And you should know that I feel the same way," she gave his hand a soft squeeze.

His eyes widened and his knees almost gave out beneath him, "Y-you do?"

Bekka nodded, her smile beaming as bright as her eyes.

At that moment, all the problems that they'd been facing seemed so distant. Brian felt the warmth in his cheeks fade away as his embarrassment—an embarrassment that he'd felt for his entire life—gave way to other, more powerful emotions.

With his heart beating so hard in his chest that it hurt, he knelt down and finally pressed his lips to hers.

RAIN

(It's easy to be soaked to the bone,
When you're in bone deep!)

Scarlet monsoon.
Ruby flood.
Entire cities,
Drowned in blood

(Drip, Drop, Drizzle)

Clouds like clots.
That burst and bleed.
That soak the soil.
Spreading death like weds

Rain, rain, come our way!
A torrential downpour here to stay!
Pain, pain, the only way.
The storm's approaching
To make us pay.

The world turns red
On the day it pours.
As lightning stabs
And thunder roars.

(Drip, Drop, Drizzle)

And the elders will pray,
And the children will weep,
But their cries will go unheard.
The rain will be too deep.

Rain, rain, come our way!
A torrential downpour here to stay!
Pain, pain, the only way.
The storm's approaching
To make us pay.

To make us...
(Drip, Drop, Drizzle)

SINKING

Hellish descent.
No time to repent.
Only as much,
As what was spent.

(Are you sorry now?)

You sent me to the bottom—
Weighted by your hate—
Bound by the sound,
Of your laughter
As you sealed my fate.

(We find ourselves sinking)
No surface in sight!
(Eternally sinking)
In the depths of our fright!
You cast aside loved ones,
For one final breath,
As you disregard,
Your impending death.

The darkness turns you mad,
As the endless drop consumes
All the sanity that remains,

In the empty vessel that is you.

(Hope you're fucking sorry now!)

Anyone could have warned you;
Could have told you from the start!
And for once you see the endless depths,
Of your own blackened heart!

Still we find ourselves sinking—
With no way left to fight—
Forever to the bottom,
Of your eternal night.

PART TWO
BEATS & BEDLAM

FIRE WORKS

This decrepit, decaying mass—
Dying, doomed and despaired;
Broken, and bent;
Betrayed;
Injured and impaired!

This rotted, clotted, horrid place,
So lacking and so lost!
Nothing but a wretched waste,
That must be destroyed at any cost.

(Fire works!)

So burn it to the fucking ground!
Let its innards melt away!
And anything that ever mattered,
Will disappear within the flames.

Watch its long-lost beauty,
Slowly turn to ash.
Or turn your back on all of it,
And let it burn down in a flash.

(Fire works!)

Astray in the ashtray of what it has become.

It's hard not to think of all the harm we'd done.
And as the incredible inferno takes it all away,
We'll watch the night sky turn as bright as day.

The rats flee the growing blaze—
Memories that cling to life—
While all that once was good and pure,
Is buried in the strife!

(Fire works!)

VORTEX

This void—
Once called my soul—
Will consume,
Will drain,
Will kill.

(Do you miss me for what I once was?)

You fear what I've become,
And where I'll go from here.
But I can't help but see you shudder,
When I am standing near.

Like the sweetest drug,
Still flowing in my veins.
I can't ignore the symptoms,
Though you may ignore the pains.
As the syringe's plunger quivers,
Consuming every drop.
The vortex inside me shivers.
And vows never to stop.

They search the shell
that I've become,
For what I used to be.

And though there are some bits remaining,
They're not easy to see.

Nothing but an empty thing,
A fuck-toy without a soul.
They can pretend to give a damn,
But it will never mend the hole.

Like the sweetest drug,
Still flowing in my veins.
I can't ignore the symptoms,
Though you may ignore the pains.
As the syringe's plunger quivers,
Consuming every drop.
The vortex inside me shivers.
And vows never to stop.

SIXTEEN

It had been nearly a week since the concert catastrophe, and in an attempt to return to something resembling their normal lives the band was at Will's for practice...

... though nobody seemed eager to begin.

"Come on!" Bekka urged them for the fifth time in an hour, "This is fucking bogus! I thought we came here to play!" The others all shifted nervously in their seats as the TV blared a random talk show. Though nobody was actually watching it, the program provided them with an excuse *not* to get started. Bekka saw through this and moved to stand in front of the big screen and planted her hands on her hips, "Well?"

Everybody turned to Brian expectantly. Since the two of them were now an item, they had appointed him as the official deliverer of bad news. He took a deep breath and hauled himself from the couch.

"Look, Bekka, we just think that, after what happened, we should take some time off."

Bekka's arms dropped from her hips and hung limp at her side, "We're back to that again?" She groaned and turned to their drummer, "Will," she pleaded, "you're still on my side with this, right? Don't you want to get back to the life we had?"

He frowned and moved his eyes away from Bekka's desperate own and shrugged, "Sure I do," he muttered as though it hurt to admit it, "But there are some things more important than our music right now."

Bekka stared hard at him and then narrowed her eyes, "They brainwashed you!" She glared at the others, "You brainwashed him!"

"Nobody brainwashed anybody," David said sternly, "We just don't want something bad to happen again."

"What's going to happen?" Bekka demanded. She looked at each of them and then sighed, "Look, what happened at the concert was a freak accident! I got too excited and the amps paid the price for it. It's not like anybody got hurt because of it!"

Brian scowled, "You did!"

Bekka shook her head and held out her arms so they could get a look at her, "Do I *look* hurt? Am I strung out in a cast and doped out of my mind to try and get over the pain? No! I'm standing here, begging you—my band-mates and *friends*—to do what we do best!"

Derek shook his head, wanting nothing more than to return to normal but knowing it was too dangerous to do so, "Just give it a few weeks, Bekka. We need a little time to figure all this out without any distractions."

"Distractions?" Bekka tossed her hands up in the air, exasperated, "So our music is a *distraction* now?"

Derek frowned and looked away, "You know that's not what I meant!"

"Sure as hell what it sounded like," Bekka growled. She shook her head before focusing on Brian, "You put them all up to this, didn't you?"

"You think I could get Will on my side by force?" He scoffed.

Bekka glared at him, "Don't you dare laugh at me, Brian!"

Brian stopped and frowned, "Look, you know I care deeply about you—"

"Then don't do this to me!" Bekka demanded.

Brian took a deep breath and continued, "You know I care deeply about you, *but* I'm not going to let you put yourself on a dangerous path just so you can feel like nothing's wrong."

"But nothing is wrong!" She argued, "Derek's spells

have kept us safe for the past week and I've learned to keep my powers in check."

Derek shook his head, "My spells are only so powerful; at some point something stronger than the barrier is going to try and break through. As for keeping the entities in check, we don't know how long they'll allow you to control them. Honestly, I'm surprised that they haven't taken control of you, yet! And that's not to say that they *won't*!"

David nodded. "He's right. This situation is too unpredictable."

"I'm with magic-man," Will said, "We all just want what's best for you."

Bekka stared at them, looking like she was about to cry, and slowly moved to sit next to Brian. Leaning her head on his shoulder, she let out a soft breath, "I don't know..." She shook her head, "Can we at least practice? No concerts. No shows. No nothing! I just want to sing again."

Brian looked down at her for a long before he looked up at the others and shrugged his free shoulder, "There's no danger in just practicing, is there?"

Will's eyes widened and he shot to his feet, "No danger? She nearly blew up an auditorium! An entire auditorium! This is my home! Do we not see where I'm going with this?"

Brian gave him a look, "She says she has it under control!"

Will shook his head, "You're going to take her word on that just cuz you two are bumping nasties now?"

Brian tensed up and glared at him.

Will saw that he'd hit a soft spot and looked away, "Listen, I want to believe she can keep this all under control, too, but that doesn't change the fact that it's still a risk!"

David frowned at that and looked at Bekka, "Some risks," he said after a moment, "are worth taking."

Derek raised an eyebrow at this and looked between David and Will. Finally he nodded as well, "There's no harm in a simple practice, I suppose."

Will growled and shook his head, "If my house is destroyed because of this, I'm going to take it out of each of your asses!"

"Threat noted," Brian said as he got to his feet and helped Bekka to hers.

"Duly," David agreed as he rose with them and headed towards the basement.

"No dispute here," Derek added as he followed.

Will sighed and shook his head, "You guys are real bastards!" He shouted after them as he shuffled across the living room and made his way to the stairs, "Real bastards!"

They had practiced for nearly three hours before they all agreed they couldn't play another note.

"We were kinda crappy," Will sighed as he set down his sticks.

"What did you expect?" Bekka shot at him, "You guys have gone a week without playing."

"Not our fault you've been out playing with your new boy-toy and too busy to harass us into practicing," Will shot back.

Bekka blushed and then stuck out her tongue, "You can thank Brian for that."

Derek laughed.

David rolled his eyes.

Will, for once, was speechless.

Brian shook his head, a slight blush spreading across his cheeks, "We all set here then?" He asked, the question directed more towards Bekka—who had more than proven at that point who was running the show—than anybody else.

Bekka, still beaming, nodded.

"Alright then!" Brian set his guitar in its case and latched it shut, "You want to get something to eat, babes?"

Will smirked, "Well it *is* kinda late. And I promised myself I'd get in a shower before bed. But if you insi—"

Both Bekka and Brian gave the vampire a look.

"Uh, right," Will hung his head in mock-shame, "Couples only."

"You got it," Brian said as he hoisted the case in his left hand and took Bekka's own with his right, "You *can* drop us off at the restaurant, though."

Will stared at him, "So *that's* the way it's gonna be, huh? I've been reduced to nothing more than a Taxi service for you kids!"

Bekka pouted, "Please?"

"God dammit! How can I say 'no' to that?" Will growled and headed towards the stairs, "Let me grab my keys." He turned to the others, "I take it you'll be needing rides, too?"

David nodded, "If it's not too much trouble."

"I was actually thinking of stopping off at the bar," Derek admitted, "My grandpa's working tonight."

Both David and Will smiled at this.

"The bar it is," Will boasted.

Derek noticed both Bekka and Brian frowned at the mention of the bar and wondered if mentioning it around them had been a mistake. Though it had been a while, the incident from their last visit might have still been a touchy subject with Bekka.

Will returned then, keys jingling in his grip as his heavy leather boots slapped down the stairs, "Alright, lovebirds, what fine-dining establishment will you be gracing tonight?"

Bekka smiled and looked up at Brian, "Mario's?"

"Perfect!" Brian nodded and smiled at the suggestion.

Mario's, a quaint Italian bistro, was conveniently located only a block-and-a-half from Brian and David's apartment. This, considering Bekka had been staying with them for the past week for—as Brian called it—protective purposes, made getting home safely less of a concern for the others as they dropped the two off.

"Thanks again for the ride," Bekka called out to Will.

Will nodded, "Don't worry about it."

"Have a good night, guys," she waved to the others.

Brian sighed, "Not *too* good."

Shortly after, the door was slammed shut and Will pulled out of the parking lot.

Derek, sitting in the passenger seat, turned his head to watch the two disappear into the restaurant. Once they were out of sight, he sighed and looked back at the others, "I need to talk to you guys."

Will frowned and gave him a look, "So what's stopping you? Talk it up, bitch!"

The week had passed like butter on a hot griddle— smoothly and all-too-quickly. While none of them had been particularly busy, Derek had found no opportunity to approach the two of them without Brian and Bekka being aware of it. With the two out on a romantic evening, the promise of alcohol seemed the best way to get the three of them in one place.

But he couldn't hold his tongue on the subject any longer.

"I want to know what that vampire wanted!" He blurted the words, eager to finally get an answer. The two looked at him for a long moment, both confusion and concern painted on their faces. He shifted his gaze between them, waiting for either of them to speak up. When neither said a word he scowled, "Look, I know a vampire when I sense one, and that guy was anything but subtle with his energies!" He couldn't hide the accusatory tone in his voice, "Now there's only a few reasons I can think of as to *why* you'd be getting visited like that, and since neither of you are dead I'd gather it wasn't because of any broken laws."

Will shook his head, "Methinks the sorcerer doth know too much!" He glanced at David, "You think we should kill him now?"

"I'm not in the mood for joking!" Derek spat at him before turning to face David, "You two assured us that all business with your kind had been taken care of! So why would you be getting a visit?"

David shook his head and looked away.

Will frowned, "Did it ever occur to you that he was just a fan?"

Derek shook his head angrily, "Really? A fan? Do I *look* stupid?"

Will smirked, reaching out and tapping his index finger against one of the wooden plugs in Derek's ears, "Well, now that you mention it, with those big, honkin' stretched doopa ears of yours—"

"Stop it!" Derek snapped, pushing his hand away.

"Maybe we should just tell him," David grumbled.

Will growled, "Look, we told that son-of-a-bitch to piss off! Why the fuck are we lingering on it? It's not like we didn't know there'd be risks!"

186

Derek frowned, "Risks? Did he threaten you?"

"Not directly," David shook his head.

Will shot an angry glare over his shoulder at him, a sound like a basket of angry snakes echoing from his throat, "He does *not* need to know!"

David glared back and countered the hiss with his an angry, snarl.

"Stop it," Derek brought his fist down on the dash, cutting off the supernatural standoff. Narrowing his eyes at Will, he spoke slowly, "If we're in danger—any of us—then we have a right to know!"

Will sighed and shook his head, keeping his eyes on the road, "The asshole wanted us to quit the band; said that there's some paranoid fucks lurking about who would like to earn some bonus points by taking out a threat."

"And what threat would that be?" Derek asked, forcing himself to calm down.

"The threat to our secrecy," David answered, "They see the human half of the band—you, Brian, and Bekka—as a potential hazard to our community for knowing too much, and…"

"And…?" Derek pressed.

"And the threat that *we* pose for letting you all know what we are," Will finished in a mocking tone as he shook his head and scoffed, "Bunch of horseshit!"

Derek turned his head to face the road, letting this new information sink in. He'd never considered the difficulties that the two supernatural members of their band faced; the constant threat to both their races and their friends. How hard it must have been to be in the middle of all that…

"So what are you going to do?" He finally asked.

Will's grip on the steering wheel was so tight that Derek was sure that at any moment it might tear right off, "We're still here, aren't we?"

Derek shrugged, "For the time being, I suppose."

"And what the fuck is that supposed to mean?" Will growled, "You think we're a couple of limp-dick pussies who would just up and run away."

"I think"—Derek sighed—"that those of your kind have survived this long by avoiding danger and maintaining your secrecy, and now both are being threatened," he shook his head sadly, "I think it's in your nature to *at least* feel compelled to escape it."

Will scoffed again, "Psycho-babble bullshit!"

"And I don't think you'd be this upset about it if you weren't considering it," Derek added.

Silence.

David cleared his throat, "Neither of us have made any decisions yet."

Derek nodded and let out a heavy sigh, "I know it probably makes little difference in the long run, but the band really needs you two."

Will shook his head, "It's *because* we're a part of the band that the crosshairs have been painted on each of your fragile, little asses! How in the hell do you *need* that?"

David nodded. "And there are plenty of guitarists and

drummers in the world that wouldn't put you in danger," he added solemnly.

"You think it's *just* about the music?" Derek shook his head at them, "We *need* you two right now! You're the strongest of us, and, like it or not, we won't be any safer if you leave! Those of your kind who see us as a threat won't consider us any less so if you're gone! We'll just be easier targets! And the same goes for you two! The damage—if you insist on thinking of it that way—has already been done! But there are greater dangers that we're facing right now, and we can't face them without you two!"

More silence.

Slowly, after a long moment, Will's lips stretched into a smirk, "You gonna kiss us now, magic-man?"

The tension that had been building erupted then and all three burst out laughing.

SEVENTEEN

Will gritted his teeth as David slammed the sliding door behind him, the van rocking from the force. He didn't bother to say anything to the therion as he sprinted up the steps and through the door of his apartment building. Taking a deep breath, he checked his mirror before turning back into the street. Though he had just spent the past few hours drowning himself in beer, he couldn't shake his nagging thirst. As he stopped at a red light, an ache in his jaw grew from a minor itch to a major annoyance and he checked the throbbing sensation with his tongue, finding his fangs fully extended.

"Damn it all to the abysmal pit and back again!" He cursed, giving the steering wheel a slap. As the light changed for him, he took a right—heading away from his route home—and drove for several blocks. Though the butcher shop he was heading towards had long-since closed, he knew that it wasn't unoccupied.

Pulling the van in behind the shop, he groaned again at both the growing pain in his gums and the incessant thirst. Before stepping from his vehicle he checked his wallet, making sure he had enough to cover the visit and silently thanked the heavens that he hadn't overdone it at the bar. With his body beginning to shake, Will freed himself from the confines of the van and started towards the butcher shop. Still several paces out, the lock unlatched and allowed the back door to creak open on old, rusted hinges.

"Come on in, William," a familiar voice echoed from within.

Will smirked at the theatrics and stepped inside, pulling the door shut behind him. The room inside was easily twenty degrees colder than the open air he'd left behind and a cloud of mist oozed and curled from his mouth as he exhaled. All around him was the metallic smell of stainless steel as well as the powerful stench of chemicals. To his right was the freezer, where he guessed his source was getting things ready.

Be right out. The psychic message rang in his head.

Will wasn't sure how to transmit his thoughts—or if he even could—and instead just nodded, hoping that his acknowledgement would be "seen".

After a moment the freezer door popped open and Xavier emerged with several frozen bags of beef blood, "William!" The auric smirked and shook his head. He was an older vampire—though Will didn't know hold old, exactly—but didn't look a day past his mid-forties. His thin, brown hair was hidden; stuffed under a black wool cap. His eyes, slightly sunken in his skull, were energetic and vibrant, glowing a bright shade of blue that bordered on purple. Though he was occupying a butcher shop, he wore an expensive-looking shirt and khaki pants with along with a pair of brown loafers. Slapping the bags down on a nearby counter, he raised an eyebrow in Will's direction, "It hasn't been *that* long since you last saw me, has it?"

"You know me," he shrugged and ran his finger along the edge of a nearby meat cleaver and inspected the resulting slit with waned interest as it sealed shut, "Is there a problem?"

Xavier scowled at this and shook his head, "Not a problem. And I'll thank you not to do that again."

Will rolled his eyes, "Oh please! Our blood is sterile! Not like anybody's gonna get sick from it. Might give 'em a hell of a pick-me-up, though," he laughed.

"Be that as it may," Xavier wiped the blade with a cloth that had been soaking in a chemical-filled bucket, "It was on good faith that I was allowed to work here and I don't want to take advantage of that trust."

Will ran his tongue across his fang, watching his source work, and nodded, "Uh-huh. So, about my blood…"

Xavier nodded and motioned back towards the bags—Will counted three in total, enough for the rest of the week if he behaved himself—before quirking an eyebrow, "Though I'm guessing you need some now, am I right?"

"You read my mind," Will chuckled.

"No, I didn't," Xavier assured him as he popped one of the bags into a nearby microwave and turned the dial. The device came to life and light flooded out and cast an eerie glow. Xavier watched this for a moment and then turned back to his friend and client, "So what's new? Are you still doing that music thing?"

Will sighed and shrugged, "It's going alright, I guess. Our lead singer's been possessed... or something like that."

"Possessed?" Xavier's eyes widened, "Don't hear that every day. So are we talking the 'fetch a priest' kind of possessed?"

"Nah, nothing that dramatic. Not yet, at least," he sighed and leaned against a counter, "Anyway, it's kinda thrown a big pile of shit all over our routine, but you know how it is."

Xavier nodded, "I do. Friends come first."

Will nodded back and sighed.

"Is something else bothering you?" Xavier raised an inquisitive eyebrow.

"What? Possession's not enough now?" Will laughed.

Xavier gave him a look.

"You really are reading my mind, aren't you?" He sighed, "Some clan-issued suit showed up the other day and told David and—"

"The therion, right?" Xavier asked.

Will rolled his eyes, "Yea, that's him. Anyway, this clan member comes to this show we're playing and told the two of us that we should quit the band for the safety of ourselves and the others. Stupid fucking bullshit really."

Xavier shrugged, "I suppose. But you wouldn't still be thinking about it if it was *that* stupid."

Will scoffed, "Now you sound like our bassist."

"Oh really?" Xavier seemed entertained by this, "And what did he say?"

"Totally called us on it," Will sighed, "Even sensed the vampire for what he was from backstage!" He shook his head, "He *is* good, I'll give him that."

"So what did he say?" Xavier asked again.

"Huh? Oh, right. Uh… so he calls us on it and gets us talking and goes on about how the band *needs* us and such. Laid on a real fucking guilt trip, if you ask me."

"So are you planning on leaving?" Xavier asked.

"Fuck that shit sideways!" Will growled.

Xavier nodded, "But you're still concerned about your friends, right?"

Will sighed, his shoulders sagging, "I guess."

"Well, you should listen to your bassist."

"Oh?"

Xavier nodded, "Absolutely! You're an excellent drummer, from what I've heard, you all make an excellent band. I'm not sure they'd recover if you left."

"There are other drummers," Will muttered, his face twisting into a frown, "I mean, if I *was* considering leaving."

"Uh huh; there *are* other drummers," Xavier said, "But there's only one of you."

"What do you mean? You think they should find another vampire drummer?"

Xavier shrugged, "That's only a small part of what you are, Will."

"Not in the eyes of our kind, apparently."

"That may be so," Xavier turned as the microwave beeped and retrieved the bag of blood. After juggling it for a moment he tossed it to Will, who caught it and ripped open a corner, "But I think our kind and their views on how we relate to humans are a bit primitive."

Will laughed, pulling away from the blood for a moment, "Try telling them that!"

Xavier laughed, "Not in a million years."

Will smirked and finished the contents of the bag and squeezed what was left on his tongue, "So what do you think?"

Xavier shrugged, "I think—especially with your singer possessed and all—it'd be really shitty to do anything but stay and do what you can for them."

Will frowned and looked down like a scolded child, "Well it's like I said before, I'm *not* leaving!"

"Then stop thinking about it!" Xavier smiled warmly, "Just keep beating the hell out of those drums and keep the band on beat. That's what you were meant to do."

EIGHTEEN

It was late when Derek and his grandfather finally left the bar. The roads were quiet and, for the most part, clear of traffic. This allowed for a quiet ride home.

Though the old man hadn't said anything, Derek knew that there was something on his mind. The urgency in his driving and the way he slowly worked his lower jaw were more than dead giveaways. Though he was eager to know what he was thinking, he knew that his grandfather was not one to discuss important matters in such a casual setting. He was certain that not a single word of it would be uttered until they were home and seated at the kitchen table.

When at last the car pulled up to their home, his grandfather gave a soft grunt as he shifted the car into park and, without turning to face his grandson, told him to meet him in the kitchen for tea.

Derek suddenly wasn't sure he was ready for what he had to say, "Aren't you tired?" He asked, hoping that he could at least delay the conversation.

"The kitchen!" His grandfather repeated.

There was no anger in his voice, but the urgency was enough to make Derek cringe. He nodded and stepped from the car and retrieved his bass from the backseat. Looking at the case, he shook his head to himself; he knew better than to try and ask if he could at least put the instrument in his room.

A short time later they were in the kitchen, his bass set down in the hallway. An old pot was already set on the stove to boil the water, and his grandfather opened a cupboard to retrieve the leaves as well as a nearly-empty and slightly-crusty bottle of honey. Derek watched his movements, noticing almost rhythmic style that the old man worked. Though well-aged, his grandfather did not show—or perhaps didn't allow to show—the rigidness and confusion that often accompanied the elderly.

Or maybe it was the magic.

Derek prayed that his own aging would be so graceful.

"I'm not surprised that you chose to become a musician," his grandfather said, his back to him as he continued with the tea. "Lots of energy and precise timing," he nodded to himself, "Very much like magic."

Derek shrugged, "I suppose."

"Not so sure I like all the holes you've put in yourself, though," he quipped, peeking over his shoulder to smirk at his grandson.

"This isn't going to be another body modification lecture, is it?" Derek grumbled, rubbing his left ear and giving the wooden plug in it a soft tug.

His grandfather shook his head and poured the hot water into a pair of mugs and began to work in the leaves, "I've come to grips with it, actually. You've made your own decisions; it's not my place to question them. I've even come to see the look as something endearing," he moved the steaming cups to the table, placing one in front of Derek and sitting in front of his own, "But, as I was saying..." He paused and looked down at his tea.

"Grandfather?" Derek bit his lip, wrapping his hands around the mug and letting the warmth flow into his palms.

His grandfather sighed, "Do you believe that everything happens for a reason?"

Derek frowned, "You mean, like, fate?"

"If you wish to call it that."

"I don't know," Derek thought for a moment, "Not really. I guess I believe that life is what you make it, not the other way around."

"Mmhm," his grandfather nodded and smirked, "I see you've thought about this before."

Derek shrugged, afraid of where this was going.

"But what if it's not that simple? What if it's a little of both?"

Derek took this in, "What do you mean?"

"What if"—his grandfather smacked his lips and took a sip of tea—"you were destined to be a musician; to be *exactly* where you are right now?"

"I don't know what I'd think," Derek shook his head, "What are you getting at?"

His grandfather shrugged and smiled, "Nothing. Just crazy old man talk." Another sip of tea and a soft chuckle followed. Then, "How's your friend?"

"You mean Bekka?"

"Mmhm."

"She's doing alright. Nothing's happened since last week, if that's what you mean."

"But you don't believe that your troubles are over, do you?"

Derek shook his head, frowning, "No. I don't."

The old man's brow furrowed, "Why?"

"Because nothing is ever that easy," Derek answered, "Besides, if the entities *had* left her body then she'd be dead. You said so yourself, they're too much a part of her now."

His grandfather nodded, "I did say that, didn't I?"

Derek nodded.

His grandfather sighed, "You haven't had any of your tea yet."

Derek looked down at his drink and stirred his spoon

into it, watching some of the larger bits of tea-leaf spin about inside, "I'm not thirsty."

"Drink!"

Derek looked up, surprised by his grandfather's tone. Nodding, he slowly brought the cup to his lips and took a long sip.

Then another.

And another.

As a calm euphoria washed over him he started to chug the contents until he'd emptied his mug. When the last drop was gone he stared in bewilderment at first the inside of the cup and then at his grandfather, shaking his head in bewilderment.

"What kind of tea was that?" He asked.

His grandfather nodded, smirking at his reaction, "It's a special blend. Good for helping one to relax."

Derek nodded, "It was delicious!"

"Bitter tea is not relaxing," the old man laughed.

Derek nodded again.

"You stress too much, m'boy. Too much of something so powerful can be dangerous."

Another nod.

"Balance is important," he went on, "You should know that if you're going to be successful with your magic *and* your music. Everything—absolutely everything!—must be balanced to function. Body. Mind. Spirit. They all need to be stable. What's happened to your friend has tilted the scales, and she needs you and the others to help push them back; to make them right again."

"But we can't exorcise that many—"

"I've said nothing of exorcisms!" The old man shook his head, disappointed, "You focus so much on getting rid of a problem that you haven't even considered working around it!"

Derek stared blankly.

"Have I taught you nothing? Heavens and stars, Derek, you are smarter than this! This Bekka-girl is *not* the problem!"

"Then what *is* the problem?"

"Those that are after her."

Derek frowned, "But they're after her *because* of the entities! If we get rid of them, they'll leave her alone!"

His grandfather shook his head, "They are after her to restore their own lost balance. To return what's inside her to their realm so that they can once again be complete."

"Exactly! They won't stop until the entities are out of her! You're not making any sense!" Derek snapped at him.

The old man looked at him for a moment and then shrugged. "Maybe you're right," he admitted, "I'm probably just tired." He took another sip of his tea, "Would you like to see a magic trick before bed?"

Derek blinked, bewildered, "What?"

A broad smile spread across his grandfather's face, "A magic trick! You always loved watching me do a trick-or-two before you went to bed."

Still uncertain of where this was going, Derek

nodded, "I guess. Sure."

"Follow me," His grandfather stood and led him upstairs to his office. The room, once reserved for guests, had been cleared out several years earlier and made into a private place for the old man to go so that he could pay bills and read in peace. Inside was a simple wooden chair and a small desk covered in random papers and trinkets. Sitting down, he cleared a spot on its surface and pulled an old, copper scale towards him—the two sides swaying like a seesaw as he did.

"I use this when preparing spells," he explained as he opened a drawer and pulled out a small pouch. Carefully, he dumped its contents—metal balls of varying sizes—onto the desk beside the scale, "Now, the smallest of these pellets each weigh a gram," he said as he rolled one forward with the tip of his finger, "The medium-sized ones are five grams, and the largest are ten." He separated the pellets by their size, allowing Derek to see that there were two of the largest pellets, four of the medium-sized ones, and ten of the smallest. The old man smiled when Derek nodded and picked up one of the largest weights and placed it on the left side of the scale, allowing it to tip to one side as he did. Then, slowly and deliberately, he picked up two of the medium-sized pellets and dropped them into the tray on the other side and the scale evened out, "As I said, balance is the most important thing in both life *and* magic."

Derek sighed and nodded, waiting for the point.

After once again illustrating the scale's condition, he pulled the two medium-sized pellets from the right side of the scale; its now-unbalanced weight forcing the left side to tilt downward under the greater weight. Again, his grandfather illustrated the condition.

"Notice that the scale is now unbalanced?"

Derek nodded, "Yea…"

His grandfather nodded as well. "The balance has been altered due to the loss of these two pellets," he held up the two mediums that he had removed, "Now we *know* that if I put them back, balance will be restored. But you and I *also* know that if I add ten of the smaller pellets, it would also be enough to balance it, correct?"

Derek sighed, "Grandfather, I'm tired—"

"Correct?"

"Yes," Derek rolled his eyes.

Sure enough, the old man individually picked up and plopped into the right side of the scale ten of the smallest pellets. With each addition, the scale tipped back until it was once again balanced.

"Ta-da!" The old man held his hands out triumphantly, "It's magic!"

Derek frowned, "That's not magic! It's simple math!"

His grandfather glared up at him, "Firstly—never assume that just because it's been explained by science that it's *not* magic! Secondly—though you and I both know that all we did was *replace* the weight, the scale does not!"

Derek frowned, "What?"

The old man shook his head, "Look, boy!" He pointed at the scale, "It doesn't know that we replaced the mediums with the smalls! It only knows that it is once again balanced!"

Derek frowned and narrowed his eyes at the scale, "What are you...?"

"The scale!" His grandfather exclaimed again, jabbing his finger in its direction, "It doesn't know the difference!"

A silent moment passed.

Derek's eyes slowly widened and his jaw slowly dropped, "It doesn't know that its balance wasn't restored by what it originally lost!"

His grandfather nodded, "Exactly! We tricked it!"

"Holy shit! I gotta make a call!" Derek was already through the door and sprinting for the phone.

"Language!" His grandfather called after him.

But he was already downstairs.

"Do you have any idea what time it is?!" Brian snapped.

Derek wasn't surprised to hear Brian's voice on the other end of the phone even though he'd dialed Bekka's number; David *had* told him that they'd both be there.

"I... I'm sorry," Derek stammered into the phone, "I'm not interrupting—uh—anything, am I?"

"Yea! Our sleep," Brian hissed.

Derek sighed and cleared his throat, his voice

changing from a stammer to something a little more solid, "I need to talk to Bekka!"

"What's this about?"

"Brian! Put her on, now!"

Brian sighed audibly and there was a pause.

"Hello?" There was skepticism in Bekka's voice.

"Bekka! It's Derek!"

"Derek? What's wrong?"

"I know how we can fix this!" Derek blurted excitedly.

"Fix... what?" Bekka asked.

"The attacks! I know how we can make them go away for good!"

"What? Really?" Bekka's voice shifted to one of excitement, "Will it get the things out of me?"

Derek paused. "Well... no," he confessed solemnly, "Like my grandfather said, it'd be nearly impossible to live through that..."

"Yea. I understand, I guess."

"I don't think there's any reason to fear them at this point, though. Our problem seems to lie with the others that are trying to get them back."

"So is this another spell?" Bekka asked.

"No, well, I don't know. I... I don't actually know *how* we're going to do it yet," Derek frowned.

"But you just said—"

"I know what I said and I'm sorry if I got your hopes up too early, but we'll have time to think about that. In the meantime, I think it may be best if you stay with David and Will."

"David and... Why? What for?"

"For safety's sake," he explained, "I'm not sure when you'll be attacked next, but it's safe to assume that there will be another attempt, and I think it'd be in all of our best interest if you were in the company of our strongest."

"I'd have to make sure it's okay with David and Will," she pointed out.

Derek sighed, "Bekka, we need to hurry."

There was a pause. When Bekka's voice started again it was shaky and concerned, "What's the rush?"

"I don't know really," Derek admitted, "I just got a bad feeling."

"I'll call them in the morning and get everything set up. Will's got a lot of extra space, so I'm sure he won't have a problem letting us stay with him. Are you going to stay with your grandfather?"

"For now. He and I need to figure out how to make this work."

"You still haven't told me—"

"It's difficult. The fast and easy explanation is that we're going to lie."

"Lie?" Bekka repeated the word, "How are we going to lie?"

"Like I said: hard to explain. You're just going to have to trust me for now until I can show you tomorrow."

"Alright. Brian and I will come over in the morning

and call the others from there."

"That'll work," Derek said.

NINETEEN

The doorbell rang a little after eleven in the morning and Derek hurried to answer it. Though he'd been expecting Brian and Bekka, he was surprised to see David standing with them. Seeing him, Derek turned to face Bekka and Brian, raising an eyebrow.

Bekka smiled, "I figured I'd get the ball rolling and called him earlier."

Derek nodded, "That's fine." He looked out the door and checked the street for Will's van, "You haven't called Will yet?"

"It's still early in the day," Brian pointed out, "Our nocturnal friend probably just went to sleep a few hours ago."

"So he didn't answer his phone?" Derek asked.

"He did not," Brian nodded and started through the door, "So what's up?"

Derek nodded and let them all pass before he shut the door and started after them, "It's in my grandfather's office, but try to be quiet. He's still asleep."

Several demonstrations and a lot of explanations later, the four scurried into Derek's room and closed the door.

"Holy hot fucking shit!" Brian clapped his hands together, "You're a genius, magic-man! A god damn genius!"

David nodded, "It does sound promising."

Derek smiled, accepting the praise. After a moment the three of them turned and looked at Bekka, who was looking down, her tracing the pattern of Derek's carpet.

"Bekka..." Brian took a step towards her.

She looked up.

"You alright?"

She sighed and shrugged, "It sounds like a great concept and all, but..."

Derek nodded. "It's still only a concept," he bit his lip, "We're not sure exactly how to replace the entities or deliver it back to the source."

Brian frowned, "So you've given us a miniature model of something that might not even be possible? What, you had to get our hopes up just as a joke?"

David frowned, "Brian, I don't think he—"

"No! This is fucked! It's a fucking twisted prank, isn't it?" He jabbed an accusing finger at Derek, "Did you just want to see what we'd look like when given a bullshit solution?"

Derek frowned and narrowed his eyes, "It is not bullshit! It's an idea in progress! There's just a lot of energy that would need to go into this; more energy than I can gather on my own."

Brian shook his head, "You fucking asshole!"

Bekka laid a hand on his shoulder, "Brian, he's trying!"

"Well fucking try harder!" He stomped across the room and walked out of the room, slamming the door behind him. A moment later his footsteps could be heard pounding down the stairs, followed by the front door opening and slamming.

Derek sighed and looked down.

Bekka frowned, "It's alright, Derek. He's just been really worried."

David nodded, "We all have." He gave Derek a pat on the shoulder, "He just needs some time to vent."

Derek said nothing but gave a slight nod. After a moment he slapped his knee and shook his head in aggravation, "But he's right! I got too excited about the possibility of this working I didn't stop to think if it was even possible!"

Bekka smiled warmly, "We'll figure it out."

"But what if it can't be figured out?" Derek asked, "What if I'm asking one and one to equal four? What if it's impossible?"

"I think if the past few weeks have taught us anything," David pointed out, "it's that there's a great deal more possible in this world than we've been giving it credit for."

There was a knock on the door then and a second later it opened and Derek's grandfather stood in the doorway wearing a faded blue bathrobe. He studied the three of them for a moment and then looked towards the stairs and nodded.

"I take it all that noise a moment ago was the angry one?" He asked.

"Yea," Bekka nodded, biting her lip, "Sorry about that, Mister Sumner."

The old man nodded again and stepped inside. "It's alright. We all have our ways of getting over stress," he chuckled, "I could give him some excellent tea."

Derek laughed.

Bekka and David shrugged to each other.

"Anyway," he relaxed, "I take it you showed them the magic trick?"

Derek nodded.

He smiled at Bekka and David, "So what'd you two think?"

"It sounds… complicated," David answered.

"Oh it's extremely complicated!" Derek's grandfather answered.

Derek frowned, "But is it impossible?"

The old man scoffed, "Nothing's impossible! It's magic!"

Bekka smiled, "Could I turn a frog into a handsome prince?"

"That's impossible," he laughed, "This is magic we're talking about! Not a cartoon! You'll have to make do with that angry punk, I'm afraid."

All of them laughed except Derek, who frowned and shook his head.

"So how can I make it work?" He pressed.

"I don't know. It isn't enough that I thought of it?" He chuckled and turned to leave the room, "Ungrateful kids!"

Brian's "venting" kept him out of the house for nearly half-an-hour. In that time, after several attempts, Derek was able to get in touch with Will and convinced him to come over. A short time later there was an angry knock on his door. Before any greetings could be fully extended, the sun-poisoned vampire on the stoop pushed past him and got into the safety of the indoors.

"What was so fucking important that I had to get up

and roast my ass for?" He demanded as he headed into the living room where the others were waiting.

Derek's grandfather, sitting in the kitchen, loudly cleared his throat upon hearing Will's choice of words.

Will sighed and shook his head, already beginning to look more relaxed, "Sorry!" He called out to him, "It's been a rough morning!"

"Would you like some tea?" The old man offered.

Will smirked, "Got anything stronger?"

"Not strong enough for you," he chuckled.

Will nodded, "I'll be alright then. Thanks for the offer."

Derek gave their drummer a look, "You seem"—he frowned, eyeing him once again—"different."

Will shrugged, "Spoke to my therapist the other day. Good session. Now what's up?" Already his sun burned skin was starting to clear, a few of the more severe spots beginning to peel.

"We need you to give Bekka a place to stay," Brian said.

"A place to…" Will frowned and turned to Bekka, "Something happen to your apartment?"

Bekka blushed and shook her head, "Derek says it'll be safer if I stay with you."

Will frowned, "Oh really? Is that what he says?" He glared up at Derek, "Do I *look* like a goddam warrior princess to you?"

Derek shook his head, "No, but you and David are

better equipped to keep her safe."

"David?" Will frowned and glanced at him, "What's he got to do with this?"

David cleared his throat and pulled himself up from the floor, "I'm going to be staying with you as well."

"Bullshit you are!" Will shook his head.

Brian frowned at the fuming vampire, "And I'm staying with Bekka for as long as it takes."

"Jesus-fucking-Christ!" Will growled, keeping his voice low enough to not be overheard by Derek's grandfather again, "I'm supposed to take you all in to my home?" He turned back to Derek, "Am I supposed to play host for you too?"

Derek shook his head, "I'm going to stay here and work on our plan with my grandfather."

"Plan?" Will's voice calmed suddenly, "What plan?"

"We think we might be able to stop the attacks and end all of this," David answered.

Will looked at Derek, "Is this for real?"

Derek nodded, "We think so."

"That's good enough for me," Will nodded, "I've got two guest rooms." He looked down at Brian and Bekka, "I'm guessing you two don't mind shacking up together?"

Bekka blushed but shook her head.

Derek smiled, "Thank you."

Will frowned and rolled his eyes, "Spare me. I'm not a total asshole."

"Language!" Derek's grandfather called out again.

Will shook his head, "Old man's got bionic ears, I swear to God!"

"Alright. We should head over to Bekka's place and pick up a few of her things," Brian suggested.

"Right," Will glanced at David, "I'm guessing we'll need to stop at your place too?"

David nodded, "If it's not too much trouble."

"Trust me," Will shook his head, "the *last* thing I want is for you to be walking around my home in the same clothes for days. That's a lot of space to deodorize."

David shot him a glare but kept any brewing comments to himself.

Derek nodded and walked the four out, "Give me a call when you get there. Let me know everything's alright."

Brian frowned and rolled his eyes, "Whatever you say, Mom."

TWENTY

"I'd give you all a tour," Will set his keys down on the coffee table in front of his couch, which he wasted no time dropping himself into, "but you've all been here before." He motioned towards the stairs, "The guest rooms are on the end of the hall. I'll let you fight over who gets which room."

A moment later the TV came on and the sound of daytime soap operas filled the room.

Brian shook his head at this, "Somehow I'm not surprised."

Will shrugged and set the remote down on the arm of the couch and laced his fingers over his stomach, "I'm not sure you're in any position to criticize my tastes."

Rolling his eyes, Brian hoisted their bags and headed for the stairs with Bekka only a few steps behind.

David lingered, absently staring towards the TV.

"What do you have to drink?" He finally asked.

Will frowned and stood, leading his friend to the kitchen, "I swear! If you down all my booze I'm gonna murder you! You hear me? Columbian-fucking-necktie!"

David turned and stared at him, "What?"

Will smirked, "Y'know, a Columbian necktie: when you slit someone's throat and pull their tongue through the opening so it hangs out like a tie."

David shook his head, "You're disgusting! Where do you learn about that crap?"

Will shrugged. "Movies mostly."

"Uh huh. Remind me never to watch a movie with you again," David turned and opened the fridge, finding only a limited selection, "It's too early for any of this!" He pointed out and moved up to the freezer, "You got any frozen juice or…" He paused, noticing the bags of frozen blood. Slowly, he picked up one of them and studied it, "Cow?"

Will frowned and nodded, grabbing it from him and putting it back with the others, "Yes, and it's not cheap so I'm not sharing!"

David shrugged, "I guess it explains a lot."

Will sighed, "What can I say? I always wait till the last minute. Makes me kind of a prick near the final stretch."

"Careful with that," David warned, "Don't want you

losing control and doing something we'll all regret."

"I think you know me better than that."

"I would hope so," David returned to the fridge and grabbed a beer.

"Thought you said it was too early?" Will chided.

"Better that than too late," David laughed, popping open the top and taking a long pull.

"Uh huh," Will rolled his eyes, "I'm gonna go check on the lovebirds."

Will knocked twice but let himself through the guest room door before he'd gotten an answer. Bekka looked up, startled by his sudden entrance. Brian scowled.

"Is David not entertaining you enough?" Brian spat as he crammed a few shirts into a dresser drawer.

Will chuckled, "We're talking about David here. Only time he's any fun is when he's shit-faced!"

Both Brian and Bekka rolled their eyes.

"But, really, I just thought I'd see how you two were doing," Will said, trying his best to show concern.

Brian looked up and crinkling his nose like he smelled something, "Bullshit. What do you want?"

Will frowned, "Why's that bullshit? Aren't I allowed to give a damn?"

Brian straightened and set the bag he'd been

unloading on the floor, "I'm beginning to wonder that too."

"Hey! That's not fair!" Will growled, "I've been there every fucking step of the way through this shit-storm of an ordeal!"

Bekka nodded slowly. "He's right, Brian," She stepped up behind him and wrapped her arms around his waist and rested her chin on his shoulder.

Will sighed and looked away. He understood Brian's reluctance to accept his concern for others; after all, his attitude around his band-mates hadn't exactly been the selfless kind. While he wished he could be more like David in that regard, he couldn't help but feel uncomfortable when things turned serious, and those moments were met with his playful joking and, moreover, selfish antics. Now, when he'd finally pulled off the joker mask, his own friends didn't even recognize him.

He sighed, "I'm sorry."

Brian looked up, his eyes narrowed and trying to excavate the punch-line before he had a chance to deliver it.

But there wasn't one waiting.

Seeing this, Brian's face softened and he nodded to him. Without the rage imprinted on his features, the guitarist looked tired and worn-out. It made sense in the long run— Brian was now the only one in the band *not* being fueled by some kind of magic or supernatural energy. Despite this, he'd been pushing himself harder than all the others; taking the task of worrying about Bekka completely on his shoulders.

Will nodded back to him and glanced at Bekka, "Try

and stay out of trouble, kid." He turned and left the room, walking several paces down the hall until he was certain that the two couldn't see him from their angle.

"God dammit, Will," he shook his head at himself, "What are you doing?"

But for the first time in his unnaturally long life, he didn't know how to answer.

TWENTY-ONE

"Fucking hell!" Will groaned as the phone woke him up for the second day in a row and snatched it off the table to answer it, "What? What the bloody-hell do you want?"

"And a good morning to you too, William"—Bill's voice was too chipper in Will's exhausted ears and he wondered—if he tried *real* hard—if he could throttle their manager through the phone line. After a moment of violent fantasizing Will realized that their manager had started talking again—"… but she wouldn't answer her phone. Then I thought I'd try Brian and David, and, again, no answer. So after giving Derek a call and finally getting the story from

221

him, I decided I'd call you, since you now seem to be harboring most of the band there anyway."

Will dragged his palm down his face, "Uh, yea. Never too old for a slumber party, you know."

"Yea, whatever. I don't even want to know."

"What is this about, Bill? I'm trying to sleep?" Will hissed.

"Sleep?" Bill laughed, "Man, you keep strange hours. You some kind of vampire or something?"

Will scoffed, "Yea, I wish! Now out with it!"

Bill cleared his throat, "Well, it's like this, there's a show in a few weeks; a big, *big* show!"

"Uh-huh…"

"Try and sound a little more excited here, Will! You'll be glad you did! Anyway, it's a battle of the bands show hosted by—are you ready for this?—Slaughterhouse Records! Turns out they're looking for fresh talent and this is how they intend to find it!"

Will sat up at this, "You're shitting me!"

"I wouldn't. Not about something this big."

"When?"

"Two weeks from tomorrow."

Will frowned, chewing at his lip, "You know I have to talk to the others about this, right?"

There was a pause, "Do you *really* see there being a problem with this?"

"I don't see why there would be," Will sighed.

"Look, if it's about what happened—"

"Bill!" Will growled into the receiver, "I just need to talk to them first."

"Whoa! Easy there, killer! Go ahead and chat it up with them. I'll keep in tou—"

Will hung up before Bill could finish and—knowing that getting more sleep was out of the question—pulled himself out of bed and threw on a pair of pants and went downstairs, finding the others in the living room watching TV.

Brian raised an eyebrow, "You're up early."

"Don't remind me," Will sighed, "I just got a call from Bill."

Everybody looked up at him.

"What'd he want?" Brian seemed as impatient as always.

"I guess there's a show coming up," Will answered.

David frowned, "I thought we weren't doing any more shows for a while."

Will glanced over at him and shrugged, "We did say that. But that was before we had an opening for a battle of the bands show with a deal with Slaughterhouse as the grand prize."

All eyes shot open.

"You're shitting us!" Brian leaned forward in his seat.

"You know, it's funny," Will smirked, "I said the very same—"

"When is it?" Bekka was shaking with excitement.

"Two weeks."

David sighed, "I don't know. I'm not sure if we should." He glanced at Bekka, "Do you think we're—"

Bekka glared at him, "I think we *have* to!"

David looked to Will for some kind of backup.

Will shrugged, "It *is* for a shot at a contract with Slaughterhouse."

David tried again with Brian, certain that he'd have some reason to say "no", but he was already excitedly talking with Bekka about a record deal. Defeated, he buried his face in his hands and let out a soft whimper.

"Fine," he surrendered, "But we need to practice until then. Every night!" He shook his head, "We can't afford another catastrophe!"

"Agreed!" Bekka's voice was suddenly serious, though she was still bouncing excitedly.

Will nodded and got to his feet. "I'll give Derek a call to meet us here for practice."

"Does he already know?" Brian asked.

"Bill said he told him," Will confirmed as he got up and started back upstairs to his room, bracing himself for another long day.

The conversation with Will lasted only a few seconds and consisted of little more than "come over for practice". Before Derek had been able to respond, the line went dead and he was left talking to himself. Sighing, he cradled the phone and headed upstairs to fetch his bass.

"Grandfather, are you free to give me a ride to Will's?"

His grandfather, busy with a pile of bills in his office, turned in the seat after a moment and frowned playfully, "When are you going to get your own car?"

"Probably when I'm out of the city and not within walking distance of everything," he laughed.

"Fair enough," the old man chuckled and stacked the papers he was working on, setting them aside, "Give me ten minutes."

Derek smiled, "Thanks."

"It's not a problem. Just make sure you remember your poor, old grandfather when you're a famous rock-star!"

Derek laughed as he hurried to his room. Though Bill had told him about the show over the phone earlier, he hadn't been sure what the others would have to say about it and, because of this, did not allow himself to get excited about it. Will's call—brief as it was—had been enough to show that the others had agreed to play. Realizing this, the pent-up excitement from earlier was allowed to surface and wash away the stress of the dead-end spell.

In the end, he realized, it just called for far more energy than he could gather and transport on his own.

Shaking his head, he took a deep breath and began the process of changing out the worn-out strings of his bass with a new set; a process that always served to relax him.

Through his years as a musician, he'd come to treat the act as a meditative one, and when the task was finished he smiled, feeling as though he'd woken up from a long nap.

Looking at his clock, he was surprised to see that a little over twenty minutes had passed. Getting to his feet, he hoisted the case, letting it dangle at his side, and headed towards his grandfather's office.

"Grandfather!" He called from his door, "Are you almost ready? I thought you only said you'd be ten minutes!"

It was quiet in the hall as he approached; no sound of moving papers or the faint scratching of pencil on paper. There was only a faint squeaking.

Already he felt something was wrong.

From the doorway, things looked as they had when he'd first passed. The materials on the desk littering its surface in a way that only his grandfather seemed to be able to work around. Behind the desk, the old man remained seated, hunched over his work; motionless.

Derek stared from the doorway for a moment, his eyes slowly drawn down to the scale as it shifted from side to side and squeaked with each pass. Stepping inside, Derek could see that it was slightly unbalanced—the two ten-gram pellets occupying the left side while nineteen grams worth of pellets offset it on the right. Beside it, his grandfather's hand rested on the desktop, his thumb and pointer finger pinched around one of the smallest pellets.

He was so still.

"Grandfather?" Derek called out, laying a hand on the

old man's shoulder and shaking him gently, "Hey! It's time to wake up..." His left eye twitched as a fresh tear welled within it and cascaded down his cheek. He shook his grandfather harder, "Grandpa! Wake up!"

The old man rocked and began to sag forward; his head dropping towards the desk. Gasping, Derek caught it before it hit and, with shaky hands, returned him to a respectable position.

"Grandpa..." The tears began to come faster, washing down his face in twin streams. His eyes stung against his efforts at holding them back and his breath caught on an inhale and he was forced to turn away so he wouldn't start hacking all over the old man. Heaving, he tried to get a lungful of air, only to choke once again on the intake. He dropped to his hands and knees, "No. Please God, no!"

He'd been raised a magician—knowing of the energies that existed in and around him that allowed for such fantastic feats to be achieved. This knowledge had kept him from being religious; had kept him from believing or praying. But there was no magic that could undo what had happened. His grandfather was too strong to die if there was any way to stop.

There was no bringing him back.

And so Derek called out, again and again, to a god he'd never even tried to believe in.

But his grandfather only grew colder.

For a long time he remained on the floor, hunched over and sobbing. Only when the phone began to ring downstairs did he even think of moving away. He looked up, hearing the first ring like a distant reminder, and by the second he was crawling for the door.

Reaching the stairs by the fourth ring and, he found himself fearful that the caller might hang up and, desperate to hear somebody's voice, he pushed himself over the edge and allowed his body to crash down the steps. Laying at the bottom of the stairs, the wave of emotions twisted in his guts and he pitched forward and threw up. Still choking on his bile, he pulled himself up and reached for the phone, pulling it to the floor beside him.

"Hello?" Bekka's voice came through, "Derek? Mister Sumner?"

Derek took in a pained breath, "Bekka!"

"Derek? What's wrong? You sound awful? Are you getting sick?"

"He's dead!" He almost threw up again as he finally spoke the words.

"What? Who?" There was a pause as Bekka pieced it all together, "Oh! Oh god! Derek! Stay there, we'll be right over!"

Derek nodded and he lay his face down on the floor, feeling the chilled wood against his cheek. Though Bekka had hung up, he continued to speak into the receiver.

"He's dead... he's dead..."

"Oh god! Hurry," Bekka was leaning forward in her seat, hands clasped around the shoulders of Will's seat.

Will nodded and swerved around a red sports car, flooring it as he did and shooting past it. He hadn't said a word after Bekka had come running into the living room with the news. What was supposed to be a checkup on when he'd be arriving had become an emergency visit. There was nothing that he could say at that point.

There was only what he could do.

He sped through a red light, ignoring the blaring horns of braking cars.

As the band's bassist, Derek and Will were expected to work together as a unit, and while they didn't always see eye-to-eye they had, over the years, developed an unspoken bond. Looking back on it, Will had never really shown him how much he really cared.

But he'd show him now!

Swerving around another vehicle—this time a patrol car—he kept his foot heavy on the accelerator and ignored the sirens and flashing lights as they started after him.

"Oh shit," Brian cursed and looked over his shoulder, "Will, are you out of your mind?"

Will shook his head, "Just shut up! Derek needs us!"

Derek's place was only a short distance away, and after leading the wailing cop car all the way to his front door they started out of the van.

"FREEZE!" The cop leapt from his car, pistol aimed

and ready.

Will turned to glare at him, face tight and serious despite having a gun aimed at his head, "There's a dead man in there!"

"I said freeze, assholes!" The cop thumbed back the hammer and focused his aim on Will.

Derek's door opened then and the startled policeman spun to face it, his gun going off as he did.

Derek was only aware of the danger on a subconscious level, but even that proved to be enough. Before he knew what he was doing he had thrown out his energies and put a magic shield up. The spell, though cast in an instant, was more than enough to block the oncoming bullet and ricochet it into his front door.

"My grandfather…" Derek croaked, pointing inside.

Bekka was the first one up the steps, her arms quickly wrapping around Derek so tight that a lingering sob was forced out of him, "Derek, I'm so sorry!"

The others worked their way up the steps to join him.

In the distance, the wail of the first ambulance—responding to the officer's call—cut through the sound of midday traffic.

TWENTY-TWO

"Derek? You gonna be okay?" Bekka was sitting beside him on Will's couch, the others standing around him.

"That cop was a fucking douchebag!" Will growled.

Brian shook his head, "Will you shut up? You're lucky he didn't arrest you!"

"There were more important things than writing me up for speeding!" Will glared back at him.

"Yes, and he took care of those things when he became aware of them," David pointed out.

Brian growled and turned around, "You were driving like a madman! You were reckless and stupid and you nearly got Derek shot because of it!"

Will frowned, "He stopped it…"

"And what if he hadn't?" Brian's face was inches from his; his hot, angry breath hitting him in the nose, "What if—"

Bekka cleared her throat and narrowed her gaze at them, "I don't know if you two have realized this yet, but you're *not* the focus of attention right now!"

Will stared at Bekka and then at Derek, who was still hunched over on the couch. He hadn't reacted at all to the argument; hadn't reacted to anything, in fact. They'd practically had to carry him from his home while the paramedics took care of the body. After that, however, he had gone quiet and still.

Brian returned to his spot at Bekka's side as she continued to talk to their traumatized band-mate. David, sitting on the floor in front of them, had his left hand lightly resting on Derek's knee, which occasionally bobbed for a moment as if to an inaudible rhythm.

"I'm gonna get him something to drink," Will announced, heading for the kitchen.

Brian looked up and shook his head, "I don't think now is the time!"

Will pivoted on his heel and took several steps back, "Whether or not you choose to recognize it, Mister Sober, people drink when they're grieving. And I happen to have some prime spiced rum waiting for a moment like this."

Derek's knee started up again.

David smirked, "I think that got his attention."

Will nodded, "I figured it would."

Brian, sighing, shrugged and nodded.

The vampire, beaming victoriously, marched into the kitchen and headed for his liquor cabinet, fetching the bottle and reaching for a couple of glasses.

"The bottle will do just fine," Derek's voice was soft and monotone behind him.

Will smirked, turning and passing the nearly full bottle of liquor to him, "Didn't hear you come in, but isn't that just like a bassist?"

Derek chuckled and shrugged as he undid the top to the bottle and took a hard swig, "Surprised the others too. Told 'em I didn't want to wait for my drink."

Will laughed, "Don't blame you. That's some good shit right there!"

Derek took another long pull and nodded, letting out a heavy sigh. "That it is," He sat down at the kitchen table.

"I'm surprised they didn't follow you in," Will said as he pulled up a seat across from him.

Shrugging, Derek ran his thumb across the label on the bottle, "I asked for a moment alone."

Will smirked, "You're not coming out to me, are you?"

Derek chuckled, though it was clearly forced. "No. I'm just thankful," he shrugged again and took another drink, "You really came through for me today."

Will shrugged, "I know how much that old man meant to you."

"Yea…" Derek sighed, "He was a good man."

Will nodded and held out his hand for Derek to pass the bottle and took a long gulp when he finally did, "So what now?"

Derek scoffed and looked up, "Are you asking me if I'm going to leave the band?"

Will shrugged, "Are you?"

Derek shook his head and yanked the bottle back, "No. My grandpa wouldn't want that, and I'm not about to insult his memory by doing something he'd disapprove of."

Will chuckled and motioned to the bottle, "Not sure he'd approve of this."

"Yea, well," Derek licked some of the rum off his upper lip and swirled the contents of the bottle, "that never stopped me before." He shook his head and reached into his coat pocket and retrieved one of his long, fat cigars, "You mind?"

Will shook his head, "Go ahead, "You've more than earned it."

Derek nodded his thanks as he focused on the tip.

"You know," Will offered, "I hear a wood match is better for—"

Derek shut him up with a look.

"On second thought," Will shrugged, "Fuck the wood match; the wood match is a dick, anyway."

Though his emotions made gathering the necessary energies difficult, after a few seconds the tip ignited and a fat plume of smoke issued from his mouth.

"I can't believe you can smoke those things," Will laughed as the cloud issued past him. "That's some kind of fucking mutant tobacco they're using in there; goddam things could fumigate a whole motherfucking circus tent!" He smirked, "Plus, they look like giant turds!"

Derek smiled and pulled the cigar from between his teeth and studied it, "Only the best."

"Well you could choke a full-grown fucking moose on the smog from that thing," he smirked. "Come to think of it, going into a show with a pair of moose antlers on my head *would* be pretty fucking metal! Smoke up, man!"

They both laughed.

The sound must have carried, because shortly after the entranceway to the kitchen was occupied by the three others, curiosity painted on their faces. David inhaled deeply and smiled, pushing the rest of the way through and heading for the table. As soon as he was close enough he snatched up the bottle from Derek's hand and took a long chug.

"Mm!" He hummed to himself and sat down between the two, "This *is* good stuff!"

Will laughed, "It does the trick."

Derek nodded and pulled the rum back to himself and cradled it against his chest.

Bekka studied the scene. "Hard liquor and cigars as thick as my wrist," She shook her head, "Some things never change."

"Could do without the booze, but still," Brian sighed as he stepped into the kitchen and pulled his cigarettes from his pocket, "Hey Derek! Light me!"

Bekka frowned, "Oh not you too!"

Brian shrugged as Derek magically lit his cigarette for him.

"Men," shaking her head, Bekka stepped into the kitchen and took her place beside Brian. Despite not being pleased with their methods, she smiled at the results and looked down at Derek as he took another pull from the bottle, which was already nearly empty, "So are you going to be alright?"

Derek looked up at her and nodded, "I'll survive. Besides, I'm willing to bet he wouldn't have appreciated it if I was out there making myself miserable over this."

Bekka smiled warmly, "I know he wouldn't have."

David took the bottle and drained it quickly—much to the distress of Will, who stared in horror as the last of the rum disappeared down his throat.

Will scowled and shook his head, "You drunk!"

David shrugged and set the bottle down, "Will you be staying here then?" He asked Derek.

He thought about this for a moment and looked at Will, "If it's not a problem. I'm not sure I could go home just yet."

"Don't worry about it," Will said, "I'll give you the guest room David's been in. He can have the couch."

David nodded and smiled at Derek, who looked concerned at the idea of putting him out, "The couch will be fine."

"Thanks guys," Derek smiled and put his cigar between his teeth again.

"So," Bekka frowned and bit her lip, "should we still go through with the concert?"

Everybody turned to Derek.

Caught off guard by the expectant stares, he paused for a moment. Finally, he nodded, smiling at them, "Yea. I think we should."

TWENTY-THREE

Practice.

It was one of the few things that the band had left that was theirs to control. They didn't know how long Derek's protective spell would hide Bekka; didn't know how long they had before they'd have to put down their instruments and bring up their fists once again.

Not that they'd done such a great job at that, either.

Derek continued to contemplate—almost to the point of insanity—how the spell could be made to work. It was an aggravating conundrum: having the solution to the equation but not the equation itself. Still, as much as the whole ordeal made him want to pull his hair out, he was sure

that the others—knowing nothing in the ways of magic—
were even more on edge; unable to do anything and being
forced to sit back and hope for the best.

And so they practiced for three days straight, pausing
only to eat and sleep. They kept the idle chit-chat to a
minimum, afraid of what the others were thinking and even
more afraid of admitting what they, themselves, were
thinking. There was little that needed to be said anyway; not
when they could let their music do the talking.

It was nearing the end of a ten-minute break, and
Brian and Bekka had hurried upstairs for a drink of water
with David not far behind them—though everybody knew
that he had something stronger in mind. Leaning in the
corner of the basement with his flask in one hand and a
smoking cigar in the other, Derek kept his eyes low and his
breathing steady. Will, not bothering to rise from his stool,
sat and stared off, occasionally letting his eyes dart towards
Derek. Absentmindedly, he swirled one of his drumsticks
between the fingers of his right hand while tapping the other
on his knee with his left.

"So what'cha thinking, magic-man?" Will finally cut
through the silence.

Derek looked up and blew a cloud of smoke through
his nose as he shrugged. "I don't know," He answered
solemnly, "I wish I could say I was thinking about how to fix
all of this, but..." He shook his head again.

Will nodded, "Don't beat yourself up for it. You've
been thinking about it a lot lately. It's good to take a break

once in a while. You know what they say, 'all work and no play' and all that jazz."

"I suppose," Derek was still shaking his head as he took another puff on the cigar and followed it up with a swig from his flask. He let out a light cough and wiped his lips, "I guess"—he coughed again—"I was thinking about my grandfather."

Will's face turned serious and he stopped fidgeting with his drumsticks and set them down. "We're all sorry about that, Derek," he assured him. "Take it from me, you can live *multiple* lifetimes and never know a man that wise. I think I speak for everyone when I say I feel the—"

Derek nodded and held up his hand so that no further sympathies would be uttered.

Will frowned and closed his mouth.

"It's just… He seemed to be on to something, y'know?" Derek pulled himself from the wall and moved towards the center of the room, "Like, I'm sure he didn't have the answer, but I just got the feeling that he was closer to it than any of us. I was wondering—if he'd just had a little more time—if we'd have gotten the answer by now."

Will scowled, "You're mad about him dying when he did?"

Derek shook his head and sighed as he slipped his bass back over his shoulders. When his instrument was secure he shrugged, "I don't know. I guess I can't be mad about something like that."

"No. You really can't," Will agreed, "Take it from

me: death is just a part of the whole process. It can be a sad thing—the loss, I mean—but it's all just another beat in the eternal scheme."

Derek frowned, "You seem pretty laid back about the subject."

Will shrugged, "Well I *am* a vampire. I've been around long enough and seen enough deaths in my time."

Derek shook his head, "But you don't kill for your blood! Hell, last time I checked you don't even drink human blood!"

"I did once. Man-oh-man! What a rush that was!" Will confessed, "But that was a long time ago, when other options weren't available for my kind. But that's not the point."

"And what's the point?" Derek asked.

Will's growing smirk exposed more than just a little of his elongated left fang, "I had to *die* to become what I am."

Derek looked down as he thought of this. Though he had already known this, the reminder served its point.

"I just don't know if I'll be able to figure it out on my own," he sighed.

Will rolled his eyes then and retrieved his drumsticks. "Quitting ain't an option, magic-man," he gave one of the cymbals a soft rattle for effect, "Besides, we all believe in you and your mojo!"

Derek smiled and opened his mouth to thank him but was interrupted as the others started to make their way down the stairs. Bekka and Brian were both chuckling at something as they reached the last step. David rolled his eyes at the two, and brought a bottle to his lips, taking a long pull and smiling as Will's jaw dropped at the sight of him.

"Is that my vodka?" Will rose from his stool, "God-fucking-dammit! You're drinking me out of my entire stash! Next you'll be raiding my wine cellar!"

David's eyes lit up at that and he licked his lips, "You have a wine cellar?"

Will shook his head angrily and held his arms, "You're *in* my basement already, retard! You see any fucking wine?"

Scowling at the realization that he'd been tricked, David took another swig from the bottle and set it down on one of the amps as he shrugged into his guitar.

"Keep the booze off the gear!" Brian barked as he slipped on his own guitar.

"Fine!" David—already starting to get drunk—picked up the bottle and took another drink before setting it on the floor by the wall.

Bekka rolled her eyes and cleared her throat, "I think our ten minutes is up, guys! Are we ready to play or what?"

"I've *been* ready!" Brian scoffed, shaking his head at David.

David swayed slightly, "Hey! I'm down here and plugged in, aren't I?"

Brian scoffed, "I'll say you're 'plugged in', you drunk!"

David growled at him.

"Uh… I'm ready too," Will held a drumstick in the air, "Just in case anybody cares."

"Derek?" Bekka's voice was soft at first and nobody noticed as she took a step towards their bassist. By the third, more concerned call of his name, however, the others turned their heads to see what was the matter.

"Yo, magic-man? You alright?" Will moved away from his setup and towards his friend.

"Shit! What's the matter with him?" Brian slid his guitar around to his back and moved to stand beside Bekka.

The liquor-induced, glassy shine in David's eyes disappeared and he moved to get a look as well.

Derek had backed up all the way to the far wall and was beginning to slide towards the floor. The color was drained from his face, leaving it gray and clammy. His mouth hung open and his nostrils flared with each breath; his chest heaving violently. As he continued to slide to the floor, the bass seemed to become heavier and heavier until it appeared to be crushing his chest under its weight.

"Oh God!" Bekka cried out, "Get it off of him!"

David was already moving towards their band-mate before their singer had finished and he began to pull the bass up over their friend's shoulders.

"I think he's hyperventilating!" Brian announced as he moved beside David to retrieve the bass. As he took it he turned to Will, who stood beside Bekka, "Do you have a paper bag?"

"I think so," Will answered, "In the kitche—"

"Get it!" Brian ordered.

Will vanished from sight.

Brian turned back to Derek, who'd begun to audibly heave. With the bass out of the way he had started to try and climb back to his feet, but something seemed to be weighing him down.

David let out a whimper as he looked around at the others, "Is he going to be alright?" He demanded.

Bekka shook her head, her right hand clutching her throat and trying to hold back the tears that were forming in her eyes, "Derek…"

"Fuckfuckfuck!" Brian pulled Derek to an upright position and came back with a sweat-drenched hand, "Oh shit! His skin's on fire!" He turned towards the stairs, "Will! Get down he—"

"Coming!" Derek coughed out, his eyes darting in his skull, "They're coming!"

Brian shook his head, "Dammit! *Who's* coming?"

"Hey, guys! I can't find any paper bags!" Will's voice echoed down the stairs, "Can I get—"

There was a loud crash upstairs and Will shot down the stairs.

"God damn!" Brian looked up, "Did a plane just hit the house?"

"Here! They're here! Run!" Derek continued to ramble.

"Oh! Ow! What hit me?" Will groaned as he pulled himself to his feet.

"What the fuck is going on up there?" Brian demanded.

Will stumbled as he looked up at the others, "I, uh... I don't think Derek's spell is working anymore."

A moment later a shrieking howl echoed down the stairs, followed by a man as he threw himself down the stairs. The sound was enough to tip Will off and before the Kamikaze attack could take him down he jumped out of its path. The still-screaming man hit the floor, all the force of the fall on his head and breaking his neck. Will stared at the corpse in confusion before turning to the others.

"Friend of yours?"

"Shut up, Will!" Brian was on his feet and got between Bekka and the stairwell as the sound of pounding footsteps on the floor above gave away their approach.

"I can feel them..." Bekka announced.

"There's too many!" Derek said, pulling himself to his feet.

David snarled, his teeth bared and his eyes narrowed at the ceiling. Every footstep that sounded above them brought another stifled growl out into the open.

"We need to get out of here!" Brian shouted over the growing racket. Turning to Will he motioned towards the garage, "We'll get Derek! You get the van started!"

Will shook his head, "Start the van with what? My keys are still upstairs!"

"What?" Brian's eyes widened, "What are they doing up there?"

Will sneered at him, "Oh, I don't know. I figured when the attack on my house came—'cuz, y'know, this shit is just so goddam typical for me!—that I might like a bit of an added challenge." He narrowed his eyes, "ARE YOU FUCKING SERIOUS? How in the seven holy hells was I supposed to know this would fucking happen?"

Brian held his tongue and stared up at the ceiling, listening to the sound of the intruders "... the hell are those bastards doing up there?"

"Making sure there are no openings," David snarled, his nose flaring as he inhaled sharply.

"No openings?" Bekka's voice was a nervous squeak.

David nodded and wetted his lips, continuing to follow the sounds with his eyes, "Cornering us; making sure there's no way out."

"But we can just bail out the fucking garage!" Will pointed out.

David shook his head, "They've probably got units stationed by there to make sure we don't try."

Will looked up at the ceiling and then towards the door that led to the garage and shook his head angrily, "Did you honestly just say 'units'? Fucking hell! How many of them are there?"

Bekka chewed her lip, "A lot."

"'A lot' isn't a number!" Will spat.

Brian glared at him, "Well it's the best answer you're getting right now!"

"So what do you suggest we do?" Will demanded.

Derek stumbled as he pushed himself away from the wall and approached the others on uncertain legs. Despite his shakiness, his face was solid and angry, "We fight our way out!"

Everybody looked at him.

"Right," Will rolled his eyes, "Let's go over our resources; we've got a tipsy werewolf, a cranky human, a demonically-possessed and scared little girl, an uncoordinated magician, and a very confused and freaked-out vampire. All of whom are lacking any sort of formal training and armed to the teeth with"—he looked around the basement for effect—"NOTHING! How do you expect this to work?"

"Maybe we should start with growing you a pair of balls!" Brian spat. With Will still staring in disbelief at him he turned to Bekka, "Get to the garage and lock yourself in the van."

Bekka shook her head, "No! I want to fight, too!"

Brian's eyes went wide and he started to shake his head.

"Trust me," she pleaded with him.

Though he didn't seem entirely convinced he nodded to her and stepped away, grabbing the microphone stand and kicking the base from it.

"Oh, this'll be good!" Will chuckled, shaking his head, "You want me to beat them to death with my drumsticks, gladiator-boy?"

Brian slammed the broken end of the metal rod to the floor for emphasis, "I want you to do what it takes to get out of here alive! And if there's any further problem with that then you can try to fight your way out with my foot lodged in your ass!"

Will narrowed his eyes at Brian and shook his head, letting his fangs extend from his gums, "When this is over, you and I are going to have a little chat on how you should speak to somebody higher up on the fucking food chain. Hey, Rex!" He turned to David then and smirked, "Might be a good idea to let your better-half out."

David smiled at this and nodded, instantly peeling his tee-shirt off and beginning to undo his belt. Without stopping he glanced at Bekka and motioned for her to turn around, which, blushing deeply, she did. With her back turned to him, he kicked off his shoes and slipped free of his pants. The change was already underway and before he had a chance to pull off his socks his body was wracked with spasms and the first pained howl emerged. The other guys watched as their guitarist's body snapped and stretched and bent in ways that made their own bodies ache. As his muscles seemed to inflate and his skin discolored, his face popped and twisted. Halfway through the change the pain of the process and the uncontrollable lurches became too much and he dropped to all fours.

Throughout the process the sound of his body breaking and reshaping and the horrible cries of pain caused the others to cringe, including Bekka, who didn't even have to see the event to be unsettled by it. Finally, as the last bone stretched and shifted, David straightened himself up, breathing heavily.

"Can I turn around now?" Bekka asked.

Will studied the creature before them—eight feet tall and covered in hair and muscle. A wicked set of teeth poked out from the parted lips of the monster and, as it flexed its new fists, he could see the long, slightly curved claws that had once been David's fingernails. At his feet, which sported claws of their own, were the shredded remains of his socks.

"Hello?" Bekka called out again.

Brian nodded, "Yea. It's over."

Before Bekka had completely turned around David— or what had emerged from David—shot up the stairs, snarling and barking as he ascended. The sight was a blur of darkened skin and fur and as he disappeared through the upstairs door the immediate sound of chaos began.

"Well, I guess he's got things covered," Will said, slapping his palms together.

Brian shook his head and used the butt-end of his makeshift weapon to herd the vampire towards the stairs, "Let's go!" He instructed.

Will growled and rolled his shoulders in a mock imitation of David's transformation. Finally, he turned to Brian and licked his lips, "See you on the other side."

"Yea, yea! Just get your damn keys!" Brian ordered.

Will nodded and disappeared up the stairs.

Derek shook his head and groaned, still groggy from earlier, and started for the stairs, "Wish I had a cooler entrance than stumbling my black-ass up the stairs."

Brian frowned, "Sure you're okay to do this?"

A soft smile crept over his face and he nodded. Before Brian could argue, he moved to the first step and started his way up.

There was no stopping him now.

TWENTY-FOUR

Derek made it up the stairs only slightly before Brian and Bekka. He still felt shaky as he stepped into the mayhem—the process of having his magical shields ripped down forcefully by the invaders was more painful than he would have guessed. His head buzzed and swam from the trip up the stairs and he steadied himself against a nearby table.

"Don't kill them!" Bekka cried out, moving past him to get beside David and Will.

The vampire and the werewolf were side-by-side, Will standing just enough behind the towering beast that David had become so that they could both fit in the narrow hall. In front of them, the horde of people—their eyes rolled back in their skulls—let out angry, inhuman groans and lashed out at the two while keeping their distance from them. As soon as Bekka came into sight, however, their motives seemed to change from one of self-preservation to an all-out, suicidal scramble. All at once their strange groans grew louder and more ferocious and the possessed invaders shot towards her. Ignoring what Bekka had just said, David snarled and swung a massive arm at the closest attacker, sending them spiraling back into the others behind them.

Bekka shook her head, eyes wide with the fear, "David!"

A whimper sounded and the werewolf's face turned towards her to give her an apologetic look.

"I don't think we should be so worried about *their* wellbeing!" Will pointed out, backing away from the onslaught. His retreat was interrupted then by a possessed boy as he launched himself over the upper level railing and came down on top of him, "Fuck!" The vampire struggled to hold his attacker's thrashing hands away from his face, though Derek could already see that the ring in his right eyebrow had been torn out. As he continued to thrash, a faint trickle of blood seeped from the wound and down his temple and soaked into his brown hair before the wound sealed over and healed, leaving only the blood trail as evidence, "God-fucking-dammit! David! Little help!"

The werewolf grunted like a gorilla, acknowledging the call for help but unable to respond as he held three of the invaders back—all of them ignoring the monster as they tried to maneuver around it to reach Bekka.

Seeing this, Brian ran into the madness, putting himself between the attackers and their target and swinging the mike-stand into the closest one's chest.

Knowing that the others would only last so long, Derek pulled himself up and approached, muttering the necessary spells under his breath to build up his energies. There was a static pop in his palms as the pools of sweat that had collected there sizzled away and the tips of his fingers began to tingle. When he was sure he'd accumulated enough power, he focused them at the floor several feet ahead of his band-mates. His head went light as he worked his magic, and he allowed himself to drop to his knees so that he could slap his palms down on the hardwood floor. As his power shot through the planks he could hear them begin to strain under the force of the magic.

David was the first to react, his ears perking up at the sound, and as the floor began to tear apart beneath him he jumped back, allowing the three intruders he'd been holding back to fall back behind the giant tear opening up in the floor.

Will's eyes went wide at the sight, "Dude! My fucking floor!"

The mass of invaders howled and cursed in an unknown language at the barrier that had opened up between them. David stood at the edge, baring his teeth at them.

Brian let out a sigh, nodding in approval towards

Derek as he kept Bekka close to him.

Derek shook his head, "That's not going to hold them for lo—"

Sure enough, one of the invaders—a tall, muscular man with a sizable bald spot on his head and wearing a brown jumpsuit—moved to jump over the gap. Halfway over the barrier, the possessed man corkscrewed his body upside-down and dug his fingertips into the ceiling and pushed forward, throwing himself the rest of the way over the chasm. Landing in a twisted handstand, the attacker's limbs bent in impossible ways as he started towards them.

David was the first to step in, letting out a heavy and angry grunt. Before the werewolf had a chance to attack, however, the man ducked down and delivered a strong uppercut into his abdomen. A sharp, pained bark was forced out and David keeled over, clutching his stomach. Without a pause, the possessed man jumped up and brought both fists— tightly clasped together—down on the werewolf's head. David made no sound this time as he collapsed in a heap on the floor.

With their greatest line of defense out of commission, the man was free to advance and lunged at Bekka, throwing Brian easily aside as he tried to get in the way. Bekka's head turned away from the threat to make sure Brian was alright and before she could turn back the man's hands were at her throat.

"Get off her!" Will appeared and pushed the man away, wedging himself between the two and forming a shield.

The man let out an angry, gargling howl and started towards the right. Will moved to counter the maneuver only to find he'd been tricked as the man adjusted to go left. Pivoting to correct the situation, the vampire was met with an elbow to the temple and a kick to the groin that dropped him to his knees. Before he could utter a pained syllable, his head was snatched in the attacker's grip and slammed down into the floor with enough force to knock the vampire out.

"Will!" Bekka cried out.

Derek kept his distance, knowing he would fare no better up close than the other two, and instead tried to collect his power for another spell. The familiar warmth and tingle of energy started to swell within him. Still mustering his powers, he began to plan out his next spell, only to be caught off guard by a foreign energy that slammed him into the wall and siphoned his power. He looked around, startled; though the man wasn't looking at him, he was certain that the attack was coming from him.

And still he approached Bekka!

The singer had no chance to plan out an escape before he was on her again. Large hands held her shoulders down before they moved to throttle her. Thrashing and struggling against the hold, her body began to twist and bend. Derek—unable to pull himself from the wall—stared in amazement as her body snapped and shifted until the man on top of her was forced to relinquish his hold.

As the attacker regained himself and prepared for another attempt, Bekka rose. Her body seemed to have snapped at the middle, and as she pulled herself up she formed a grotesque, upside-down "V". She lingered in this position a moment before pushing off with her feet and doing a back handspring. Her body, still oddly twisted, jerked and shifted as it righted itself again.

Though unnatural and unsettling, the man was not in the least bit impressed with the display and moved to attack again, throwing a punch at Bekka that was easily—though abnormally—dodged. Rather than stepping out of the path of approaching fist, she cocked herself to the side, balancing on her left leg and letting the rest of her body fall to the side until the rest of her was parallel with the floor. From there, she pulled her right leg in abruptly and threw it into the lower belly of the man. A series of inhuman cries sounded then as the attacker dropped to the ground and began to writhe.

Bekka returned to an upright position, her face twisted with fury, and stomped over to glare down at the attacker. Her eyes narrowed, "Leave him!" She commanded. As she spoke, the same, inhuman language that the others had been speaking leaked through at the same time in several different tones.

The attacker's body jerked several more times and Bekka sneered and lightly pressed the toe of her shoe to his throat and applied enough pressure to elicit an audible wheezing. She repeated the command again and again, each time with the same strange, overlapping translation echoing through her mouth, until finally the body went still.

The magical hold on Derek loosened then and lifted

at that moment, and as quickly as his energy had been taken from him it flooded back. As he pulled himself together, he watched as the others seemed to be granted the same lift from their own invisible binds. David and Will, though clearly still in pain, rose up on staggering feet. Brian jumped up, eager to get back into the fight until he saw that it had already ended, and looked in astonishment at Bekka, who blushed under his gaze and shrugged.

Will shook his head, "Well this is..." He knelt down and poked the man in the ribs, jumping when a pained groan sounded, "... well, it's fucked up is what it is."

Brian frowned down at the man before turning towards the hall where the other attackers had been, finding the space was vacant.

"Where are they?" He asked.

Bekka's eyes fluttered before she looked up at him, "We need to get out of here!"

Will shook his head, "No! They're gone! We're fine! See?" His voice was desperate, "Why would we have to leave now?" His pleas for an answer were punctuated by the shattering of a nearby window and the roaring hiss of fire, "You can't be serious!"

Brian clapped a hand down on his shoulder, "We need to go!"

"They're trying to burn down my house!" Will shouted, throwing the hand off of him.

Derek nodded, hurrying to retrieve the keys, "And it would be better if we weren't inside it when they succeed!"

"But it's *my* house!" Will roared.

"Get over it!" Brian spat.

"Please!" Bekka looked up at him, "We need to get out of here! There are more important things to worry about right now!"

Another window broke on the second floor and Will paused to stare upward, pained as his imagination painted the picture of the destruction. Finally he nodded, growling as he did, and moved with the others towards the basement.

"What about the gear?" Derek asked.

"Shit!" Will cursed, "We'll never get it all out in time!"

"Grab what you can!" Brian called out as he scooped up David's pants and tossed them to the werewolf.

David was already beginning to shrivel and shrink into his human form as he pulled the pants on, stumbling on his morphing legs as he tried to get through the pain of the transformation and become decent at the same time.

Several minutes later the van peeled out of the garage with everyone crammed inside. Will, fuming about the loss of both his home *and* his drums, didn't bother to slow the vehicle down on the way out of the driveway, forcing the possessed arsonists to dive out of his way.

"Oh God!" Bekka clapped her hand over her mouth as her eyes widened in shock and concern, "Don't hurt any of them!"

Will rolled his eyes at this and jerked the wheel abruptly, "No! We wouldn't want to do that, would we?" He growled, his tone dripping with sarcasm.

Everyone turned their heads towards the flaming wreckage of their drummer's home, taking in the horrific sight of the horde of attackers as they stumbled over one another to try and futilely catch up to them. Bekka squealed in terror as one of them, a younger woman clad in an expensive-looking blouse, slapped at the side of the van.

"So"—Will began, his voice trailing for a moment—"where to?"

TWENTY-FIVE

Bekka's apartment.

It had been a unanimous decision on where to stay—
the guitarists' place was too small (they'd already found that
fact out the hard way) and Derek was certain that his place
was probably already up for rent again by an "asshole"
landlord. It wasn't hard for the others to see that their bassist
was more reluctant than unable to go back, but nobody took
the subject any further.

While still exhausted from the spells he'd cast back at
Will's, Derek wasted little time in beginning to put up
another barrier, this time promising that Bekka would be
harder to find. As the bassist stood, eyes clenched shut and

fingers rapidly tracing glyphs in the air, his body swayed and shook from the energy.

Will watched this for as long as he could, feeling a sense of obligation since he had nothing else to do besides *not* complaining about the lack of beer. Finally, however, he grew bored with watching his friend gyrate and turned on the TV.

"Got nothing better to do than watch soaps?" Brian scolded him.

Will sighed and leaned forward and rested his arms on top of his knees, toying with the idea of standing but finally thinking better of it, "As a matter of fact, no, I don't! I just watched my house get fucking torched! TORCHED! Gone for-fucking-ever! I think—and this is just a personal opinion—that after everything I've just lost I've earned a little down time."

"'Down time'?" Brian shook his head, "What the hell is all this to you? Some fucking inconvenience?"

"I'd call it pretty fucking inconvenient," Will scoffed as he turned the channel again.

Brian growled, "Inconsiderate blood-sucker!"

Bekka waved her hands in front of her in an attempt to calm the situation, "Brian, please!"

Will vanished from the couch and appeared behind Bekka, baring his fangs at the momentarily startled Brian, "Blood-sucker, huh? You trying to tempt me?"

Derek sighed heavily as he paused, "Trying to concentrate over here."

Will snarled, "Shut up, magic-man! Brian seems to

think that just because he's fucking the star of this twisted little show that he can—"

"SHUT THE FUCK UP!" David snarled and whirled his head around with the ferocity that the others had come to expect from the guitarist's animal-side. He stood, glaring at the two for a long moment before continuing: "We are in the middle of a crisis—something that could mean life or death for one or all of us—and you're arguing over television? Grow up! Both of you!" He shook his head and focused on Will, "So you've lost a house? So what? How does that compare to the loss of one of us; one of your band-mates?"

Will frowned and looked down, ashamed.

Brian smirked, "That's what I sai—"

"And you!"—David bared his teeth at Brian, shutting him up—"You talk like you're the only one who's trying to keep Bekka safe! Like nobody else here is putting in any effort!" He reached out his hand and pointed towards their bassist, "Derek's been busting his balls time and time again and since this started, in the midst of a royal ass-kicking he's at it again, but you're interrupting him over—what?—a grudge you have against a *friend* who's just watched his life burn to the ground?" He shook his head again, "Both of you need to pull your heads out of your asses!"

Everyone stared at him for a moment, stunned and amazed. Both Brian and Will stared down at the floor for a long while, too proud to be the first to apologize but too afraid to try and start up the argument again. Finally they both looked up at one another and shared a single nod.

"Can somebody pass the noodles?" Will called out, sending several grains of white rice flying from his mouth.

"Not sure," Brian teased as he grabbed the box, "Can you keep it inside your mouth?"

The others laughed.

Will rolled his eyes and reached out, accepting the carton of Chinese food. As he dumped a generous portion onto his plate he smirked and mumbled something about using blood as a condiment.

"There goes my appetite," Derek set down his fork and pushed his plate away.

"Not mine," David smirked and pulled the rejected food towards himself, dumping what had been left on the bassist's plate onto his own.

More laughter.

Derek shook his head, still chuckling, and reached forward, "Anybody else ready for their fortune cookie?"

David—mouth still stuffed with stolen food—perked.

Will cackled, "I think Fido here is always ready for a cookie."

Another bout of laughter.

Despite most of the plates at the table still having unfinished food on them, everybody moved in to grab one of the plastic pouches. Soon the room was filled with the crinkling as they were torn open, followed then by the breaking of the cookies themselves.

Then everybody read.

"'Silence is golden'" Brian chuckled, "Hey, Will, I think I got yours."

"Har har," Will rolled his eyes as he read his own, "'Time is on your side'…?" He shook his head, "'Time is on your—' what the fucking hell does that mean?"

David smirked, "How 'bout this one, 'a level head makes all the difference'?"

Derek shook his head, "These things are all really more statements than fortunes."

"Well what's yours say, magic-man?" Will prodded.

Derek shrugged and passed the tiny slip of paper over to him.

Will scanned it for a moment and laughed.

Brian raised an eyebrow, "Well?"

"'Brush your teeth after every meal'!"

"No way does it say that!" Brian cackled.

"Swear to God!" Will passed the slip over and was met with further laughter.

"What about yours, Bekka?" Derek finally asked when the hysterics had died down.

There was no answer. Instead, Bekka simply stared at her own slip of paper analytically, frowning as she read and reread the words thereon. A short while passed as everybody waited for a response, and when none came Brian reached out and touched a hand to her shoulder.

"Bekka?"

She looked up at the contact and looked around the table at the others.

"What is it?" She asked.

"Your fortune?" Brian pressed, "What's it say?"

Bekka bit her lip and looked back at the little piece of paper before passing it over to him and getting up from the table to scrape her plate into the garbage. Brian picked up the slip and scanned it for a moment before sighing and setting it down again and rising to his feet to join her.

"Look, it doesn't mean anything," he told her quietly, though the others could still hear, "It's just a stupid fortune cookie."

Bekka nodded, though she didn't look convinced.

Slowly, Derek picked up the fortune and scanned it and frowned.

"What's it say?" Will asked.

Derek started to read it aloud but was cut off as Bekka turned towards the table and recited her fortune to them.

"'Rough times await'."

Nobody spoke for a long while.

"Well, it's like Brian said, it's just a stupid fortune cookie," Will finally offered.

Bekka nodded again, still not looking convinced. "Uh... I'm kinda tired," she looked to Brian and smiled slightly when he nodded in return.

David pursed his lips, "Bekka, you know it's going to be—"

"I know," she interrupted, smiling weakly at him, "Thank you."

There was little left for the others to say as the two retired to her bedroom.

TWENTY-SIX

Bekka hung up the phone and let out a heavy sigh.

"What was all that about?" Brian asked.

"Apparently Bill heard about the gas leak at Will's house," she explained.

Will raised an eyebrow, "A gas leak?"

Bekka nodded.

He shook his head in disbelief, "A gas leak? Are you fucking serious?"

David growled, "Calm down! It's better than getting Bill involved in the *truth*!"

"That's for goddam sure!" Will sighed and relaxed,

"Twitchy bastard fucks up enough *without* bringing life and limb into the equation."

"So what did he want?" Derek asked, turning back to Bekka.

"Well," Bekka sighed, "he wanted to make sure everyone was alright first and foremost."

Brian scoffed and shook his head, "I bet! Gotta protect that investment of his!"

Bekka shot him a look and his smirk faded away, "He was also wondering if we wanted to come over to his place and get some recording done."

"How am I supposed to do that when my drum set went up with the"—Will air quoted—"gas leak?"

"So buy a new one!" David rolled his eyes, "We all know you're rich enough and it's not like you broke the bank on the first one."

The others waited while David helped a sun-poisoned and cranky Will get his new drum set into the back of the van. The process took several trips back and forth from the store, but when they were finally done Will climbed into the driver's seat and shook his head.

"Fucking hell! Is it too much to ask for a goddam cloudy day for once in this piece-of-shit town?"

"Spare us your temper and get us to Bill's!" Brian

called from the back.

"Yes, please," David added as he climbed in.

Will growled and rolled his eyes, "Oh yessa, mastas!" He shook his head as he threw the vehicle into drive and lurched out of the parking lot, "Bunch of fucking assholes!" He muttered.

Bekka pouted, "Even me?"

Will sighed and shook his head, "No, not you. You're our little demon-possessed princess."

Bekka frowned but shrugged it off a moment later, accepting it as the closest thing she was going to get to a compliment from him at that time.

The drive to Bill's was quiet after that. Will turned on a CD—the deep, bass-filled voice of the lead singer of "Moonspell" playing through the car's speakers.

They were only five tracks into the album when they pulled into Bill's. The front gate was already open in anticipation of their arrival. From there, they rolled onward down a long, paved driveway that ended in a circular path that wound around an intricate garden. The house itself was a cream color—Bill himself had corrected them in the past when they'd called it "white"—and the front door was framed in a large, two-story window that domed off at the top and gave the band a clear view of a crystal chandelier inside that hung over the main entrance.

"All this *and* a recording studio!" Will grumbled.

Bekka stepped out behind Brian and stretched when she was no longer confined, "Looks like he's doing well for himself."

"Yea, well, let's hope he doesn't have any gas leaks while we're here," Will scoffed as he slammed the door shut and walked around to the other side.

"That's not funny," Derek stepped out and slid the door shut behind him.

"No," David nodded, "it isn't."

Will shrugged and smirked, passing off the inappropriate comment as just another failed joke.

Derek sighed and stared analytically at the house. "I don't sense anything," he finally offered.

"That supposed to make us feel better?" Brian mumbled, shaking his head.

Bekka gave him a look and, after she'd made her point, looked to Derek and smiled.

David seemed less convinced, "Is there any way you can cast another protection spell?"

Derek shrugged, "I could, but it'd take a while."

"How long?" Brian asked.

Derek shook his head, mentally calculating, "An hour or two probably. We'd be done and gone before it even made a difference, and I think Bill might notice if I was sitting around doing nothing for that long."

David sighed, "Then we're doing this unprotected?"

Will smirked, "As unprotected as a prom night hotel visit!"

Nobody laughed.

Bekka frowned at the idea but shrugged, "I guess

we're not going to be *that* long."

Brian shook his head and waved his hands in front of him. "Whoa! No way are we going in there without some kind of protection! Those things have been there at every turn and now we're just going to take a chance on it?"

David nodded, "I agree."

Will rolled his eyes. "Big fucking surprise there."

David shot him a menacing glare.

Derek looked down and shook his head, "There's no way I can just whip up an instant protection spell! It doesn't work that way!"

"Well think of something, magic man," Will sighed. "Before Brian and his dog both shit on themselves."

Will was rewarded with another hateful glare, this time from both David and Brian.

"You're skating out on thin ice, leech!" Brian growled between clenched teeth.

Bekka frowned and stepped between them, "Stop it! This won't get us any—"

At that moment the front door to the house swung open. Bill stood on the other side, a large bottle of scotch in his left hand.

"Glad to see you could make it," their manager said as he stepped out, his shoes slapping against the welcome mat on the front porch. The others quickly stopped talking, afraid that he might have already overheard something. Bill, oblivious to the tension in the group, held up the bottle, "Anybody want a drink?"

Will smiled widely, "Where have you been all my life?" He started up the steps to join their manager, accepting the bottle and reading the label, cooing happily as he did.

Derek wasn't far behind, though he was far more polite about his enthusiasm as he made his way up with his bass slung over his shoulder.

"I was so sorry to hear about your house, William. *And* your grandfather, Derek," Bill shook his head sympathetically.

"Uh huh," Will mumbled, still staring at the bottle, "Where are your glasses?"

"Oh, yes. You'll find them with the rest of the liquor on the shelf over the kitchen sink."

"Oooh! The *rest* of the liquor? You hear that, David?"

David rolled his eyes, but couldn't control the curl at the corner of his lip as he set down his guitar and followed him into the kitchen. For a moment the other three stood in the doorway, both Brian and Bekka frowning at their band-mates, before Derek licked his lips and shrugged.

"Maybe I'll go see what he's got," he said before heading towards the kitchen as well.

"Oh, c'mon! Not you too," Brian groaned.

Bekka chuckled and shook her head, giving Brian's arm a squeeze. "Come on. I want to see the studio."

As Derek stepped into the kitchen he was surprised to find how large it was. The others were shuffling through the various bottles on the top shelf at the far end, on the other side of a large island-like countertop that housed the stove and a marble cutting board. A decorative chrome faucet glistened to his right and he paused to admire the intricate design in the metal before joining the others to raid Bill's liquor cabinet.

As they started in, Brian's voice came from the other room, "When you guys are done getting plastered, join us in the attic!"

Will smirked and cupped his hands around his mouth as he called back, "You got it, boss!"

A moment passed as they continued, and then Bekka's voice called out, "And don't forget to bring up your instruments!"

Will thought about this for a moment before realizing that he would have to lug his new equipment up three flights of stairs and started a cursing fit.

David and Derek laughed.

Though he was strong enough to easily carry the entire drum kit up the stairs in one trip, Will was forced to take it up piece-by-piece to maintain appearances with their manager.

The studio, as it turned out, was much nicer than anyone would've guessed. While not incredibly spacious, what room was available had been well utilized. The recording area itself—separated from the rest of the studio behind a wall of sound-proofed glass—was large enough to fit two or three people. The rest of the space had been set up with a sound-mixing station along with the recording equipment, which was all modern and top of the line. Both Brian and Bekka were still examining the equipment with enthusiasm as their drummer kept up his illusion of humanity by grunting and groaning as he got the last of the kit up the stairs.

"Jesus-fucking-Christ, Bill! What were you thinking?" He shook his head and bent over, faking another heavy breath, "The fucking attic! Really?"

Bill smirked and shrugged at him, giving an innocent chuckle, "What can I say? The acoustics up here are excellent!" He paused, giving Will a moment to catch his breath before motioning with his chin towards the recording booth, "You can set up in there. We should probably get your samples done first."

Will nodded at this, seeming to recover faster than he should have as he started moving his drums once again. The others cringed slightly as Bill's eyebrow raised in curiosity only to settle a moment later. David shook his head and gave the drummer a smack to his lower back as he passed. Will didn't have to ask what it was for and let out another pained grunt and cursed under his breath.

When everything was ready and Will was seated behind his setup Bill let himself fall into an office chair in front of the council, slipped on a set of headphones, and began to toggle the knobs as the others watched.

"Alright," Bill spoke into a nearby microphone and Will looked up as his voice echoed in the recording studio, "Let's just go through some basic sound tests to—"

Will laid down a heavy drum beat at that moment that had their manager jumping in his seat. Seeing his reaction, the drummer let out a silenced cackle from the other side of the sound-proofed glass and started talking inaudibly to his band-mates.

"Dumb shit doesn't know we can't hear him," Brian scoffed.

Bill groaned, adjusting his headset, and shook his head, "I can hear him just fine."

Will let out another silent bout of laughter.

"Alright, to Hell with the sound tests," Bill's voice was stern as he spoke into the microphone. He released the button on the council that connected him to the recording booth and looked over his shoulder towards Bekka, "What song do you want to start with?"

Bekka smiled thoughtfully and rubbed her chin for effect, "Um... how 'bout 'Spiders'?" She looked towards the others for their opinions and smiled when they all nodded in agreement.

"Okay, Will," Bill was back on the intercom, "we're going to start with 'Spiders'. Ready on my mark," With that he held up three fingers, adjusted some controls, and began a visual countdown.

It was the strangest thing.

Or, at least, that's what they kept telling Bill.

For the tenth time their manager replayed Bekka's recordings, and for the tenth time they found it scratchy and accompanied by several underlying whines. As everyone stood there, looking nervously at one another, the digital recorder ran through the track once again with the same results.

"That *is* so bizarre," Will offered, shaking his head.

Bill groaned, resting his chin in his hand, "Doesn't make any sense! I built these walls to be soundproof, but I swear to God I can hear other voices in the track!"

"Voices?" Will spoke before thinking, "What are they saying?"

"I can't tell," Bill kept his eyes glued to the computer monitor as he started the track over for the eleventh time, "But it sounds like somebody's crying."

Bekka frowned, "Can we still use it?"

Bill shook his head, finally turning in his chair to face them, "I'm afraid there's too much static. We're going to have to record it again."

Brian frowned and looked back at the others with a concerned scowl.

David finally cleared his throat, glancing at the clock on the wall as though they had suddenly remembered a prior engagement, "Actually, we have to be getting back soon."

Bill frowned and narrowed his eyes skeptically, "But we haven't even finished recording the *one* song!"

"And we're not going to until you get these walls fixed!" Will cut in, jabbing his finger in the direction of the recording studio, "How in the hell do you expect us to work under these circumstances?"

Bill stared at the drummer but finally nodded, "Alright. Leave your equipment here for the night and I'll have somebody come and take a look at it. And tomorrow I expect you guys to come back here and actually get some work done!"

Brian nodded, placing a hand on Bekka's shoulder and starting to lead her towards the stairs, "You got it, Bill."

Bekka barely had a chance to say goodbye as she was led away from the studio, the others close behind. They were back in the van and heading down the stretch of driveway towards the road before Bill had made it to the front door to see them off.

"What the hell is going on?" Will demanded, "Now your little demonic friends are going to fuck up our ability to record?"

Bekka looked down sadly, her cheeks turning bright red.

Brian scowled, "Don't yell at her, asshole! You think she *wants* all this to happen?"

Will started to open his mouth again but a deep growl echoed through the vehicle from the passenger seat where David sat; his eyes narrowed and shimmering with animalistic fury.

The vampire shook his head and brought his eyes back to the road.

Brian sighed and looked over towards Derek, "What does all this mean?" His voice was drenched in desperation, "Are these things trying to tell us something?"

Derek frowned, "It's certainly possible."

Bekka whimpered, her body shivering, "But *what*?"

Nobody had an answer.

WINGS

You stripped my wings,
And left me falling,
With your laughter in the distance.

You cut the strings,
And I've been calling
For your blood ever since.

Futile flaps and thunder claps.
The ground comes at me quick.
My life with you goes flashing by,
And it makes me so fucking sick!

You horrid fuck!
I'll find you!
If I have to climb the sky!
I'll get to you amongst the clouds
And there I'll make you die!

Futile flaps and thunder claps.
Down into the earth.
I'll keep falling to the core!
My return: a Hellish birth!

Here I fall!

(The descent of the decent)
So shall I fly...
Again!
(The rise of the wrath)

WHERE THE UNBORNS GO

(I walk this barren desert.
Broken glass beneath my feet.
I'm afraid.
So very, very afraid.)

I'm crossing over thresholds
I'm not meant to overcome.
And I can't help but be terrified,
Of where I'll be when I am done.

And the voices keep on calling...

(They ask...)

"Where is it that you came from?
Why did you come to this place?
Your body's not misshapen,
And you still have all your face!

Is it for someone else you've come here?
Or do you simply wish to see,
The sad and the decrepit,
Trapped in eternal misery?"

In the land where the unborns go.

Be they lost or trapped in sin.
Their cries entrap me in their woe,
As they're torn limb from limb.

(They cry…)

"Why do you taunt us, newcomer?
Why show us all your skin?
This is not a place for you!
This broken land we're in!"

In the land where the unborn go.
Where none would dare to tread.
A place of soulless torment,
And never-ending dread.

PART THREE:
MELODIES & MAYHEM

WEEDS

Tangled in my own regret.
I can't see through the vines.
I fight and tear and yet
I'm far too entwined.

Tearing to see sunlight,
Though I'm already underground.
They strangle as they hold me tight,
And I cannot hear a sound.

Life's a fucking weed
That refuses to be torn!
Flourishing from need
And choking all who're born!

Trapping every creature!
Consuming every breath!
They drain everything that is pure
Leaving only death!

Life's a fucking weed
In the garden of what's pure.
Blindness is our one true creed.
And death's the only cure!

PARASITES

How do we justify,
Our wasted lives?
How do we explain,
A purposeless existence?

How do we motivate,
Our broken machines,
When all natural forces,
Demand that we cease?

The revolution of our race—
The evolution of a farce—
Is that confusion on your face?
Or a target on your ass?

(We...
... Are...
... Parasites!)

Where is there to go,
When everywhere is the same?
Who are we to punish,
When everyone's to blame?

The evolution of our kind—

The revolution of a beast—
The marching of the blind,
Stomping on the deceased.

We've all fucked up the definition of life;
We've butchered the purpose of being!
We've created a hellish path,
Completely free of seeing!

(We...
... Are...
... Parasites!)

TWENTY-SEVEN

It was late.

Nobody slept.

Instead, everyone had packed themselves onto the couch to stare at the TV. Though all eyes were focused on the flashing lights and moving pictures, none were really absorbing any of the program; their minds far away from the promise of sleeker abs or a five-second guacamole-maker.

Bekka was especially unsettled.

What had been on those recordings?

Were the entities inside her trying to say something… or possibly warn her of something?

As the time passed, she became more and more aware of the impatient, raspy breathing that was issuing from David.

"Is everything okay?" She asked, patting his knee softly.

He nodded, but after several more minutes he let out a heavy sigh and got up to stretch, "I need to go for a run."

Bekka heard Brian sigh and as she looked over her shoulder at him she noticed his eyes rolling.

Bekka frowned and looked back to David, "Where do you run?"

David shrugged, "In the woods… past the park."

Bekka thought about this for a moment. What was this strange urge she had to…

"Mind if I join you?"

Both David and Brian looked over to her, their eyes burning into her and making her blush.

Had she really just asked that aloud?

"You… want to go running?" David asked, skeptic.

Still blushing, Bekka nodded.

"Since when do you run?" Brian asked.

Bekka shrugged, giving him a reassuring smile, "I don't know. I just thought it would help me to relax."

Brian stared at her and then looked up at David analytically before nodding slowly, "You'd better make sure she stays safe."

David nodded, "You have my word."

Bekka smiled and watched as David went through his

suitcase, pulling a tattered, bleached wife-beater as well as a pair of torn sweatpants. Taking the hint, she hurried to her room and raided the dresser for a sports bra, a light-blue tank top, and a pair of black shorts that she'd only used at the gym several times before never going again.

When she was done getting changed, she left her bedroom, finding Brian waiting in the hall for her.

"Is everything okay?" He asked, taking her hands into his own.

She smiled and nodded, "Yea, just feeling a little anxious."

Brian stared, his eyes piercing into hers, "Be careful out there."

She nodded. "I will."

With nothing left to say, Brian moved his face to hers and kissed her. Though it was not their first kiss—not by far—there was something extra in it that made it feel new to her. Bekka couldn't tell if it was fear or admiration or something else, and at that moment she didn't want to look any further into it than she had to.

It was what it was.

Brian cared deeply for her, and she knew that he always would.

Finally they separated from one another, the lingering warmth seeping into her moistened lips and making her pause to enjoy the effects. His eyes were already on hers when they opened and she smiled at their gaze and blushed.

"I won't be too long," she promised him.

He nodded and reluctantly let her hands go.

David was waiting by the elevator outside the door to her apartment. He didn't ask any questions or seem impatient when she finally stepped out. Instead, he smiled warmly.

"You going to be warm enough?" He asked her when he caught sight of her outfit.

She smirked at him and made note of his own getup, "Are you?" She blushed and let out a soft chuckle.

The park wasn't a long walk from her apartment. In fact, tenants on the other side of the building had the pleasure of having a view of it and the surrounding forest. Despite this, Bekka was embarrassed that she had never visited there.

The late-night city was, for the most part, empty and allowed for a quiet and peaceful walk. They kept the talking to a minimum, both having their own thoughts to tangle with and understanding this of the other. Slowly, as the not-so-distant park grew more and more near, the small-talk began to grow as well.

"So do you go running often?" She asked, looking up at him.

David shrugged, "Whenever I have the chance."

"What made you start?"

"Not sure," David shrugged, "I've done it for as long as I can remember."

Bekka frowned. Though she'd known David for a long time, she had not known this about him, "Why?"

"It just feels right for me. The only times I ever feel right are when I'm playing guitar and when I'm running."

Bekka nodded slowly, biting her lip, "So what's it like?"

"What? Running?"

Bekka blushed, "No. Being... what you are."

"Oh," David looked down at that and chuckled, "I guess I don't know how to explain it."

Bekka smirked and looked up at him, "Oh come on! At least try!"

David shrugged, "It's like... having two people inside you—one that's always in control and rational, and another that's just raw emotion."

Bekka smirked, "Like split personalities?"

David shook his head, "No. It's always me in control. It's more like..." He thought, "it's more like being bipolar, I suppose. With the animal in me being my manic side."

"Does that mean you're depressed in your human form?" Bekka looked over at him.

"Sometimes," David admitted.

Bekka looked down sadly, "Why?"

"Because it's only half of who I really am, and I know that very few will accept the other half."

"But we accept you!" Bekka pointed out, "All of you!"

David nodded, smiling, but Bekka could tell it was forced.

"What aren't you telling me?" She finally pressed.

"It's just… very lonely," he confessed. Bekka frowned at this and was about to say something but was interrupted when he smiled suddenly, "We're here."

She looked up, startled at how fast they'd seemed to make the trip to the edge of the forest, and nodded. Though she wanted to talk to her friend more about his situation, he had already begun to stretch and prepare. Unsure of the process, she watched for a moment and mimicked his movements as best she could, finding herself more flexible than she had remembered. As she flexed her knees, something suddenly occurred to her.

"Do you think I'll hold you back?"

David looked up at the question and frowned. For a moment he was silent, and then he shrugged, "Maybe I'll just run in this form tonight."

Bekka frowned and shook her head, "But…"

"Don't worry about it," David smiled warmly, "I'm just happy to have the company."

Bekka smiled back and soon after David finished his stretches and stepped into the woods with her close behind. As they moved in deeper, Bekka was surprised to find that the darkness—which had grown with the density of the surrounding coverage—was becoming less and less foreboding. Instead, her vision seemed to shift until she could make out almost every detail around her.

"David…" She called out.

He stopped and turned to face her, "What?"

"I can see."

He smirked, "I would hope so."

"No!" Bekka blushed, shaking her head excitedly, "I can *see*! Like, *everything*!"

David studied her and his own eyes widened, "Bekka! Your eyes!"

She bit her lip then, nervous, "What? What is it?"

"They're... they're glowing!"

"What? Really?"

David nodded.

Bekka frowned and raised her hand in front of her face, surprised to see that every curve and contour was crystal clear.

"The entities! They're helping me see," she gasped.

David nodded and studied her a moment longer, "It doesn't hurt, does it?"

"Not at all," she shook her head.

He smirked, "Then let's see what else they can help you do."

Before she could question what her friend meant, he was off like a bullet, disappearing deeper into the forest.

"Hey! Wait!" She called after him.

He didn't stop.

Bekka frowned, afraid that she'd lose him and be left alone in the wilderness. Before the fear could overwhelm her, however, she was overcome with the drive to follow; to catch up to him. Though she wasn't sure how she intended to do this, she began to run after him.

Soon she was surprised to see David in the distance, becoming clearer as she closed in on him. How was this possible? She'd chased down a werewolf in its own element! And he'd even had a head-start!

Her foot came down on a twig and the sound caught David's attention and he turned his head, his eyes widening when he saw her. Startled, he didn't notice a tree root jutting from the dirt and stumbled over it, giving Bekka the chance she needed to catch up and get side-by-side with him. He smiled at her and shook his head as they raced through the trees together.

"Your friends seem to be helping you with more than just your sight," he pointed out.

"I know, right?" Bekka exclaimed, the sensation of it all drawing out an intense euphoria. It continued to push her forward, demanded more and more speed from her, but she felt that her body had already reached its limit, "Can you run any faster?" She called out as she hurdled over a hedge.

David landed not far behind her and stumbled as he slowed to a stop, forcing Bekka to do the same.

"Run... faster...?" He spoke between heavy breaths.

Bekka nodded, blushing as she realized that her own breathing wasn't at all labored, "Is that bad?"

David took a deep breath and shrugged. "I could, but I'd have to transform," he smirked and shook his head, "And then you *definitely* wouldn't be able to keep up."

Bekka's eyes lit up at that and her lips curled into a ferocious grin, "Try me."

David chewed his lip for a moment, studying her. When he finally came to the conclusion that she wasn't joking, he moved to pull off the wife beater.

"I think the elastic in the waistband should hold," he told her, referring to his tattered sweatpants, "But I'm not making any promises."

The warmth in Bekka's cheeks flared up and she nodded and turned her back to him. For a moment there was silence, the sounds of the sleeping woods carried on a light breeze, but these were soon interrupted by a pained grunt. Bekka started to turn to see if her friend was alright and quickly regretted it as she saw that one of his legs had warped and elongated to be nearly a foot longer than the other. Deciding she didn't want to see the rest of the transformation, she turned back, flinching at the series of grizzly sounds that picked up behind her. Through it all she was forced to listen to the stifled cries of agony that came along with the process.

As the sounds slowed and stopped, the process finished with a series of wet noises that made Bekka start to heave. Finally, after a moment of silence, a heavy, clawed hand touched down on her shoulder and beckoned her to turn. The image was like something out of a horror movie, but Bekka knew better than to be afraid as she turned to face her friend in his beast form.

While intimidating, he was strangely beautiful. His eyes shifted over her, once again studying her expression. Though most of the humanity was gone from his face, she could see that he was nervous.

Smiling reassuringly, she nodded to him, "Ready to run?"

David cocked his head and let out a barking cackle as he shook his head.

Bekka smirked, "What? Don't think I can do it?"

A massive shoulder shrugged and he shook his head again.

"Well you're not the only one with a trick up your sleeve, I'll have you know!" She teased.

Even in his new body, she recognized the confusion in his eyes.

Bekka couldn't blame him. Even she wasn't sure what the entities inside her had planned, but something deep inside pushed her—urged her—to run faster; to push her body harder than she already had. So, with nothing to lose and no reason left to doubt herself, she gave herself up to the urge.

She knew it should have hurt like hell when both of her arms suddenly shifted and separated from her shoulders, but she felt nothing more than a soft tug. Her eyes went wide, but at that moment her knees gave way and bent backwards; her ankles rotating in their sockets until they faced in the opposite direction. Thrown off balance, she toppled backwards, but before she could hit the ground her warped arms swung around and caught her so that she was supported on all fours and staring up at the night sky. David let out a startled whimper and started to advance, reaching out to help her. Before he could get any closer Bekka's neck elongated and swiveled around, changing her perspective from the sky to the forest floor. Though she still felt no pain she cried out, terrified as her body bent and twisted like a hellish pretzel. When it was all over she turned around—stepping on all fours like an animal—to face her stunned friend.

"I…" She began, shaking her warped head. The drive to run remained, and though she was startled by the effects she somehow knew there was a purpose to the transformation. Taking in a deep breath, she finally nodded to herself and smiled up at David. "I'm alright," she assured him before smirking cockily, "Let's do this!"

Before the werewolf had a chance to react, she was off like a wildcat. Her new speed caught her off guard and she cried out as she saw a tree approaching like a missile and banked to the left, missing it by several inches. Behind her, David barked excitedly and the sound of his running started up. Not long after, he caught up, though Bekka could see that he was putting more effort into it than he was used to and she tried to force her body to slow down for him.

It was like pulling the needle away from a heroin addict.

Her body ached for more, and as she sprinted on all fours she felt, for the first time in a long time, complete relaxation. Unable to keep up on only two feet, David dropped forward and began to use his arms, as well and Bekka cackled as they continued deeper into the woods.

After nearly half-an-hour they stopped. Their running had brought them alongside a stream that meandered through the woods like a liquid serpent; its water burbling around the rocks that jutted out from its depths. David approached this and began to drink, stabbing his massive hands into the water and bringing it to his mouth before repeating the process. Bekka watched, suddenly aware of the burning of her own thirst, and finally approached the water and dipped her lips to the surface to drink. When they had both quenched their thirsts they moved away.

With her body's need for speed satisfied it began to revert back to her human shape. Her head swiveled back to its rightful place as he arms shifted and reattached to her shoulders. All of this left her lying on her back as her knees and ankles righted themselves, her body frozen as the process was reversed.

David watched this, sneering in his own way until she was finally herself again and then stepped back and reversed his own transformation. Bekka, too dazed and exhausted, simply stared up into the night and let the sounds of her friend's transformation pass over her. When he was human once again he let out a sigh and rolled his shoulders before sitting down next to her and casting his own gaze towards the sky.

"Well *that* was weird."

"Yea. It was," she agreed, yawning.

David turned his head to face her, "You're not hurt, are you?"

Bekka shook her head.

He nodded and was silent for a moment before he

finally smirked, "At least my pants stayed in one piece."

Bekka laughed, "Yea, at least there's that."

Another silent moment followed and Bekka began to hum softly to herself. With no complaints from David her humming quickly turned to gentle singing, which grew in volume. Though she was sure that at any moment he would ask her to stop, he instead stayed quiet and listened until the song was over.

At that moment he let out a sigh, "I wish I had that kind of talent."

Bekka looked up, "What are you talking about? You're a brilliant guitarist!"

"I suppose," he shrugged, "But to use your voice as an instrument; to have the artistic and poetic insight to create the lyrics..." He shook his head, "I envy you."

Bekka smirked and shook her head. "What I do is nothing without the rest of your guys to back it up," she shrugged, "It's like the human body, all the parts need the other parts to work as a whole."

"The human body?" David looked at her quizzically.

"Well," Bekka thought for a moment, "Take the drums, for example. They're like the heart of the body; supplying a rhythm and a beat for the rest of the body to go by."

David nodded slowly, "Go on."

Bekka blushed, "Okay, well, the bass... well the bass works closely with the drums and carries that beat out to the rest of the band to coordinate on. So it's kind of like the pulse."

"And the guitars?" David smirked.

Bekka nodded, smiling, "The guitars wrap around all of it, creating the shape and movement. So I guess they're like the bones, muscles, and skin."

He nodded, smiling at the thought, "So if Will's the heart, Derek's the pulse, and Brian and I make up the skeleton, muscles, and skin, what does that make you?"

Bekka beamed, "I'm the spirit."

David chuckled, "Aren't we the modest one?"

They both laughed.

TWENTY-EIGHT

The trip back into the city took a while.

Bekka was afraid to try her pretzel routine again, leaving David to pick up the slack. He didn't seem to mind, however, and as he carried her in his monstrous arms through the woods she felt herself beginning to doze.

When she woke up again, she found herself in her own bed next to a snoring Brian. She frowned, looking around the room before finally lying back again.

Had somebody been talking to her?

She shook her head, passing it off as a crazy dream, and shifted closer to Brian and closed her eyes. Despite his snores—or perhaps because of how they reminded her that she wasn't alone—she soon began to drift off again.

And then it was there again!

Whispers!

Bekka wasn't sure if she'd fallen asleep yet, but nonetheless forced her eyelids to stay closed in fear that the voices might disappear again if she opened them. Instead she lay and listened. Though they weren't in English, she could somehow understand them; understand their plea to keep them safe as well as their promises to make her stronger and better equipped to protect them.

As they spoke to her, she was suddenly shown another realm. In this place—an infinite dimension occupied by only one being—the spiritual remains of all those who died passed over. There they became a part of the one; joining to it and adding to it. To be a part of this being was the fate of all living things; it was inevitable. But, inside of it, it was hectic, chaotic, and, for those that now occupied her body, terrifying.

Fearing the assimilation, they had somehow escaped that realm and crossed back over.

And there they had found Bekka.

Knowing that the being on the other side wouldn't happily let a part of itself go, it sent others out to retrieve them. Those energies—those entities—remained loyal to the greater being, and would do whatever it took to appease it.

Bekka's eyelids fluttered.

She understood.

All of it.

There was one last, unified whisper in the back of her mind, begging for help, and finally her eyes shot open and she sat up in bed with such force that Brian was woken up.

"Hey," he laid a hand on her shoulder, giving it a gentle squeeze, "Everything alright?"

"I see now," Bekka whispered, staring off into the darkness, "They showed me."

"They? They who? And what did they show you?"

She turned her head to face him and smiled, "The things inside me. They showed me everything."

Brian frowned, "So are they going to leave?"

Bekka shook her head, "No. They can't."

"Can't"—Brian growled—"or won't?"

Bekka bit her lip softly, "Both."

Brian scowled and looked away, "Don't they understand that they're putting you in danger; that they're the cause of everything bad that's been going on?"

Bekka nodded, "That's why they're giving me these powers."

Brian looked up, confused, "Powers?"

Bekka nodded again and explained what had happened in the woods, how her body had painlessly twisted and bent in impossible ways to allow her to simply run faster. When she was done, Brian shook his head.

"So—what?—you're a comic-book character now?"

She smirked and shrugged, "Something like that, I guess."

Sleep came easier for Bekka now that she better understood everything. What she'd been shown had confirmed a great deal of the group's suspicions, and when she told the others the next morning they, too, seemed to be relieved to actually *know* something.

"So does this change anything?" David asked, turning to Derek.

Derek frowned, "What do you mean?"

David began to speak but Will cut him off with, "He means: can you fix her now?"

David scowled at the interruption but didn't disagree with him.

Derek frowned and shrugged, playing with his stretched earlobes for a moment, "Then 'no'. It doesn't really change anything."

"Well what the fuck?" Will threw his hands up in the air, "What's the point of knowing anything if it still lands us in the middle of fucking nowhere as to how to fix it?"

Brian glared at Will and stood up and stepped beside Bekka. "It tells us that these things aren't trying to hurt her," he defended. His eyes shifted to Derek and he smiled softly, "Be that as it may, I'm confident that you'll find a way to fix it."

Derek shook his head, "I'm not sure you're getting it! This isn't something that magic can make go away! Magic is about energy and balance, and this has upset the balance!"

"But there's got to be some solution!" David growled; his hands balled up into fists.

"Yea!" Will cut in, "There's always a way! I mean, your grandfather showed you that scale thing before!" He stopped himself from going any further.

Derek's eyes drifted down and he shook his head. "I just don't know," he confessed, shaking his head. "It doesn't matter! We can't make the entities leave without killing Bekka and I don't see how we can get enough energy to make the switch and trick them!"

Bekka pursed her lips and crouched down in front of him, setting a hand on his knee, "Please. Just try."

The softness in her voice seemed to relax Derek and he sighed, nodding. "I'll see what I can do," he told her in a near-whisper.

Bekka smiled at him. "Thank you," standing up, she jumped as the phone rang and startled her. Recovering, she hurried to the counter and answered it, "Hello?"

"Rebecca, it's Bill. I've got some great news!"

TWENTY-NINE

Bill was already waiting at the concert hall with the band's instruments when they got there. While Bekka was curious as to how he'd gotten all the gear there from his place, she was sure that he had his ways and kept her questions to herself.

As it turned out, the opening act for a Hellish Torment concert had been forced to cancel, leaving an opening that Bill had been more than happy to fill. Though the others had been skeptical about going out on such short notice, Bekka had been quick to point out that it would be good practice for the Battle of the Bands. And while Brian and David insisted that the battle was not at the top of their lists of priorities, even they couldn't hold themselves back in the end.

"Hey! Who's been man-handling my shit?" Brian demanded as he slipped his guitar over his shoulder.

Derek frowned as he inspected his bass, "Obviously not somebody who can tune worth a damn!"

David scowled, plucking a few strings and finding them out of tune as well.

"Take it up with our do-no-wrong manager," Will scoffed as he sat behind his drum set.

"Is something wrong?" Bill walked out onto the stage, running his hand along the closed curtain that hid them from the audience—still in the process of being seated—on the other side.

Brian nodded and held up his guitar, "Yea! You mind telling me who the fuck's been dicking with our instruments?"

Bill frowned, "I paid a couple of kids to help me bring them downstairs and set them up. Why? Is something broken?"

Brian scoffed, "Yea! My trust in you!"

"Whoa!" Will stood up and glared at Bill, "You're telling me you paid a couple of little shits to load up our gear? Aren't there professionals who can do that?"

Bill blushed, "I figured I'd save a couple of bucks on a simple job."

"Well next time don't try to 'save a couple of bucks' with our gear!" Brian barked.

Bill frowned and nodded. "Y-yea. No problem," he turned and started off the stage, "Break a leg out there!"

"Uh-huh. You too, Bill," Brian muttered as their manager scampered off.

Bekka gave him a face but couldn't hide her growing smirk as he caught her eye. Realizing the slip-up, she looked away, double-checking some of the equipment's connections and levels before nodding to the stage crew.

"Looks like everything's all set," she called to them.

One of the men backstage gave a nod back and signaled to the others that they would be ready soon.

As the others finished re-tuning their instruments Bekka got into position, getting ready for the curtain to rise and beginning to bounce on her toes; pumping herself up.

"Alright boys," she called out, "we all know the set, right?"

Four thumbs went up in her direction.

She smiled and gave a single nod in their direction before turning to face the curtain; the audience waiting on the other side beginning to chant.

"Mikes go live in ten... nine... eight..." Bill called out to them from backstage.

Bekka continued the count-down in her head. As she reached the five-second mark, the curtain started to rise and there was the thumbs up from the crew as the speakers squealed to life in the auditorium.

"Ten seconds my ass," Bekka grumbled as she found the power switch on her microphone and ran her thumb across it and flipped it on. The speakers crackled to life as she raised the microphone to her lips.

"ARE YOU ALL FUCKING READY TO BLOW THE ROOF OFF THIS BITCH?" She cried out. The resulting roar grew quickly in volume; the impact of their stomping feet shaking the stage. Bekka smiled at the response, "THEN LET'S DO THIS SHIT!"

Brian came in heavy at that moment on his guitar, the rapid, high-pitched squeal ranging back and forth as his fingers flew along the frets. As the intro's tempo grew more rapid, Bekka heard Derek's subtle bass line as it worked its way in. After another few seconds Will came in, slow at first, but racing along to match the others' pace. When their combined efforts seemed unable to get any heavier, David jumped into the mix.

As the sound go nice and heavy, Bekka began to rock back-and-forth onstage. In front of her, hundreds of metal-lovers began to jump and gyrate to their music. She matched their movements for a moment, enjoying the connection that was being made, before stepping over to the keyboard that had been set up behind her. Sliding her microphone into an attached cradle, she assumed her position and got ready. Right on cue, all the others stopped playing, throwing the auditorium into an abrupt silence. Before the crowd could react, however, Bekka's fingers began to work the keys, issuing a rhythm that was much softer and slower than what had been built up. The audience's violent thrash-dance calmed at that moment and they began to sway in response.

Bekka smiled to herself.

This is what she lived for.

Their time on stage ended too soon in Bekka's opinion.

The show was going perfectly—every member in top form—and as the last song of their set drew to a close she took in a heavy breath before howling excitedly and holding the note until she was red in the face and felt like she might actually pass out.

A hard cymbal crash sounded from Will and the others slapped their hands over their instruments' strings to silence them.

Bekka thrust one hand into the air, her pointer and pinky fingers extended as she gasped for air and smiled, "THANK YOU ALL FOR COMING OUT TONIGHT!" She called out to the screaming crowd, "ARE YOU ALL READY FOR SOME HELLISH TORMENT?"

Despite the irony of the statement, the crowd's cries doubled in volume. The sound faded as the curtain dropped and the crew rushed out to help prepare for the main attraction. David, Brian, and Derek quickly unplugged their instruments and carried them offstage as Bekka unlocked the legs to the keyboard and folded them up. While it wasn't her instrument, she was well aware that Hellish Torment had no need for it on the stage and figured she'd help in the process of preparing for them.

Will worked with two members of the crew to break down his drum kit while others began to haul in the pieces of a much more elaborate-looking one. Scowling at the expensive components, Will shook his head.

"Showoffs," he muttered.

Bekka giggled as she stepped offstage.

The members of Hellish Torment passed by them quietly, each nodding and smiling as they did. There was very little to be said and even less time to say it in, but this didn't stop the lead singer, Ian Drull, from stopping and giving Bekka a massive grin.

"Quite the show," he offered, "I was very impressed."

Bekka blushed and smiled back. "Th-thank you," she stammered, honored by the compliment.

Ian looked as though he wanted to say more, but with time pressing down on them to get the curtain back up he simply gave another complimentary nod and continued past.

Brian, watching the exchange a short distance away, set down his gear and hurried to Bekka's side when the exchange was over.

"Can you believe that?" He whispered to her, "Ian-fucking-Drull!" He shook his head, beaming, "What an honor!"

Bekka blushed and nodded, "I know! He actually thinks we were good!"

"*Good*?" Will scoffed, "We were fucking *spectacular*!

I'd like to see those hacks try to win the crowd over after the show we just put on!"

Derek smirked but shook his head, "I don't think they'll have a problem. They are, after all, who the audience paid to see."

David nodded, putting his guitar in his case, "True. But you gotta admit, we weren't bad tonight."

"Was there ever any doubt?" Will laughed.

The others couldn't think of any reason to disagree.

"I'm just glad that we got through it without any incident," David said as he slung his guitar over his shoulder.

Brian nodded, "Tell me about it! I was sweating bullets the whole time."

Derek nodded, "We got lucky," he explained. Though their bassist *had* had the opportunity to put a small barrier up, he'd made it clear that it wouldn't be hard to break through, "I wouldn't suggest taking another risk like this, though."

Bekka nodded.

Will shook his head, "What's all this talk about? We're fine! So we took a small risk? Isn't that what life's about?"

Brian shook his head, "Not life-threatening risks."

Will scoffed at him, "Oh come off it! We needed this and you all know it!"

"Be that as it may," Derek's voice was calm and collected, "we shouldn't assume that future endeavors will be so uneventful."

Will smirked, "Listen to our boy, captain-dictionary!" He nodded, holding his hands up in defeat, "I'll admit it, we were lucky. But can we *please* not ruin this evening with talk of what could have happened?"

Everyone stared at him for a moment.

"I think that sounds fair," Derek finally nodded.

Will smiled, "Great! Now we celebrate!"

THIRTY

Celebrating, as it turned out, involved going to the bar and getting wasted.

Bekka took Brian to a corner booth at the far end of the bar where they sat and smiled at one another over glasses of soda water and cranberry juice while the others sat up front over pitchers of beer and shots of tequila. The drinks were on the house, courtesy of the sympathetic bartender who had been close friends of Derek's grandfather, and as the night drew on the three—with the exception of Will—became more and more inebriated. Despite being immune to the alcohol's effects, the vampire seemed to have no problem acting the part.

"Best. Show. Ever!" He barked out, slurring his speech before letting out a heavy belch and washing it back down with a fresh shot.

Brian looked over his shoulder at his band-mates and sighed, shaking his head in disgust, "Still don't understand why anybody would want to do that to themselves."

Bekka took his hand and smiled. "Don't worry about them," she whispered, "Will's more than capable of keeping them in line."

"So who's going to keep him in line?" He glanced over his shoulder again.

Leaning over the booth, Bekka cupped her hand on his cheek and forced his gaze away from the others and back to her, "Please," her eyes were filled with desperation, "try to be happy."

Brian sighed, letting his eyes lock onto hers and take in their depths before nodding and smiling. "I'll try. For you, I'll try," he took a sip of his juice and sighed again, this time trying to relax, before looking back up at her, "So what's on your mind?"

"Actually," Bekka thought for a moment and looked down, "I've been thinking about the contest."

"You mean the Battle of the Bands?"

She nodded.

Brian tilted his head, "What about it?"

Bekka shrugged, "Just wondering if it's a good idea or not; if we'll even win. That sort of thing."

Brian frowned, "You want to cancel?"

She didn't answer at first, but finally, eyes focused on her soda, she shook her head, "No, I don't think that'd be fair to the others. Besides, it *is* a great opportunity if we do win."

"That's a pretty big 'if', y'know," Brian pointed out.

Clucking her tongue, Bekka shrugged again, "I don't know. We *were* pretty good tonight."

Brian nodded, "True enough. But do you think it'd be enough? I mean, there's going to be a lot of bands in this competition who want it just as bad as we do."

"But that's not the only part of it," Bekka explained.

"What do you mean?"

"I mean that with everything that's been going on, we all need to feel that we're still a band; that we're not as doomed as everyone seems to think we are."

"Nobody said we were doomed," Brian argued, "We just need to be careful until we find a solution."

Bekka frowned and looked down, "There's already a solution."

Brian looked up questioningly.

Bekka nodded, "They came here to escape that other place," she pointed out. "They chose me and gave me these powers so that I could help keep them from having to go back. If there was no other way…"

Brian nodded, his eyes going wide, "Then they wouldn't have bothered coming in the first place!"

Bekka nodded.

"So they must know how to fix this!" Brian's sour face

began to melt into a wide smile, "They must know how to stop the attacks without killing you!"

Another nod, "Otherwise it all would've been pointless!"

"Well they've been 'talking' to you, haven't they? Have they told you the secret or given you any hints?"

She shook her head, "It doesn't work that way. They only seem to be able to express emotions and give me flashes of their world."

Brian frowned, "Well can't they 'flash' you some fucking blueprints or something?"

Bekka pursed her lips as she thought, "Maybe they already have…"

"Bill? Yea, it's Bekka. I was wondering if you still had those recordings from the other day?"

There was a pause on the line.

"You mean from the botched session?" Bill asked.

"Yea! Those! I was hoping to maybe take a closer listen and see if I could… uh, find the problem with them."

"There's no need," Bill explained, "I had some guys come in and look over the booth. They found a few places where the sound could've seeped through and sealed them up."

Bekka sighed, shaking her head, "I'd still like to have

a copy of those recordings."

"But why?"

"Dammit, Bill! I just want a copy of the—"

"Whoa! I'm sorry, but I already deleted them!"

Bekka frowned, "What?"

"Yea. They *were* corrupted, after all," Bill explained, "I didn't see a point in wasting computer memory on something that couldn't be used."

Bekka groaned as her arm dropped from her ear, letting the phone hang at her hip for a moment before slowly bringing it back to her ear, "Is there any way…" She thought to herself as she asked the question, knowing there was no way to get the samples back.

"Would you like to come in and re-record them?" Bill offered.

"Huh?"

"Re-record? I mean, you guys kinda blew me off the other day and now that the booth is all fixed up it shouldn't be a problem to—"

"We'll be right over!" Bekka hung up the phone before their manager could get another word in.

The others looked at her expectantly.

She shook her head, "He deleted them."

Brian's eyes went wide, "What?"

David shook his head, mumbling.

"Why would that idiot—" Will began.

"It doesn't matter," Bekka held up her hands to stop any further comments, "He offered to have me come in and re-record."

Will scowled, "What good does that do us?"

Derek nodded, "I hate to say it, but just because they came up on the track last time is no guarantee that it'll happen again."

Brian glared at them, "What other choices do we have?"

"There are none," David sighed, "We're going to have to re-record and hope for the best."

"Hope for the best?" Will looked around the room in disbelief, "You can't be serious!"

David turned an angry eye towards him, "Wasn't 'hope for the best' your anthem last night?"

Will inhaled sharply and growled, shaking his head, "I'll get my keys."

"You didn't bring your instruments?" Bill narrowed his eyes at the band as they stepped from the van and headed towards his front door.

Will smiled, patting him on the back, "This is our girl's time to shine. We're just here to support her and drink your booze!"

"Didn't you drunks already get enough liquor in your systems last night?" Brian asked as he slammed the van door behind him and jogged up the steps.

"Funny thing about last night," Will rubbed his chin thoughtfully, "can't remember a damn thing."

"Oh please," Brian mumbled, staying close to Bekka.

She laughed and shook her head, turning to Bill. "We don't have much time," she explained to their manager, "We just wanted to test out the booth and get some recordings for the song we started."

Bill sighed, his shoulders sagging, "I was really hoping to have something more substantial than *one* song by the end of the week."

"And you will!" Will lied, pausing on his way to the kitchen, "Tomorrow we'll be here bright and early to start recording."

Rolling his eyes, Bill nodded and motioned for Bekka to head up the stairs towards the studio. Brian wasn't far behind and Derek, surprisingly, started up behind them as well. When they finally got to the attic, they found all the equipment already turned on and ready to begin.

"Seems like a wasted effort now," Bill whined as he sat down behind the console and made a few adjustments. Finally he nodded towards Bekka, "All set."

Smiling warmly at him, Bekka stepped into the recording booth and slid a pair of headphones on before giving Bill the thumbs up. Without another word, he brought up the combined tracks from the others' recordings and played them back. The music began to play in Bekka's ears and she signaled for him to turn up the volume as she began to bob on her heels to the rhythm. Behind their manager, she noticed Derek pulling a flask from his pocket and taking a quick pull from the end; something that Brian scowled at. As her cue approached, she let out a heavy metal howl into the microphone. Holding the note for several seconds, she willed the entities inside her to speak to her the way they had before.

She did not want this visit to be in vain.

"God dammit all," Bill sighed and shook his head as they listened to the track over again. Sure enough, the recording was littered with the sound of voices, "I swear! It's like you're demon-possessed or something!"

Bekka chewed her lip nervously.

Brian let out a laugh, "If only it was that simple, huh?"

"Could be cell phones," Derek offered.

Everyone looked at him.

"Cell phones?" Bill repeated.

Derek nodded, "You've sound-proofed the recording studio, but your equipment might be picking up interference," he shrugged, "I've heard of stuff like that happening before."

Bill narrowed his eyes, "But just on Bekka's tracks?"

Brian shrugged, "It makes more sense than demons."

Sighing, Bill nodded, "I suppose that's true."

Bekka twisted at her hips for a moment, swaying

innocently in an attempt to elicit the desired response, "Bill, do you think I could get a copy of this recording?"

Bill sighed and shrugged as he grabbed a blank disc, "I don't see why not. I'm just gonna end up deleting this one, too. Might as well have something to show for all this wasted time."

The disc whirred in the burner for a moment before sliding back out and Bill grabbed it and popped it into a case, handing it over his shoulder to the first person who would take it.

Brian snatched the case and smiled politely, "Well it *has* been a blast, but we have some errands to run."

Bill shrugged, "Just make sure you're here tomorrow and ready to get some work done."

"Sure will," Brian took Bekka's hand and led her down the stairs; Derek trotting down after them. When they'd reached the first floor, he stuck his head into the kitchen where David and Will were passing a bottle back and forth, "Hey, stooges! We're off!"

THIRTY-ONE

The neighbors had already visited twice, the second time with the threat of calling the police and filing a noise complaint. With no other option, the five were forced to plug a pair of headphones into the stereo and take turns listening to the recorded track over and over again in hopes of deciphering the entities' message.

"I got nothing!" Brian growled as he stepped away from the stereo, handing the headphones over to David as they passed.

Bekka was sitting, hunched over with her head rested on the palms of her hands. She was tired. While the day hadn't been eventful, she'd been hoping for some quick and productive answers from the recording, and after nearly forty-five minutes of playing and replaying the track she was beginning to lose hope.

Brian sat down beside her, noticing her agitation for what it was and an arm around her. "We'll figure it out" he assured her.

Will sighed and shook his head, "Or we could just blast our damn ears to shit and wear the disc down to nothing in this futile attempt at—"

"Just shut up!" David growled before putting on the headphones.

"*Please*," Brian nodded.

Will shrugged, "I'm just saying, if we haven't gotten it by now, we're not going to at all!"

Bekka looked down sadly.

Seeing the effect his words were having, Will's tone quickly changed, "But maybe we don't have to. Maybe we can take it to somebody who speaks their language… or whatever."

Brian looked over, surprised to hear something productive emerge from his mouth, "Like who?"

"Hell if I know!" Will forced a laugh, "Maybe Derek's freaky aunt?"

"You mean the one you knocked out during our last visit?" Derek glared back at him.

Will shrugged, "It was an idea."

Brian thought for a moment, "Maybe we should."

All the eyes flashed in his direction, and though
Bekka knew he hated having that kind of attention on him,
he didn't seem to notice as he continued to think.

"Maybe," he went on, "she'll know how to decode the
message."

Derek frowned and shook his head, "It doesn't work
that way!"

Brian turned and glared at the bassist, "I'm getting
tired of you telling us what's not going to work! How 'bout
you give us something productive to work with for once!"

Bekka laid a hand on his shoulder and applied a light
amount of pressure, "Brian…"

He pulled free from her and shook his head, "No!
This is bullshit! I'm getting tired of hitting nothing but dead-
ends!"

Derek looked down and shook his head. "I'm sorry
that the laws of magic aren't bending to your whim, Brian,"
he grumbled. Finally he looked up, eyes fierce and angry,
"But it *does not* work that way!"

"Then how the fuck does it work?" Brian took a step
towards him.

Derek didn't back away and instead balled his fists,
"The only person now who can understand what they're
saying is Bekka! They chose her! And now they're a part of
her! Whether or not Bekka chooses to understand them, they
are speaking a language that only she can decipher!"

The room went quiet and, slowly, everybody started
to turn towards Bekka.

Under the heat of their stares, she blushed and shook her head, "But I've already tried!"

"Have you?" Derek challenged her.

She frowned and looked away, hugging her arms around her torso. She knew she'd been caught. It wasn't that she hadn't tried—she had!—but she hadn't put her heart into it; hadn't wanted to admit to herself that the entities were and always would be a part of her. That they would always be a part of her until the day she died. She frowned and turned away from the others; it all seemed so futile—both for her and for the beings occupying her.

"I don't want to…" She muttered to nobody in particular.

Brian, standing the closest to her, frowned and stepped around her to face her, "Bekka, we need to know what they're saying. It could be the key to stopping all of this!" He cocked his head at an awkward angle so that he could look into her eyes, "Don't you want that?"

She had started to cry; overwhelmed by the hot sensation in her eyes and the tight lump in her throat that she couldn't swallow away. She tried to hold it for as long as she could, but as she inhaled her body betrayed her wishes and she sobbed and collapsed. Brian caught her and held her against him as the tears began to flow freely down her face.

"I'll try," she finally said between sobs.

Days passed as Bekka listened again and again to the recording. She kept a notebook close by, writing what she could and sketching anything that she "saw". Though she was putting a great deal more effort into understanding the message, she still felt that a part of herself was holding her back; a part of her that Derek seemed to see all-too-easily. Though the bassist didn't say anything to the others—or to her, even—she knew what he was thinking whenever he walked by. The tension didn't help matters any, nor did the ever-growing cabin fever. On the third day, during a lunch break, she finally decided that she'd had enough.

"I need to get out of here!" She said as she slammed down her tuna sandwich, startling the others.

Brian frowned and set his own food down on the plate and shook his head, "You know it's too dangerous, Bekka."

David nodded as he finished chewing a bite of his sandwich, "He's right. Derek's been doing a good job of keeping us protected, but out there—with all those people..."

Bekka glared at them and shook her head as she pushed her chair away from the table, "That's easy for you to say! You can go out whenever you want! I've been stuck in here for days listening to myself over and over and over again; hoping to get some hidden message out of a bunch of whines and static!"

"But Bekka—" Derek started.

"Whines and static!" She slammed her hands down

on the table, rattling it on its uneven legs, "You tell me I should be able to understand them? Then why haven't I yet? Huh?"

He didn't have an answer.

Bekka nodded and pursed her lips, "Exactly!" She turned away, "I'm going out."

Brian was on his feet in a flash, "Then I'm going with you!"

Will laughed, "And what will you do if shit goes down out there?" He shook his head at him, "Like it or not, you're the least equipped to protect her! I mean, even she has powers! What can you do?"

Brian's eyes widened at this before he turned to Bekka, who, biting her lip, nodded.

"I'm sorry, Brian," she said, "but I don't want to see you get hurt."

"To Hell with that!" He growled, taking a step towards her, "I'm not letting you go out there alone!"

She smiled at him but slowly shook her head, "I can take care of myself."

Brian's eyes darted across her face.

"If it makes you feel any better, I can go with her," David offered.

Brian frowned as he looked over at him. At the other side of the table Will shook his head but said nothing.

"Fine," Brian nodded, "But I'm trusting you to—"

"I'm sure wolf-man will go all hot-and-hairy at the single sign of a threat," Will said with a laugh.

Brian glared at him but said nothing as David worked his way around the table to Bekka's side.

Smiling up at him, she nodded her thanks before getting up and starting for her room, "Great! Let me go get changed!"

She didn't need to look behind her to know that Brian was following. As she stepped through her bedroom door, she paused to hold it for him as he stepped through before closing it. He remained silent, keeping his back to her as he looked at the poorly-and-temporarily-mended window. Sighing, she slipped her shirt over her head and tossed it in a nearby hamper.

"I'm sorry," he finally said, turning around as Bekka reached back to unhook her bra, "I wish I was stronger."

She frowned as she casually freed herself from the confines and shook her head, "What do you mean?"

Despite her exposed breasts, Brian kept his eyes firmly locked on her face, "I mean I can't protect you! I'm the *only* one who can't protect you!" He looked down at the floor; ashamed, "What good am I to you?"

Bekka frowned and stepped over to him. "You do so much for me, Brian," she said as she reached her arms up and laid them on his shoulders, cupping her hands behind his neck, "You've always been there for me; always cared. And though I haven't always seen it, I know now that you've always been looking out for me.

"I don't care that you're not a vampire or a werewolf or if you can't cast a spell. You're still you and you're who I need the most during all of this!" She kissed his cheek gently, "And that is why I can't have you endangering yourself for me. Brian, I..."—she shook her head—"I don't know what I'd do if something happened to you!" She paused and kissed his cheek again, getting her lips close to his right ear as she whispered "I love you."

Her soft, airy breath in his ear made him shiver and he wrapped his arms around her naked torso and pulled her in tight against him. He'd waited so long to hear those words from her, and now that she was finally his he still wasn't getting tired of hearing them. He took in a sharp breath, getting her scent in his nostrils.

"I love you, too."

It was nearly forty minutes before Bekka and Brian finally emerged from the bedroom; the others glancing knowingly—but saying nothing—as they stepped into the living room. Bekka blushed under the heat of their stares while Brian ignored them and plopped himself on the couch. David, who had been sitting on the floor, stood as she approached.

"You still going out?" He asked.

Bekka smiled at the question—remembering what she had gone to her room for in the first place—and nodded.

David smiled and waited till she was closer and then

turned to head for the door.

"Be careful," Brian called over his shoulder.

Bekka smiled and looked back to him. "We will be," she made sure the door closed quietly before they headed down the hall. After a short while she turned her head to David, "Too bad it's so early."

David frowned, not understanding, and raised an eyebrow, "What do you mean?"

"Well, don't you usually run at night?"

David nodded, "Is that why you wanted to go out?"

Bekka shook her head, "No. I just needed a break from sitting around listening to myself sing the same song."

"Hard to believe anybody could get tired of that," David laughed.

Bekka giggled as well and hurried her own pace to stay beside him. As they made it to the elevator David pressed the call button.

"So have you been able to decipher any of the messages?" David asked as they waited.

Bekka frowned and looked down. After finally getting away from the stereo and the repeating sample it was the last thing that she wanted to talk about.

"Not really," she admitted, "Just what they've shown me so far. The rest is pretty garbled."

The elevator sounded shortly before the doors opened.

"So what is it they've shown you so far?" David asked as he stepped inside.

Bekka shrugged and followed, pressing the button for the first floor as she did, "They keep telling me about the balance of energy and how the things after them won't stop until it's been restored."

David frowned, "But we already knew that! Isn't there anything else; anything *new*?"

"Not really," Bekka chewed her lip.

"Bekka," David turned to her as the elevator continued its descent, "This is important! What aren't you telling us?"

Bekka scowled and looked at the buttons light up as they passed each floor, "I'm not sure, David. I can feel them inside me; I can feel them getting angry at me. It's like I know exactly how it's all supposed to work—like they've already spelled everything out for me—and I just can't quite put the pieces together."

David sighed, "Well I know that Derek's doing his best, but is there anything that the rest of us can do?"

Bekka paused and looked up at him, "Us?"

"Yea," David nodded, "you know: your band-mates? We're all behind you on this. Each and every one of us is ready to do what needs to be done to make this work."

Bekka frowned, her eyes studying David as she recited the word over and over again in her mind. Something in what he'd said...

"Everyone... does their part," she mumbled.

"Yea. That *is* what I just said," David frowned as the elevator stopped at the lobby and the doors started to open,

"Is everything alright? You look a little pale."

Bekka nodded and pressed the button for her floor and tapped her foot impatiently as the doors slid shut again. Suddenly she didn't want to go out anymore.

"I GOT IT!" Bekka screamed triumphantly as she burst through the door.

"HOLY FUCKING TITTY-SPRINKES!" Will was suddenly at his feet, though nobody had actually seen him leave the couch. After several deep breaths he shook his head and glared at Bekka, "Scared the shit out of me, girl! What's wrong with you?"

Derek furrowed his brow and looked up, "Did you just say 'titty-sprinkes'?"

"Yea, and what of it?" Will took another deep breath and settled back into his spot on the couch, "Not like I'm gonna let Morgan Freeman have all the fun with that one."

Brian had already climbed out of the couch and was making his way across the living room to get beside her. She nodded to Brian, letting him know that she was alright, and locked her gaze on Derek, who was turned at the hip on the sofa, looking back at her.

David stepped in behind her, calmly shutting the door.

Brian looked up at him, "What's all this about? You

two were barely gone five minutes!"

"Tell me about it," David answered, "We made it as far as the first floor and then she suddenly went all wide-eyed and bushy-tailed and *had* to come back."

Bekka's already painfully-wide smile grew and she looked up at David, "Remember what I told you about 'the body of the band'?"

David nodded slowly, "Yea, I guess."

"Wait, the WHAT of the band? What are you babbling about?" Will crossed his arms over his chest.

"I hate to say it," Brian said, "but Will's right. What *are* you talking about?"

Bekka smiled and looked around at them. "All of you—each and every one of you—has a role to play in both the band and in solving this," she thought a moment longer and shook her head, "It's all so perfect!"

Derek frowned, "What do you mean?"

Bekka looked at him and nodded, "I can hear them clearly now! It's like we're sharing the same thoughts all of a sudden! They didn't choose me! They chose US! All of us! Together we have what they need to be free!"

"What the fuck are you talking about?" Will was shaking his head at her.

"I'm talking about being a band!" Bekka squealed in excitement, "I'm talking about being the perfect body!"

TWISTED ROMANCE

Metal wrapped 'round metal.
Glass pressed to glass.
Fluids mix and drip and flow.
And it's all over so fast.

(There's nothing left that we can do)

The car crash is the passion.
The explosion is our love.
The burning is the climax.
And I'll see you above.

(I can't help but get lost in you)

It's not enough to get lost
In the fear and chaos.
And we'll all writhe and dance
In this twisted romance.

(And I know you want it, too)

With the fenders bending
And the chorus ending,
Two bodies become as one.
And to those depending

There will be no mending.
The horrific deed's been done.

(Though my eyes are clenched, I see)

Metal wrapped 'round metal.
Glass pressed to glass.
Fluids mix and mingle.
But the excitement never lasts.

(As you crash into me)

The collision is climactic.
All will stop and gaze.
As the chaos and the disorder
Dims in the dying blaze.

(We are united eternally)

TORMENT

He wears his smile in his pocket.
Where no one else can see.
And since none have seen him happy
They're convinced he'll never be.

His laughter's in a fist.
So tight, no one can hear.
With no joy in his voice at all,
They're sure he's filled with fear.

All they see is torment.
They don't look for what he was.
All they see is torment.
Nobody ever does.
All they see is torment.
They're not sure what the cause.
All they see is torment,
And all his other flaws.

The world's so filled with judgment.
It won't stop to find the good.
But when time is so goddam precious,
It's a mystery why it should.

All they see is torment.

His soul's as dark as night.
All they see is torment.
They can't see his plight.
All they see is torment.
All ignore the fight.
All they see is torment.
He can never set things right.

PART FOUR:
BATTLE OF THE BANDS

CAN YOU HEAR ME NOW?

It was quiet on that faithful night.
So quiet my ears bled.
Now every silence I come across
Is the cause of so much dread.

(Did you mean to hurt me like you did?
I imagine it must be so)

You clearly didn't hear me then—
The night I can't forget—
My lips felt stitched; my throat was parched,
And I wonder if you even regret…

The night you didn't hear my cries
And you tore my soul like a plow.
Now I can't help but wonder:
Can you hear me now?

(Can you hear a fucking thing?)

So quiet on that horrible night.
You must have known; somewhere,
That what you did was dreadful
And unfair.

(Did you mean to hurt me like you did?

You best believe it'll come back at you!)

My silence was a siren.
My silence was a call.
But you ignored every moment,
That I made no sound at all!

I'm hoping that you'll see your fault,
Though I honestly don't see how.
But you can start by telling me:
Can you fucking hear me now?

(Listen! Listen! Listen!)
Maybe you will hear...
(Listen! Listen! Listen!)
My voice in your dead ears.

I REMEMBER...

Your death's still fresh!
Like a newborn,
Everyday
Emerging into my mind!
Blossoming!
Forever here to stay!

Recollections of your murder—
Oh! What a blessed time!—
Keep me warm at night
As I relive that treasured crime!

Memories of that moment;
Of your long awaited demise
Always are a part of me,
And replay in my eyes.

I remember how you cried.
I remember all your screams.
I remember when you died.
I relive it in my dreams.

You twisted fucking piece of shit
I hope you rot in Hell.
And when I die and descend
I'll torture you as well!

I am what you made of me.
You were the birth of your own death.
And the monster that I've become
Was born of your last breath.

I remember…

THIRTY-TWO

"The body of the band," Bekka explained, trying to remember how she'd worded it before, "starts with the drums—the heart," she nodded towards Will. "Next comes the bass, which carries and maintains—the pulse," her gaze shifted to Derek. "Then there's the skeleton and the muscles—rhythm guitar," she turned to Brian, her eyes lighting up as they met his. "And then the outer layer—the skin—represented by the lead guitar," she smiled up at David, "Finally there's me, the singer: the mind and spirit."

Except for David, who'd already heard it, they all stared in confusion.

Wetting his lips, Will let out a heavy sigh, "That's

really quite clever and will probably make a lovely poem, but how the fuck is it supposed to help us?"

Brian frowned and shook his head, "Do you have any ideas?"

Will frowned, "Well no, but—"

"Then how 'bout you shut your hole and let her tell us hers?" Brian growled at him.

He licked a fang but said nothing.

"That's what I thought," Brian turned back to Bekka, "So how does all that work into your plan?"

Bekka nodded, "Just like we work as a body with our music, we have to unify our talents and abilities to create the solution."

"So we're going to jam-out until the bad things go away?" Will scoffed.

Brian growled, "I swear I'm going to bust you in your fucking teeth if you don't shut-the-hell-up!"

The vampire smirked, "You could try."

David growled and stood straight, making himself taller, "How bout I try, then?"

Though he didn't stand down, Will frowned and stayed quiet.

Brian sighed, shaking his head, and looked to Bekka, "Still, it's not like we have very many abilities outside of our music that would help with this problem."

Bekka smirked, "What are you talking about?" She looked at Will and David, "We have a vampire and a werewolf"—she turned to face Derek—"and a magician…"

Brian frowned, "And an anchor-of-a-human."

Bekka shook her head, "Don't sell yourself short, sweetie. The entities chose us because we all added up to what they needed!"

Brian raised an eyebrow, "So what *am* I supposed to—"

The phone rang and Bekka sighed, hurrying over to answer it.

"Hello?"

The others watched, unable to hear the other side of the conversation.

Bekka's eyes went wide after a moment, "Oh! Was that tomorrow? We completely—"

More silence.

"Um, well, we're kind of busy at the—"

Brian frowned and started to step towards her. As he did, she covered the mouthpiece and mouthed "it's Bill" to both him and the others behind him. At that, they all frowned, their minds racing as to why their manager would be calling them.

Almost all at once it came to them.

The Battle of the Bands!

It was tomorrow!

Bekka shook her head, "Well I'm not so sure—"

Brian growled and held out his hand to take the phone.

Bekka shook her head as she listened and finally sighed, "Alright. We'll be right there."

The others groaned—their shoulders sagging—as Bekka hung up the phone.

Will was, unsurprisingly, the first to speak up.

"All the shit that's going down and—"

"Stop!" Bekka's voice was hard and angry. She sighed and shook her head, "It's not like he was giving me much choice."

Brian nodded slowly, "He did seem a bit pushy."

Bekka shook her head, "That's one word for it, I suppose."

"So let's just not go!" Will suggested.

"Not an option," Bekka said, "He said he's tired of us breaking our promises to him and blowing him off all the time. He's threatening to bail on us if we don't show up at his place to discuss tomorrow's concert."

David frowned and shook his head, "We can't deal with this right now! We've got bigger, more serious situations to—"

"But if we don't, it could be the end of our music career," Will pointed out.

Brian growled, "Well that's a risk we're just going to have to take!"

"No," Bekka shook her head, "We can't just abandon everything we've worked for!"

Will nodded, "Exactly! If we don't do this, our band might be good for nothing more than birthday parties!"

The others sighed, looking down.

"Come on," Brian argued, "We can't honestly be

considering putting this on the back burner to play some concert!"

Bekka frowned up at him, "Look at us, Brian! What are we going to do with our lives if we don't have our music!"

"But..." Brian's mouth hung open for a moment before sliding shut and he looked down, nodding, "Will, get the van ready."

"So did the selfish son-of-a-bitch have anything else to say besides 'come over and help me change my tampon'?" Will growled as he navigated the busy city streets.

Nobody had it in them to tell him to shut up; after all, they were all bitter towards the situation, as well. Bekka sat beside Brian, shaking her head to herself and "listening" to the entities within her. It seemed, since stumbling across the answer to their problem, they had become more talkative. Though they weren't necessarily speaking to her, it was nevertheless interesting to eavesdrop—if that was the right word for it.

Brian frowned as he noticed her odd behavior and set his hand on her leg, "Everything alright?"

Bekka looked up at him and smiled. "Yea," she paused and listened a little more, "They're excited."

"They?"

Another nod and she patted her chest softly, "They

know that we've figured it out."

Will sighed from the driver's seat, "I really don't think we've got it all figured out. I mean, sure, we understand that we all have a role to play in finding and sending out replacement energy, but do we really know how we're going to do this?"

"I've been thinking about that," Derek nodded, "First we're going to need to get a vast amount of energy, then—"

"So how do we get the energy?" Will asked, "All I'm saying is that we don't have all the answers yet."

Bekka bit her lip and looked to Derek, "Is it possible?"

Derek nodded, leaning forward in the back seat so he was closer to her and Brian, "Theoretically, yes. It would just take a lot of time and effort to build it up. And then there's the problem of where to store it all."

Will chuckled, "Too bad you're not all vampires."

Brian frowned and looked towards him, "Oh? And why's that?"

"Because, if you think about it, all a vampire is *is* an energy-stealing battery," Will turned onto Bill's driveway, "Anyway, we're here."

Derek was silent for a moment, his eyes locked on the back of Will's head as the others started to get out of the van. It wasn't until Will stepped out as well that he was shaken out of his trance and started out, as well. Once grouped together, they started for the front door, where Bill was already waiting for them.

"Shit!" Brian frowned, "He looks *pissed*!"

Will was the first to start up the steps, eager to be out of the sunlight, "Hey! What is up, Bill? Mind if we raid your—"

Their manager swung his arm out then, catching Will in the throat and sending him over the railing and into the bushes that lined the front of the house.

Everybody stopped and stared. It was startling enough that Bill had just attacked one of them, it was downright wrong that he'd been able to knock their vampire drummer down so easily. David, who had been right behind Will and halfway up the steps, let out a soft, nervous growl and took a step away from their manager just as Derek's eyes went wide.

"He's been taken!" The bassist shouted to the others, just then seeing the dark, spectral traces around him.

Bekka flinched and whimpered; grabbing her head as the entities nervously rioted within her.

Brian frowned and stepped protectively in front of her.

"*So nice of you all to come,*" Bill's voice was laced with multiple tones and crackled like a broken radio. The sound was enough to make everyone flinch. His eyes rolled in his head—each independent of the other—as they took in each of the remaining band-mates before finally locking onto Bekka and widening excitedly, "*Yes! There you are!*" He reached out his hand as if ready to accept an offering, "*Give me the girl!*"

"Like hell!" Brian growled between clenched teeth.

*"**We** will **have her!**"* Their possessed manager threatened.

David snarled and began to pull off his shirt and kick off his shoes. Bill narrowed his eyes at this in confusion and started to advance just as the werewolf's shoulders exploded outward with inflating muscle.

It was the fastest that David had ever transformed! The ordinarily painful process becoming an agonizing moment that felt like his entire body had just been hit by a flaming truck. The others all gasped and stepped back as, in the span of half-a-second, he had gone from his human form to his raging, bestial one.

The bushes beside them rustled and a pained groan emerged. Will growled as he stood, a series of scrapes and gashes rapidly healing over as he did.

"What the fuck was that?" He demanded, rubbing his throat and coughing, "God-fucking-dammit! I think I swallowed a bird's nest!"

"Bill's been possessed!" Bekka called out to him.

Will smirked, "That mean we can kick his ass?"

Brian glared at him, "We'd prefer it, actually."

The vampire's smirk widened and he leapt into the air, soaring over the railing and landing gracefully on the steps, "It is about fucking time!"

Bill sneered at the scene and opened his mouth, letting out a strange, clucking laugh before charging down the stairs at the two supernatural creatures that stood in his way. David roared, swiping at him as he approached, only to have their possessed manager leap over the attack and deliver a spinning kick to the side of his head. As the werewolf toppled over, whimpering in pain, Will dove into the air and collided with Bill, knocking them both down the steps. The vampire groaned in pain as one of the stone steps caught him in the side, the interruption giving Bill enough time to drive a knee up into his stomach. Will hissed as he was thrown overhead and landed hard on his back.

David pulled himself up, staying on all fours and using his bulk to block their manager from getting to Bekka.

Brian scowled, looking to Derek, whose eyes were already half closed as his mouth moved silently, "Isn't there some spell you can cast?" He demanded.

Derek glared back at him, "What do you think I'm doing?"

"Taking too damn long!"

Derek shook his head, "And what would you have me do?"

"Anything!" Brian thought for a moment, "Get me in there! Give me the strength to help them!"

Derek shook his head, "Your body wouldn't be able to handle it!"

Brian looked back at the fight and shook his head, "God dammit!"

Bekka whimpered sadly, seeing Bill throw a hard kick into David's chest before twisting impossibly around to grab the recovering Will and swing him around into the railing with enough force to snap it in half.

"Somebody do something!" She cried out.

Derek frowned and held out his left hand, pushing what energy he could into David and Will to strengthen them. With his right hand, he directed another wave of energy at the broken railing; hurling the metal fragments at their manager.

Bill growled as his attacks were interrupted by the projectiles and bent backwards—his spine audibly cracking as he did—and slipped between his own legs. As the railing fragments crashed into his front door, Bill shot down the steps and tangled himself under David, tripping the werewolf and driving his head into the steps.

Will cursed and vanished from the others' sight before reappearing at the bottom of the steps between Bill and Bekka and brought his foot down in an attempt to crush their manager's skull.

In a bizarre acrobatic feat, Bill curled around to save himself from the attack and corkscrewed on both hands before balancing upside-down on his head and pulling Will's legs out from under him while, at the same time, kicking out and catching the vampire in the chest.

"Motherfucker!" Will cursed as he crashed into the driveway.

Bill was on his feet along with a chorus of sickening, bone-crunching sounds and swung his leg around to come down on Will's sternum, pinning him. Will cried out in pain and thrashed about, trying to free himself from the increasing pressure on his chest.

"Oh my god!" Bekka cried out, "He's going to kill him!"

"Like hell!" Brian shook his head and charged, driving his shoulder into Bill's back…

… only to be thrown away. His eyes spun in his skull and his shoulder ached.

And Bill remained upright; standing over Will.

"What the…?" Brian stammered, trying to stop the world from spinning.

"Brian!" Bekka cried, starting to run to him.

"No!" Derek held her back, "He'll be fine!"

David, pulling himself up, let out an angry breath and charged down the steps, driving the top of his skull into Bill's back. Their manager cried out in surprise as he was thrown forward—off of Will—and over the fallen Brian.

"Get down!" Derek pushed Bekka out of their manager's path and rolled to the side, allowing him to sail past and crash into the side of the van with enough force to dent and cave in the sliding door.

Will bared his fangs and hissed, "My van!"

Brian shook his head as he pulled himself to his knees, "Get over it!"

Turning to face the threat, Derek muttered under his breath just as Bill pulled himself from the mangled vehicle and lunged at Bekka. At that moment, a shimmering wall of energy appeared around her as Bill came down on her. The smell of burnt hair and flesh filled the air as Bill was thrown back several yards, howling in pain. Derek's face contorted with effort as he maintained the spell. David, seeing his chance, jumped in and yanked their manager from the ground as Will shot forward and grabbed him by the head. Working together, David yanked Bill's body to the left as Will twisted to the right, snapping their manager's neck.

For a moment things went quiet, but as David let the body fall from his grip it suddenly supported itself and stood upright. Bill's body staggered, his eyes darting about in confusion before he finally reached up and gripped his twisted head and righted it.

"Shit on me!" Will gasped, breathing hard and sprinting towards him again, "How the fuck do we kill him?"

Derek scowled, studying their lumbering manager, "You've gotta stop his heart!"

"And how the hell do you expect us to do that?" Will ducked under a left-hook that he was sure would've taken even his head off.

There was no answer as both Will and David struggled with their own attempts. Every attack that they delivered went either unnoticed or was easily dodged. Bekka frowned, trying to step forward only to have Brian stop her and shake his head.

"It's too dangerous!"

Bekka's body was shaking.

She *needed* to do something!

"Please!" She tried to get past him again, "They need my help!"

Brian shook his head again, fighting harder to keep

her back, "They're fighting to keep you out of this!" He argued.

There was no changing her mind, however, and before Brian could stop her she gripped both his shoulders in her hands and somersaulted over him.

"Bekka! No!"

But she was already in the middle of the fight, weaving between her vampire and werewolf comrades and throwing her fist into their manager's face. Everyone stopped at the sound of his jaw breaking—a surprising feat considering how small Bekka's fist was—and they stared in disbelief as she bobbed fluidly around him to deliver another blow to the center of his spine.

"Oh shit!" Will cried out, "She's wrecking him!"

David let out a grunt and motioned for Will to move forward. Slowly and deliberately, they advanced; not wanting to distract Bekka and potentially give Bill the upper hand. Will nodded to his friend as he and the werewolf continued to creep forward while Bekka and Bill fought. It was easy to see that Bekka had the upper hand as she easily swayed and countered every attack with one of her own.

Brian's eyes were wide as he watched them, several times trying to move in to intervene only to have Derek hold him back.

"Dammit! Let me go!" He demanded.

Derek shook his head, "She's equipped to handle this. You're not!"

Growling in frustration, Brian took a step back and

went back to watching in silence.

Bekka moved to duck under a wide swing then and was startled when Bill caught her by the throat with his right and lifted her off the ground. Their manager's face twisted in glee, looking horrifically cartoonish. Gasping for air, Bekka kicked out and struggled to free herself from his grip.

Brian continued to struggle against Derek's hold, "No!"

David looked up at Will and gave him a nod. Smirking, the vampire narrowed his eyes vanished, appearing a moment later behind Bill and yanking him away from Bekka.

"What do I do now?" He asked, looking past Bill to Derek.

"Drain him!" Derek cried out.

Will's eyes went wide, but as his captive's thrashing became harder to overcome he finally set aside his restrictions and opened his mouth and extended his fangs.

Bekka's eyes widened as well and she looked back at Derek in shock, "What?"

Derek shook his head, "It's the only way to stop him short of ripping out his heart!"

David let out a grunt and started to advance towards Bill.

"No!" Bekka cried.

David whimpered and stopped.

Will was already feeding. As Bekka turned to watch, their wide-eyed manager shook and began to cough up his own entities as they rejected their dying host.

David was already turning back to his human form, groaning and whimpering in pain as he shrank down.

"No!" Bekka cried.

"Don't stop!" David instructed when his mouth was able to form words again.

The vampire gave a slight nod and pulled Bill in tighter as he continued.

Unable to watch, Bekka turned and ran straight into Brian, burying her face into his chest and letting out a sob. Without looking away, he ran a comforting hand across the top of her head, assuring her that it would be alright.

Finally, Bill's eyes went hollow and dead and the body slackened and collapsed at Will's feet. The band, frozen where they stood, stared down at their manager's body for some time before Will looked up, his own eyes shimmering with the stolen energy and a slight trickle of blood running down his chin.

"So," he wiped the excess away with the back of his hand, "Does this mean we don't need to record?"

THIRTY-THREE

"I cannot believe how passive you are about this!"
Bekka went on, "We just killed a man!"

Will shook his head as he drove, "I don't know what
you expected from us! It was either going to be us or him!
Would you have rather had the alternative?"

Brian frowned but didn't say anything. Because of the
damage done to the van's door he was now forced to hold it
shut from his seat. While he wasn't resentful for this, he was
nonetheless irritated by the circumstances.

David sighed from the passenger seat and nodded,
"Will has a point. We weren't about to reach a peaceful
negotiation with him."

Derek nodded but remained silent.

The bite wounds from Will had, fortunately, healed over in the matter of several seconds—one of the "benefits", as he'd called it, of being a vampire—before the last ounce of life had seeped from their manager. With no evidence of how he'd truly died and almost every bone in his body broken, the band had struggled to carry him into the house and leave him sprawled at the bottom of the staircase. Though it wasn't a respectable way to go, anybody who found him would simply believe that he'd fallen.

Tears were slowly beginning to form in Bekka's eyes, and though Brian would have liked to have been able to comfort her he was well aware that the door would not stay closed on its own if he moved away from it.

"It's alright," he assured her, craning his neck to see her from his position.

Bekka shook her head and wiped her eyes, "It doesn't *feel* alright!"

Derek sighed and leaned forward, "It's like Will said, it was either him or us. You can't feel guilty for protecting yourself."

Bekka whimpered and looked down, still crying.

Nobody tried to stop her. Though their actions made sense, there was no denying that it was a traumatic experience.

"If it makes anybody feel better," Will smirked, running a free hand through his hair, "I feel like a million bucks!"

David sighed and shook his head, "Shut up, Will."

"Yea, really," Brian shook his head and sighed.

The band-mates went silent after that, letting their own thoughts occupy them as they put as much distance between themselves and Bill's house as they could. Nobody moved or said a thing.

Nobody but Will, who bounced in his seat and slapped his hands on the steering wheel.

"For Chrissake! Can you settle down?" Brian finally demanded when the racket had gone on for too long.

Will's body shook and his head tossed from side to side, "I can't help it!" He confessed, "I haven't had human blood in so long! I just feel so fucking jacked-up!"

Growling, Brian shook his head, "I don't care! You're acting like a damn crack head!"

Derek's eyes suddenly went wide, "Wait! That's it!"

Brian turned, "What? Crack?"

"No!" Derek shook his head and directed his eyes to the back of Will's head, "Will! You say you feel energized?"

Will nodded, "Damn straight!"

Everyone was seated patiently in Bekka's living room while Derek paced back-and-forth in front of them. Next to David on the couch, Will continued to twitch from the excess energy, and it was more than clear that it was beginning to irritate his neighbor.

"What is all this about?" David finally asked. Derek stopped in mid-step and glanced at his band-mate but continued to think. David growled as Will's bouncing knee knocked against his once again, "Well?"

"Energy," Derek said the word as though it explained the whole situation. The others looked at him expectantly. He sighed and shook his head, "Our current problem is about getting the energy required to make this all work."

Brian sighed and nodded, "We know that! Get to the point!"

Derek rolled his eyes, "Look, it's like Will said earlier, vampires are all *about* energy storage! 'Like batteries', remember? And now"—he motioned to their jittery drummer—"we can *see* that energy," he smirked.

"But it's in Will! How can we use it?" Bekka asked, frowning.

Derek smirked, "Energy is energy no matter what the source or how it's stored! Vampires convert life force—be it from blood or psychic energy—into magic energy to sustain themselves. And, like any other form of energy, we can harness it!"

Brian looked at the bassist skeptically, "But he only gets this kind of energy from blood. *Human* blood!"

Derek nodded, "Yes…"

David frowned, "You're saying he'd have to feed *again?*"

"Actually…" Derek bit his lip as he did some mental

calculations, "He'd have to feed a lot more than once."

David was on his feet so fast it startled even Will, "No! No way! Do you have any idea what kind of thin ice we're already on with our kind? The fact that we're associating with humans right now—just being your band-mates—has got members of the supernatural community gunning for us! And that's *without* any violations against us!"

Bekka frowned and looked at David nervously, "What are you saying? I thought you'd settled things with The Council…?"

David frowned and nodded. "We did. But the ones after us aren't working under The Council's orders," he shook his head, "They already see us as a threat, and they'd be more than happy to take us out if we gave them an excuse to."

"Assuming they even *need* an excuse," Will nodded, "We've been thinking about leaving to try and keep all of you safe."

Derek frowned.

Brian glared at the two.

"You were going to leave us?" Bekka's lip quivered.

David shook his head, "We haven't yet."

"'yet'?" Bekka's eyes began to water.

Brian wrapped an arm around her, not moving his angry gaze away from the two, "So why haven't you?" He growled, "It's not like you're irreplaceable!"

Bekka inhaled sharply and looked up at him, "Brian! No!"

Brian quickly shut his mouth and sighed, shaking his

head, "Sorry."

David was still frowning, but gave a short nod, "It's alright."

Will growled and slumped back in the couch. "If he wants us gone so much, we can be gone," he snapped his fingers for emphasis, "Just like that!"

Derek sighed, "He said he was sorry!"

Bekka nodded, "Yea! C'mon, guys, this isn't the time to fight! We're so close to figuring this out," she looked expectantly at Derek, "Aren't we?"

Derek smiled and nodded, "It's just like you said, I'm the pulse, Brian's the skeleton-slash-muscle, David's the skin, you're the spirit and"—he turned to Will with a smirk—"Will's the heart."

David frowned, "I'm not sure I understand."

Derek smirked and began to explain.

THIRTY-FOUR

Less than twelve hours till the Battle of the Bands...

... and the group's plan was still in development.

Will had left earlier that morning in search of human blood, and while nobody was particularly happy with that fact, Derek was certain that it was the only way.

The others played out their roles to themselves in his absence, making sure that when the moment came they would not come up short. Bekka, on the other hand, was too nervous to focus on anything, let alone something so important. After talking about it with Derek, she was painfully aware of the dangers that everyone faced; dangers that could easily take the lives of any or all of the band-mates.

With this thought haunting her, she stayed in her bedroom, unable to bring herself to feel anything other than guilt and dread.

Back in the living room, Derek went over the plans again. "The energy starts with Will," he explained just as much to himself as to the others, "There's going to be *a lot* of it—more than I think a vampire has ever tried to stockpile before—and it could potentially overwhelm his system. Assuming that this doesn't happen, it'll then be up to me to transfer that energy from his body to Brian's—assuming that the transfer doesn't rip him apart and-slash-or consume all of my powers and kill me in the process. If all works out and the introduction of the energy into Brian's body hasn't destroyed him, we should have a perfect imitation of Bekka's situation: a human body saturated with an abundance of life-energy."

They all nodded.

David sighed. It was already known that the process would attract a great deal of the wrong kind of attention. Derek had made it clear that, while the plan was being executed, the band would be overwhelmed with possessed attackers drawn to the increased energy signatures, and it would be up to him—and *only* him—to keep all of them safe while they did their part.

"Now, Bekka's the key to making this all work," Derek went on, "It will be up to her to infuse the energy in Brian's body with cloned signatures of the entities within her, creating copies. This will, hopefully, ensure that the energies will be accepted when we send them out."

"And how exactly does that work?" Brian asked.

Derek nodded, understanding his band-mate's unsteady nerves, "We fake your death."

Brian sighed and nodded, "And how do we do that?"

"I'll use a spell to convince the energies that you're dying. When they no longer have any reason to hold on to you, they'll begin to cross over."

"So what's to stop my own energies from leaving me in the process?" Brian frowned.

Derek nodded slowly, "There is that chance. But you're going to have to trust me not to let it get that far."

David looked over at Brian and smiled reassuringly, giving him a friendly pat on the shoulder, "It'll be alright."

Brian rolled his eyes.

Derek took a deep breath and offered a lame smile, "And, if all goes according to plan and nobody gets killed, we'll all be good to go to the Battle of the Bands tonight."

It had been decided, mostly by Bekka, that if everything worked out then they would perform. Though the others saw it as a lesser priority, they understood her need to return to their normal lives as soon as possible.

"So where are we meeting Will?" David asked.

"At ten; his place," Derek sighed, sounding doubtful.

The others glanced at the time one-by-one, confirming that it was still only eight in the morning.

Brian frowned, "His place?"

Derek nodded, "It's the largest area we know of that won't attract attention."

Down the hall, Bekka's door opened and shut and the sound of her footsteps started towards them. Soon after, she was standing at the entrance to the living room.

"Are we ready?" She asked.

Derek nodded, "Everyone's clear on their roles and the dangers."

Bekka bit her lip at that and looked at them, "And you're still alright with it?"

Both Brian and David nodded.

Bekka bit her lip and looked up at Derek, "And you?"

Derek smiled and gave her a tight hug, "Of course. You know that we're all here for you."

Bekka's lip quivered. "Thank you," she whispered to them, "Thank you all so much."

He'd been out for more than three hours and still Will had found not a single person who he felt deserved to die. Looking at his watch he scowled—it was already past eight and he didn't have anything to show for it! What would he be able to do in less than two hours?

As desperation set in, he decided that a trip to Xavier's might be in order and U-turned the van in the middle of traffic—ignoring the angry honks and curses—and headed east. While his source was good for a bag of beef blood when the time called for it, Will wasn't sure how reliable he'd be when it came to human blood—*fresh* human blood.

"C'mon, Xavier!" He prayed to himself, "Be there! Just fucking be there!"

The van was barely in park as he jumped out, leaving the engine running. As he approached the butcher shop he noticed that the door was already open and waiting and he frowned.

Was it a neglectful worker?

Or could it be an invitation?

Cautiously, he stepped inside and looked around.

Ah! William! I was wondering when you'd be around! The voice in his head startled him and he almost knocked over a cutlery set.

"Son of a bitch, Xavier!" He swore, steadying himself. Though he was ecstatic that his source was still available, he couldn't help but curse his name at that moment.

My apologies. The auric spoke in his mind, *I'm out front.*

"Of course you are," Will rolled his eyes as he passed through a set of doors.

On the other side, the sterility of the backroom ended and the serenity of the front began. Will paused at the change in scenery and worked his way to one of the booths where his source sat over a cup of coffee.

"I was beginning to wonder if you'd even show," Xavier smirked, taking a sip from the faded green mug.

Will frowned as he sat down across from the auric, "How'd you know I was coming?"

Xavier scoffed, "Please! Your panic and quest for human blood is reeking up the entire city! I'll admit I wasn't sure what it was at first. Even came close to leaving shop, but when I realized it was you I figured you'd be paying me a visit sooner or later."

"It's not what you think," Will assured him, "I need it for my friend."

"Your friend, you say?" Xavier raised a skeptical eyebrow.

Will rolled his eyes, "Well, no. It is *for* me, but I need it to help my friend!"

"I know what you meant," he shook his head, "My-oh-my what a predicament, eh?"

Will nodded, realizing that the entire story had been read from his mind. He sighed, "It really is."

"So you're going to stay with the band, I take it?"

Another nod.

Xavier smiled, "Good to hear."

"Look," Will's patience was wearing thin, "Can we just move this along to whether or—"

Xavier's face grew stern and angry. "Don't you rush me, young-blood," he growled, "I know what you're here for and I know your purpose and I know of the urgency it all represents, so I would suggest you don't talk to me like I know nothing! Time is against you—yes—but you must come to grips with the severity of the order you're placing!"

Will blushed and nodded, "I understand."

"No," Xavier sighed and leaned back, "I know for a

goddam fact that you don't."

"Okay, fine. I don't. What-the-fuck-ever, man," Will sighed, "Can you help me through this *now* and lecture my ignorance later?"

Xavier chuckled, "Of course I can."

Will let out a relieved sigh, "Oh thank the god of fuck!"

"Yes. Thank him, indeed," Xavier laughed.

THIRTY-FIVE

"Where the hell is he?" Brian demanded.

They'd just gotten to the remains of their drummer's old house, most of which had either burned down in the fire or been destroyed by water damage from the fire fighters' efforts. The group had been forced, in Will's absence, to use a cab to get to the meeting place. Upon their arrival to the destroyed home, the cabby had given the four of them a skeptical look, starting with Derek—who had ridden shotgun—and swiveling back to the others in the backseat.

"You sure this is where you want to be?" He asked in a gruff voice.

Bekka had nodded, smiling pleasantly as the others started to get out on either side of her. After handing him the fare and thanking him again, she'd crawled out as well.

Shortly after the cab turned away, they had realized that their vampire companion, and a very crucial element in their plans, hadn't gotten there yet.

"He must be on his way," David offered, though his voice gave away his own doubt.

"Bullshit!" Brian growled, turning to glare at him, "That fucker probably got scared and hightailed!"

Derek frowned and shook his head, "He'll be here! It's not even ten!"

"What's your point?" Brian demanded, starting to turn red with rage, "He's had *hours* to do this! He should've been here by now!"

Bekka looked at him sadly, "Brian, he's not late yet. Just give him a chance."

He frowned, looking down at her. She pouted slightly as she read the desperation on his face. He was scared for her; terrified. There was nothing at this point that he wouldn't do for her, and the fact that he wasn't able to make everything all better that very minute was tearing him apart inside. Seeing this, she nodded and gave him a soft smile.

"He'll be here," she promised, "He has to be."

Brian could only bring himself to nod.

"What should we do in the meantime?" Derek asked a moment later.

David frowned, looking around, "We're too obvious

out in the open like this. We'd better go inside."

Brian scoffed, "Right, 'inside'. Into the dilapidated, burnt-up and falling-apart house," he shook his head, "What the hell's wrong with you?"

David growled and glared at him, "Look, I know that you're on edge about all this—trust me, we all are—but if you don't chill out then this is going to go someplace you don't want it to. Besides," he looked back towards the house and took a step closer, "I was talking about the basement."

Blushing slightly, Brian nodded; Bekka coming up behind him and guiding him forward as the others started towards the underground garage. As they drew nearer, David squatted down and gripped the massive, sliding door and began to pull. At first it lifted easily, then snagged on something and stopped suddenly halfway up. David grunted against the pressure and continued to force the door upward against the blockage. Struggling, David continued to force the garage door upward until, finally, it became too much and the obstruction broke, releasing its hold on the door and allowing it to rise the rest of the way.

"Does Will use you as a jack when he's changing the tires on his van?" Brian joked as he patted David on the shoulder and moved past.

Bekka followed him in, stepping gingerly over and around the piles of junk. When, at last, they'd reached the door to the basement, Brian was the first to turn the knob and step through. Inside, it was dark and dusty and reeking of stale ash. The four instantly began to cough on the thick, smoky air. Soon it became clear that there was no adapting to the unbearable nature of the room and Derek waved his hand in a circular motion, creating a small whirlwind that collected all of the wandering particles and cleared them from the air.

David smirked, letting out one last cough, "Thank you."

Derek shrugged, "I do what I can."

With the dust—along with some of the smaller debris—cleared, the four moved deeper into the basement. As they stepped through the basement—where they had held their practice for several years—they all thought back to the times they'd spent in that room. Now, however, it was nothing more than an empty, ashy mess.

"Kinda depressing," Bekka murmured.

Brian nodded, staying close to her. As a shudder crept up Brian's spine, he growled.

Bekka frowned at this and rubbed the center of his back with the flat of her palm and gave him a kiss on the cheek.

David, in the meantime, had reached the other side of the room and, with nothing left to, started back towards the others.

"I can't believe how much different it seems," he spoke softly, as though the very foundation would crumble if he talked too loudly. The only thing that remotely resembled its former self was the remains of Will's old drum kit—still resting in the spot where he'd been forced to leave it. The others turned to face him, watching as he ran a fingertip across one of the warped cymbals and studied the resulting ash residue. Finally, stepping away from the old set, he gave it a soft kick and sent it tumbling to the ground.

Bekka winced at the sudden clamor, as though an army of the possessed might have been waiting for a single sound to spark their entrance. When nothing appeared she relaxed her shoulders and let out a deep breath.

"I hope Will gets here soon," she said.

Brian nodded, smiling softly. "He'll be here," he assured her.

Will had had no idea that such a place existed, or that humans could be so deranged and masochistic. He'd had his suspicions, and from time to time he'd gotten a glimpse of their potential, but, as he drove away from the underground "sanctuary", he couldn't help but shudder. Nevertheless, he had what he needed.

Xavier had taken him to an abandoned church the next town over with the promise of all the human blood he'd need. At first, he hadn't been sure if his source was bringing him to a prison full of death-row inmates or something less conventional. In retrospect, he would have preferred something a little less guilt-inducing.

The old church was boarded up, and the only way in was through the cellar door in the back. He'd been surprised to find this was guarded by a post on the other side who would only unlock the door if one was to first provide the correct series of knocks and a password that had been kept hidden from him. Once granted access, the two vampires were hurried inside and sent down a flight of stairs; the sound of orgasmic moans and cries growing louder with each descending step. At the bottom, Will had been surprised to find the room filled with humans—male and female alike dressed scantily in bondage gear and hooked up to intricate tubing networks—and vampires that drank freely from them. When one of the human feeders began to turn pale from blood-loss, they'd be unhooked from their tubing—most, assuming they hadn't already passed out, complaining and promising that they still had a pint to spare—and replaced by another from a seemingly endless stockpile in the next room.

The pleasured sounds that had caught Will off guard in the first place, he was surprised to find, came from the donors and *not* the vampires they were feeding.

Engrossed and more than just slightly disturbed by the whole situation, Will had watched for a moment while this went on, some of the vampires casually greeting Xavier as they passed them. After a time, Will's source made it known to the clientele that they would need to leave, offering his sincerest apologies and assuring them that this would not be a prolonged situation. Once the other vampires had gone, Xavier called out a fresh batch of the human donors and had them hook themselves up to their blood-letting tubes— something that made Will's flesh crawl and forced him to look away.

He was sure that what he'd witnessed could inspire the most metal song ever written.

From there, Xavier helped Will to collect as much blood as each donor was able to give, filling jug after jug until they were positive they had more than enough to fuel the spell and began to haul it all up to the van.

"Does The Council know about this?" Will had finally asked, positive that the supernatural government would never allow such a place to exist.

Xavier shrugged, seeming all-too calm as he set down another two gallons of blood by the van and turned back for more, "They're aware that places like this exist, yes."

Will had been startled to hear this, "And they allow it?"

"They do not so much allow it," Xavier replied, "as they do not oppose it."

"What? But why? How?" Will was dumbfounded.

Another shrug, "They have better things to do than try to sniff out these sorts of places. If the location of one becomes public, a clan is issued to shut it down. If a donor becomes talkative and threatens our secrecy, they're dealt with. The truth of the matter is that this will happen one way or the other, and to put precious time and manpower into trying to fight it is simply illogical on their part."

Will nodded slowly, not liking the response but unable to argue against the logic. When they were done he'd thanked his source for the help and gotten into the van and started for his old house.

He only hoped that the atrocities he'd witnessed had not been in vain.

The four band-mates sat in the basement, passing whatever bit of conversation they could back-and-forth until it became tired and useless and they were forced again into silence. It had been nearly an hour—just ten minutes before eleven—and even Bekka's patience for Will were beginning to waver.

Nobody said anything, of course, but all of them could see the doubt lingering in each other's eyes.

For the time being, all hope seemed to be lost.

Will was, after all, the spark needed to make the whole spell work!

Without him there would be no way to start the process; no way to even hope to mimic it!

Bekka let out a soft, worried sigh and Brian, without looking up, casually reached his hand out and rubbed her back.

"It'll be alright," he echoed robotically.

David smiled—a weak-looking gesture—and nodded.

Derek started to smile as well, only to suddenly scowl and look towards the ceiling. His eyes drifted, swimming back-and-forth in his head. The temperature in the room started to grow cold and as the frigidness peeked his stuttering breath came out as a mist along with the others.

"Something's here," he informed the group, not bringing his eyes back to look upon them.

Bekka tensed, "Is it Will?"

Derek shook his head, his voice becoming a whisper. "I don't think so," he stared towards the ceiling a moment longer before leaning towards David, "You should probably—"

David nodded, already climbing to his feet and pulling his shirt and pants off.

Bekka blushed and looked away and Brian scowled but remained silent, averting his gaze as well.

Finally undressed, David took several steps back into the darkness and stretched his limbs, taking a deep, calculated breath. A loud, wet crunch echoed through the basement and, like before, he suddenly stood before them a second later in his hulking werewolf form. His height was emphasized in the cramped space and he was forced to stoop down to avoid hitting his head on the sagging ceiling.

Brian frowned up at the creature before them, "We need to find you some clothes that stretch."

David cocked his head, looking down at himself and shot a ferocious look at Brian, letting out a snarl.

"I'm just saying," Brian shrugged casually. A moment passed and he turned to Derek, "So, why did he need to transform again?"

"I already told you!" Derek whispered through

clenched teeth, "Something's—"

He was cut off as the ceiling groaned collapsed at that moment. It did not come down in parts, but rather it dropped down from above them in a single, massive piece. The only warning they'd been granted had been a series of strained creaks and groans that had given David enough time to jump into action.

Despite having been forced to crouch down, his speed had been incredible. One moment he'd been several yards away, and the next he was standing over the other three, straining to hold the roof above their heads.

Brian saw the pained effort in the werewolf's eyes and grabbed Bekka's hand and motioned to Derek, "Garage. Now!"

Moving as fast as they could, they made their way to the door. Behind them, David shimmied under the roof, moving slowly after them while keeping the bulk of the roof held up. When the others were safely in the garage he used all his strength to push the weight over his head long enough to jump through the open door; the roof coming down and crashing loudly behind him.

Brian, breathing hard, shook his head, "What the fuck could've done that?"

"Magic," Derek answered.

"Well then who's the wizard whose ass I need to kick?" Brian demanded.

Derek turned, shaking his head, "I don't know?"

Before Brian could say anything else he was hurled

back by an invisible force; yanked from Bekka's side and thrown hard into the furthest wall of the garage.

"Brian!" Bekka cried out and started to run in his direction, only to fall back as something blocked her path.

Above them, the already-collapsing ceiling was ripped away. As they watched, the floating mass lifted and crumbled into dust, the remains raining down on them. There, through the haze, a tan-skinned brunette woman in a tight-fitting red dress came into view above them; staring down with a pair of pale-white eyes, her long, dark hair whipping violently about her head.

"*Give them to us!*" She demanded, her voice, like Bill's before, coming out in a creepy, echoing growl, "*Or all of you will die!*"

Brian, struggling against the wall, cried out and cursed at the woman, "You can't have her, bitch!"

The woman's head only slightly shifted as she turned her gaze to him and sneered, "*You speak for all of them, then?*"

Derek narrowed her eyes at her, clenching his now-glowing fists, "You bet your ass he does!"

David, now standing at his full height, growled.

Bekka backed away from the woman, letting out a soft whimper at the immense power she felt emanating from her. As she retreated, their new enemy slowly descended and landed on what remained of the floor above them.

Though she spoke softly, her words were intimidating, "*Then so be it. You'll—*"

There was the roar of an overworked motor in the

distance and the repeating honk of a horn that grew louder and louder. Everyone looked up, startled, as Will's van came into view, hurtling past the driveway and rocketing headlong into the wide-eyed woman. There was a brief cry of surprise and a loud crash as she and the vehicle tumbled through the gaping hole she'd made over the basement.

"Will!" Bekka cried, running towards the door but finding it jammed from the rubble on the other side.

Ignoring the door, David picked up Bekka and leapt over the wall to the other side. As they went to check on Will, Derek hurried to Brian.

"Are you hurt?" He asked him, studying the magic that still held him to the wall.

"No," Brian responded, "Who is that bitch! How is she so much stronger than the others?"

Derek shook his head, "They sent in a bigger bill-collector, I guess."

Brian scoffed, "I guess so."

As Derek reversed the spell Brian pulled himself from the wall and the two hurried to join the others. As they approached, David helped them both up, lifting them over the wall with ease.

On the other side, in the demolished basement, the tires of the van—now on its side—still spun, grinding against the rubble on the floor. There was a series of loud, metallic bangs and the door to the driver's side—now facing towards the sky—flew open and Will climbed out, growling as he was bathed in sunlight.

"Son-of-a-fucking-bitch!" He swore. "I can't leave you kids alone for a goddam second, can I?"

"Apparently not!" Bekka laughed and clapped excitedly.

Brian smirked and nodded, "Holy shit, dude! Did you just save our asses?"

Will cocked his head, smirking, "You mean that wasn't a Jehovah's Witness I just took out?" He snapped his fingers in mock-defeat.

"Hardly," Derek smirked at the joke, "Did you get the blood?"

"Oh shit, did I!" He smiled widely, then frowned, "But don't you dare ask how I got it! I've been chugging down the stuff by the gallons for nearly forty-five minutes! I feel like a coked-up bolt of lightning!" He jumped down to join the others, "We doing this shit or not?"

Derek nodded, "Backyard."

THIRTY-SIX

The group settled under the shade of a large tree in Will's backyard; someplace where they were hopeful the sun's rays wouldn't be too much of a problem for their vampire drummer.

Will had carried with him several gallon jugs—three in total—and as the others watched he began to drink.

Brian smirked, "Damn! And I thought you only drank like that when alcohol was involved."

Will's eyes drifted, still gulping the blood. When one of the containers was empty he tossed it aside and quickly started in on the next.

Derek frowned and glanced over his shoulder in the

direction of the house.

"She's coming back."

David grunted and started back towards the house on all fours.

Brian growled, "How can she be coming back? Will ran her over with the damn van!"

Derek shrugged, not taking his eyes off Will and his progress, "Bekka survived getting run over by a truck. Anyway, it doesn't matter! David's got it covered!"

"David can't—"

"David's role is to protect us!" Derek quipped, "He is to keep us covered while we do this, just as you are to receive this energy and make it your own! Now are you ready to do your part or not?"

Brian frowned but nodded, "I am!"

Derek nodded his approval and looked back to Will as the vampire emptied the third container and shuddered.

"Oh, God! It's getting cold!" He complained, retching.

"Do you feel the energy or not?" Derek pressured.

Will nodded, "Shit yea! I'm feeling it!" He let out a laugh, "And then some!"

Derek nodded again and hurried to stand beside him, "I need you to focus on all of the energy—imagine it being the size of a baseball that you're holding in your hand."

Will raised an eyebrow, "A baseball? Really?"

"Just do it!"

The vampire sighed and nodded, closing his eyes and

holding out his hand.

Derek squinted at his palm, focusing on it, and slowly a smile grew on his face, "That's it! Just like that!"

Bekka frowned, looking as well but seeing nothing, "What is it?"

"The energy! It's immense!" Derek frowned suddenly and shook his head, "But I don't know if it's going to be enough."

Will scowled and opened his eyes, "Don't you dare tell me—"

"Be quiet and focus!" Derek commanded.

Will did as he was told.

David bolted towards the house, sprinting on all fours to be sure to get to the possessed woman before she had a chance to fully recover. If she was anything like Bekka, she'd be able to regenerate from almost any injury, but it would take time.

Running up what remained of the side of the rear-facing wall, he leapt over the collapsed foundation and landed inside what had been the kitchen. From there, he sprinted through the door to the living room—or what had been the living room when it had had a floor—and allowed himself to drop gracefully into the garage. From there, it was a simple leap over the next wall into the remains of the basement, where the van had been pushed aside and the woman lay, bent and twisted like a ragdoll.

"*Give... them... to... us!*" She demanded as her body jerked and snapped and reformed.

David roared out and lunged, swiping at the woman with his claws. Despite her injuries, she was not beyond dodging the attack and bent over backwards at an impossible angle and jutted her leg out at the last moment to catch David off guard and send him toppling.

Not letting himself be kept down for too long, he pushed off with his hands and landed back on his feet. The woman let out a strange, bird-like sound and lunged at him; driving her fist forward. David dodged as best he could, but still wound up catching most of the force of the attack in his side. Letting out a pained howl, he kicked out and struck the woman in the chest, sending her careening into the wall and baring his teeth.

The woman glared at him for a moment before she lunged from the wall and shot into his chest like a missile, knocking him down and standing over him, beginning to kick him in the head.

"*Give them to us!*" She demanded between attacks.

David took a moment to get his bearings, caught completely off guard by the tremendous strength of the woman despite her sleek, small stature. As she went to drive her foot into him again, he snatched her by the ankle and sank his teeth into it.

The warm, sweet spray of blood filled his mouth,

tempting him to rip further into the meat. After an alluring moment, however, he pulled her away from his jaws and hurled her across the room and through the weakened wall with all the force he could muster, burying her body in a pile of brick and mortar.

Satisfied, David wiped his snout with the back of his forearm and nodded to himself, turning away just in time to see five possessed strangers drop down on him...

There were several loud crashes and a pained roar and a moment later, David—still in his werewolf form—sailed through the air and crashed to the ground a short distance from the others. As he let out a soft, pained whimper, Bekka knelt down over him.

"Oh god..."

Will frowned, shaking from the excess energy, "Are we doing this or not?" He demanded.

Scowling, she turned to face him, "Can't you see he's hurt?"

"Not as bad as you think!" Will pointed out.

As if to illustrate his point, David let out a groan and started to rise to his feet. Bekka frowned, shaking her head in disbelief as the werewolf stretched out his joints and started back towards the house, slowly at first, but soon dropping down into a full gallop.

Will smiled at that and nodded. "There ya go, big guy," he turned to the others, "Now let's do this!"

Derek nodded, holding his hands—which started to shimmer and glow—out in front of him. As he chanted something under his breath, Will seized; a pained grunt emerging from his slightly parted lips.

"What's happening?" Bekka started to move forward only to have Brian catch her by the shoulders and hold her back.

"None of this is going to be pleasant for any of us," Brian explained, remembering what Derek had told him.

Bekka frowned up at him and then looked back at Will, her eyes wide with worry. She didn't' say anything, but Brian could tell she was feeling guilty and gave her shoulders a light squeeze. After a moment she looked back up at him, a faint and phony smile painted on her lips.

"Thank you," she whispered.

Brian shook his head slightly, "Don't thank us until it's over."

A pained grunt interrupted the two and they looked up at Will, who was now floating several inches above the ground, his body ramrod straight and his head pitched back—eyes clenched and mouth hanging open in agony.

Derek, they noticed, seemed to be having his own problems as well. Though he'd only been working his magic for two minutes his face was already drenched in sweat and his body shook with pained effort.

Behind them, the sounds of the battle between David

and the others waged, and they turned to watch. There were
five possessed attackers coming at them, sprinting in whatever
twisted, demented form served their purpose best. Though
they were fast, David was faster, and as each got a step further
he advanced by four and cut them off. Each time one of them
attacked, he was quick to parry and retaliate, going so far as to
grab one of them by the ankle and use their own body as a
blunt weapon.

Brian smirked to himself as he watched this, "Way to
go, buddy!" He whispered before turning back to the vampire
and the magician and, as though beckoned by a silent call,
began to step forward.

Bekka, still entranced in the battle, didn't notice him
leave her side and, after another moment, she turned back
and was startled to find him with the others.

Will let out one final blood-curdling shriek before the
spell released him and he fell to the ground. Derek's hands
were now glowing as though he held the sun between them.
His face continued to drip with sweat and his body still
shook, looking like he might, at any moment, collapse under
his own weight.

As Bekka watched, she was stunned to find that the
light in Derek's hands was growing brighter and brighter.
Finally forced to look away, she shielded her eyes and focused
instead on Brian who, despite the intense light, continued to
approach. When he was close enough, Derek gave him a
slight nod before swinging his arms around in a wide arc and
smashing them into his chest and knocking him back into the

grass; the last of the glowing-white energy disappearing inside of him.

Derek stumbled slightly and nodded to Bekka. "It's up to you two now," he spoke softly before falling forward and passing out a short distance from Will.

A nervous tear welled and fell from Bekka's eyes.

Up to her?

Brian lay on the ground, writhing and crying in pain while laughing hysterically; the energy coursing through him beginning to drive him insane. Bekka frowned and knelt down beside him, pressing a hand to his still-warm chest.

"Please! We've got to make it through this."

THIRTY-SEVEN

Bekka couldn't tell if Brian was in pain or somehow pleasured by the immense energy inside of him. His reaction from it was a mystery—his body writhing and seizing in a strange orgasmic, agonizing dance. Finally, his eyes shot open and locked on to hers, his pupils contracting and dilating randomly.

"Brian!" Bekka gasped.

Brian's voice was scratchy as he smiled up at her, "You've got to finish it!"

Bekka frowned, "But how?"

But it was too late for answers, Brian's eyes widened as his body arched and twisted, his mouth opening in a silent cry. As she watched, his body seemed to twist and bend in ways that she'd only recently become accustomed to, and that's when she realized it: the energy *was* killing him!

There wasn't much time!

And then, suddenly, she knew the answer.

Pushing her left palm to his chest and applying enough pressure to softly pin him to the ground, she moved her face closer and pressed her lips to his. At that moment, Bekka felt a warmth begin to grow within her chest. She started to pull away from Brian, afraid that her nerves were making her sick, but was suddenly overwhelmed by the beings inside of her to continue and she returned her lips to his. The warmth turned into a burning that slowly crept up her throat and into her mouth and passed on into Brian, whose eyes flew open as he received it.

Behind her, Bekka heard David roar a warning and she pulled away and turned just in time to see one of the possessed attackers slip by him and sprint at her.

"*Give them to us!*" it demanded.

Bekka cried out as the attacker pulled a switchblade from his back pocket and sprung the blade from its handle.

Bekka flinched as she watched the knife come down at her, closing her eyes tightly to the reality of what was coming. Even if the stabbing wouldn't kill her, surely the attacker would know how to finish the job from there.

But nothing happened...

Uncertain, she opened her eyes and was surprised to see Brian standing over her; his face twisted in pain. Eyes widening, she realized then that he had rolled in front of her and blocked the attack—the possessed attacker straddling over him and growling in agitation.

"*Give them to us!*" it snarled again, pulling the knife free of Brian's back and yanking his hair back and stretching his neck, "*Give them back!*" With that, the attacker dragged the blade across his throat.

Brian's eyes widened as his blood began to pour from the growing wound. As his life left him, Bekka watched as the energy poured out from him.

The possessed attacker frowned, seeing this as well, and paused, looking from Bekka to the dying Brian and back again in confusion. Finally, after a long moment, the body of the attacker collapsed as the entity possessing it left. Behind them, David snarled and swiped at another attacker, who fell lamely under the attack as it, too, was freed.

Brian's body remained upright; supported by the waves of energy pouring from his body.

"Brian! No!" Bekka cried out.

David, looking around at all the unconscious people, shrugged off the anomaly and turned to join the group. When he saw what had happened his casual approach turned into a desperate sprint to Bekka's side. By the time he was next to her and kneeling down beside Brian, he was in his human form.

"What happened?" He demanded.

Bekka shook her head, crying, "They tried to get me and he jumped in front of... oh, God, no! They killed him!"

As she watched, the last of the pale-blue energy that they'd magically infused Brian with bled out, and as it did his own auric energy began to leave his body.

"No!" Bekka cried, seeing the last bits of life leave his body and she grabbed at it as it seeped out of him. As she did, her hands began to glow, and as she reached to grab at the tail-end of Brian's life-energy she was surprised to find that she was able to hold it. Her body grew hot at the contact, feeling as though she was inside an oven, and, for a moment, she was afraid that she might pass out from the heat. Fighting to stay conscious, she struggled with Brian's aura and wrestled it back into his body, "Dammit, Brian! I won't let you die!" She promised him, "I won't!"

Brian's eyes fluttered slightly as she worked to keep his aura inside his body. Seeing this, she pushed onward, refusing his aura's attempts to escape over and over again.

Though she had willed it, Bekka was startled when a wave of energy stretched from her chest and began to seep into Brian's nostrils and mouth. As they did, she felt herself growing tired—the vitality that the entities had given her starting to fade slightly. With several of the energy signatures that had occupied her body for so long beginning to flood into Brian, the wounds in his back and throat began to close up, leaving behind a mess of caked blood.

Bekka's eyes widened at the effects and her tears began to dry up as she took Brian into her arms and started to help him up.

It took almost twenty-five minutes to revive Derek and Will from their nearly comatose slumbers. When they were both finally awake, they were ecstatic to hear that the spell had worked.

Derek smirked, looking around and noting the unconscious bodies strewn about the lawn, "And the entities?" He asked

Bekka shrugged, "They're still with us."

Will frowned, looking up as he rubbed the back of his sore neck, "Us?"

She nodded and motioned towards Brian.

The two looked at Brian for a moment, who still swayed on unsteady feet.

"Wait? Now *he's* possessed too?" Scowling, Will shook his head, "Well don't think I'm going through *that* again to save his ass!"

Bekka giggled and shook her head, "You won't have to."

Will looked up at that and smiled, "So it's really over? Like, for good?"

Bekka smiled and nodded, "Uh-huh!"

Will smiled and was suddenly in front of her, lifting her easily off her feet and spinning her in celebration, "We did it!" He cried out happily, "We fucking did it!"

Bekka giggled and smiled as he let her down, Brian

smirking as he finally steadied himself.

"So now I'm a freak, too?" He asked playfully.

"Welcome to the club," Derek groaned, stumbling towards the group, "You'll get your tee-shirt in two-to-four weeks."

The others laughed as David helped their bassist remain upright. When she was done giggling at the joke, Bekka looked up at Derek.

"I guess your grandpa was right."

Derek nodded, "He usually was."

She smiled and raised a questioning brow to him, "You feel up for the concert tonight?"

"After everything we've been through?" Will jumped in, sounding angry, "After all of this horseshit that we've been dragged through?"

Bekka blushed and bit her lip, "I'm sorry! I just thought—"

"You thought what?" Will smirked suddenly. "That we *didn't* want to go through with our plans," he shook his head, laughing, "Of-fucking-course we're doing the concert!"

Derek smirked, nodding to Bekka, "Isn't that what all of this was about?"

Brian nodded, wrapping an arm around her shoulder. "That's what I thought!"

Bekka blushed and smiled, "Thank you—all of you— so very much."

Will smirk and shook his head. "You're crazy! It's not like we would've just left you high-and-dry!"

David nodded, "You know we'd do anything for you, Bekka."

"Including wreck the van," Will joked.

Bekka frowned and looked back towards destroyed house where the van had been buried, her cheeks turning bright red, "Oh my... I'm so sorry, Will!"

He shrugged, "It's fine. I'll just get a new one."

"Did mister frugal just utter those words?" Brian teased, "Must be nice to have so much money!"

Will smirked, "You have no idea."

David shook his head and laughed while Derek tried to stifle his own.

Brian frowned suddenly, still looking in the direction of the van, "I don't suppose our instruments were still in there, were they?"

Will opened his mouth to speak but stopped as a thought occurred to him, "I guess I'll also be buying everyone some new gear, as well."

Derek frowned, biting his lip, "Hey guys. How far are we going to get now that we don't have a manager?"

The others frowned as they considered this for a moment, all except for Brian, who smiled and took a step over towards their bassist.

"Y'know, magic-man, I think we *do* have a manager?" He said, putting an arm over his shoulder.

Derek's eyes went wide and he looked up at him.

Will nodded, seeing where Brian was going, "Totally!" He smirked at Derek, "Congratulations, buddy!

You've just been promoted!"

Derek blushed, shaking his head in disbelief, "I... you guys want *me* to manage the band?"

Bekka smiled and nodded excitedly, "Mmhm! We know you can do it!"

"I... I don't know what to say!" Derek stammered.

Will smiled, "How 'bout you say something along the lines of 'let's go celebrate with a drink after the concert tonight'!"

David's smile grew wider at that.

Bekka frowned and glanced at Brian for a moment, "Guys... maybe we should do something el—"

Brian stopped her and shook his head. "No, it's alright," he looked up at the others, chewing his lip nervously, "I think I should tell you guys something."

"Brian!" Bekka's eyes widened.

He smiled at her and nodded, "It's alright. I think they're ready to hear it."

Bekka raised an eyebrow and smiled, "Oh? Does this mean you're going to quit smoking, too?"

"Let's not push it," Brian chuckled.

Everyone laughed.

Bekka blushed and nodded, finally feeling that everything was going to be alright, "Well, we should probably get ready then. We *do* have a show tonight."

The group started off, uncertain of what the future had in store for them but nevertheless comforted with their newfound faith in one another. With this certainty driving them forward, they were finally able to rid themselves of all their fears and focus on their passion.

FLESH

Slowly, deliberately, I score my flesh with razors.
Slowly, deliberately, I scorch my flesh with flame.
And through it all,
The rise and fall,
I find myself within the pain.

A puncture marks the juncture,
Between the anger and the angst
And where I heal,
'Cuz now I feel
I owe the agony my thanks.

I'm empty on the inside.
Filled with nothing more than the need,
To see itself on the outside
And so I let it bleed.

There's nothing left to bleed, you see.
There's nothing left to flow.
All my pain.
All that fucking shame!
And I've got nothing left to show...

... But my scored, scorched flesh,
And seeping soul,

Like ribbons from the rips.
Through tears and tears
I see no one's there.
And my body pays the toll.

HIDDEN

Tear out your eyes.
Cut off your hands.
Believe my lies.
Accept my demands.
You'll never find me!
I'm hidden!

You're blindness is your only strength!
Never look beneath the surface!

(Beneath the surface!)

Break all ties.
Sever all bands.
Hear my cries.
Obey my commands.
You'll never find me!
I'm hidden!

Beneath the surface!
Never look beneath the surface!

(You're blindness is your only strength!)

EPILOGUE

"Bloodtones?"

Bekka smiled and stepped forward. "That's us," her voice was shaky with excitement.

The program director smiled and nodded behind his clipboard, taking a quick look back at the others behind her. Except for Will, everyone had their guitars strapped to their backs, and behind them a few members of the stage crew were helping with the new drum kit. When he was sure that everyone and everything was accounted for, he nodded his head towards the stage.

"You guys are on after this set. You're going to have to haul balls, 'cuz you've only got five minutes before the curtain's going back up, and if you guys aren't hooked up and tuned by then, it's your time on the line."

Bekka nodded, "We understand."

"Fuckin' A we do!" Will howled.

The band onstage started to wrap up their set, the drummer going ballistic while the bassist laid down a steady rhythm. The guitarist, an attractive-but-talentless young man, repeated the same riff over and over. It didn't take a trained ear to notice that he was also half-a-second behind.

Bekka sneered at them from backstage, knowing that they at least had them beat, and turned back to her band-mates.

"Alright, guys, you all tuned?"

"Bekka," David smirked and shook his head, "give us some credit."

She blushed and nodded, "Okay, you're right. Sorry. It's just been a while since I've been able to focus all my attention on—"

Brian interrupted her with an arm around her shoulder and smirked, "We know. But you've gotta be chill now. It's all good."

Everybody stared in disbelief at him.

Will's jaw dropped playfully, "Did I just hear the always down-and-depressed Brian say something positive?"

"How bout I get 'down-and-depressed' on your face?" Brian smirked wickedly in his direction.

"Oop! There he is again," Will laughed.

"Bloodtones! You're on!"

Bekka hadn't even noticed the mediocre music wrap up and the band start to pass them as they left the stage. As they did, the heavy black curtain fell, cutting out the sound of the audience.

"Holy shit!" Will started up, heading onstage with the others, "If they liked that load of crap they'll love us!"

"Hey!" The lead singer of the previous band, still onstage, complained.

Will's eyes narrowed and he stared down the young man expectantly, "What?"

The singer—probably a few years younger than them and sporting a series of neon-green spikes in his hair and a pair of tight pants of the same shade—stared back at him for a moment before seeing something in the depths of his eyes that made him nervous. Realizing that it wasn't a conflict he wanted to be a part of, the punk quickly finished wrapping up his microphone cable and scurried away.

"Well that was anticlimactic," Brian laughed.

Derek nodded, hooking his bass up and quickly testing out the chords, "Tell me about it."

David scoffed and shook his bangs from his eyes, "No backbone, whatsoever."

Bekka frowned, "Can we focus, guys? We're here to outplay them, not scare them!"

Brian sighed and nodded, hooking up his guitar, "I don't see why we can't do both."

Bekka shook her head. "Anyway," she looked around the stage to make sure they were all hooked up, "Are we clear on the set?"

"Crystal clear, babes," Brian smirked, getting into place.

"Ready and willing," Will nodded, testing out his new drum set.

The others all offered a reassuring nod just as a voice came over the loudspeakers and introduced them. At that moment the stage director signaled that the curtains were going up. As they did, Bekka turned to Brian and gave him a nod.

Nodding back, Brian stepped up to the microphone in front of him and wetted his lips before letting out an earth-shattering growl.

"IT'S IN THE NATURE OF THE BEAST TO RUN!"

With that, Bekka let loose a crazed howl into her own mike just as the stage lights came on and illuminated them all. Will matched their singer's enthusiasm with an impossibly swift and ferocious intro that cut out just as Bekka pulled away. The music calmed down, the beat slowing to a steady rhythm as the two guitarists set the mood and Derek laid down the groove.

"WHAT IF WE COULD RUN AWAY,
JUST YOU, ME AND THE BEAST?
WE'D TAKE TO THE STREETS ONE NIGHT,
AND HEAD FOVREVER EAST!

"THE HILLS WOULD BARELY SLOW US!
THE MOUNTAINS: NOT A CHANCE!
JUST YOU, ME AND THE BEAST, YOU SEE,
ON OUR ROAD TRIP ROMANCE!"

The drum beat kicked in again, and this time Derek followed along on bass while the guitars continued. Bekka, finally free of the burden that had been dragging her down for so long, let herself loose to the sound and kicked about wildly onstage. As the next verse approached, Brian started in with Bekka.

"WHAT LINGERS ON THE INSIDE,
WILL CONSUME US IN THE END,
BUT WE COULD BE AWAY FROM HERE,
WHEN ALL OF THAT BEGINS!
IT WILL WREN ME FROM THE INSIDE,
UNTIL THERE'S NOTHING LEFT!
THEN COME FOR YOU, I KNOW IT'S TRUE!
AND STEAL YOUR FINAL BREATH!"

The song drove on, David picking up the pace while Brian kept the rhythm going steady. As they all played their hearts out, the audience went berserk; screaming and tossing their hands excitedly in the air. Bekka smiled at the intensity as she pulled the microphone back to her lips.

"BUT WE CAN CHASE THE FREEDOM,
THAT WE KNOW WE'LL NEVER CATCH!
RUNNING FROM WHAT WE KNOW WILL COME,
TO MAKE OUR MOMENT LAST!"

Brian smirked as he growled over Bekka's vocals.

"IT'S IN THE NATURE OF THE BEAST TO RUN!"

At that moment, the others all leaned towards their own microphones and added their vocals to the mix.

"AND WE'LL KEEP MOVING FORWARD,

UNTIL THAT EVENTUAL FEAST!
PEDAL-TO-THE-METAL; HAND-IN-HAND!
JUST YOU, ME AND THE BEAST!"

As the last, lingering notes simmered away into the air, the only sound in the stadium was the overwhelming roar of the audiences. As the band stared back out into the crowd, it suddenly dawned on all of them that the outcome of this competition would mean little to their path.

This was what they were meant to do.

They were simply possessed by the music.

~CURTAIN CALL~

SCARS

Years ago I was cut.
So very fucking deep.
And now they claim my wounds have healed,
But they could never see...

How my skin has hardened.
Like a shell I'm trapped inside.
Unmovable!
Untouchable!
Unfor-fucking-givable!

OH!
How far do these scars run?
Can anybody see?
My life has grown so calloused,
I've forgotten the real me.
And for every passing moment,
The malicious hands of time,
Take every bit of myself,
Till none of it is mine!

The pale-pink trails of razors.
The shiny trails of tears.
The wide, treacherous trails of hatred.
And the sharpened trails of fear.

OH!
How far do these scars stretch?
I'll reach inside to see.
Digging till there's nothing left,
Then they'll all agree.
And for every passing moment,
They rip apart my mind.
Fucking stealing all of me.
But they say the pain's sublime!

All scars to be remembered.
All scars to be embraced.
All scars that sting and linger.
Just beneath the surface.

SHUT UP!

(Tienes que cerrar la boca!)

Keep it shut while I speak my piece!
Let me get a word past your verbal disease!
You've had your time, now it's my turn.
Just shut the fuck up and learn.

(Cierra la boca!)

You never let me speak my mind.
You never hear me out.
I guess if I want to be heard
I'm gonna have to shout.
I'll bust your fucking eardrums
With the sound that you've ignored
I won't be your silent one!
I'm done being your whore!

(Cierra la boca!)

Keep it shut or I'll take a piece
Of what you tried to take from me!
'Cuz once I've had my final say,
I'll finally be free!

(Debido a que estoy hablando!)

The Bloodtones will take to the stage again in the Crimson Shadow/Death Metal series' crossover, "Crimson Metal" and the second installment of the Death Metal series, "Encore".

ABOUT THE AUTHOR

Nathan Squiers (The Literary Dark Emperor and the author formally known as "Prince") is a resident of Upstate New York. Living with his loving fiancé/fellow author, Megan J. Parker, and three incredibly demanding and out-of-control demon-cats, Nathan lives day-by-day on a steady diet of potentially lethal doses of caffeine and bacon. When not immersed in his writing, he often escapes reality through movie marathons, comics & anime, and gnarly tunes. While out-and-about, The Literary Dark Emperor can be found in the chair of a piercing studio/tattoo parlor, at the movies, or simply loving life with friends & loved ones.

Learn more about Nathan's work and join The Legion at www.nathansquiers.com